THE VOICE TRAILED OFF, BUT KATE WAS SURE THE LINE WAS STILL OPEN . . .

She hung up the phone and stood next to it, trembling. This was the second time someone had called with the same kind of twisted version of a nursery rhyme. The whispering voice was masculine, she felt certain, but she couldn't tell if the speaker were young or old. Was it just someone with a sick sense of humor? Somehow Kate didn't believe that. But then what could these calls mean? As she looked across the kitchen at Jessica, who was pondering which two cookies were most full of chocolate chips, she felt a shiver of apprehension.

Books by Beverly Hastings
from Jove

DON'T TALK TO STRANGERS
DON'T WALK HOME ALONE

DON'T WALK HOME ALONE

Beverly Hastings

A JOVE BOOK

DON'T WALK HOME ALONE

A Jove Book / published by arrangement with
the author

PRINTING HISTORY
Jove edition / November 1985

ISBN: 0-515-08390-9

Jove books are published by The Berkley Publishing Group,
200 Madison Avenue, New York, N.Y. 10016.
The words "A JOVE BOOK" and the "J" with sunburst
are trademarks belonging to Jove Publications, Inc.

PRINTED IN THE UNITED STATES OF AMERICA

PROLOGUE

Frigid February wind rattled bare branches and swayed the boughs of small evergreens on the hillside. A small figure picked his way along the overgrown path, thorny branches catching at his heavy jacket.

Part way down the hill, the boy stopped and adjusted the straps of his backpack that bulged with second-grade schoolbooks and half a peanut butter and jelly sandwich left over from lunch. His eye was caught by a movement in the bushes and a moment later a small brown dog emerged onto the path below.

The boy squatted down and held out a mittened hand. "Here, boy. Come here," he called.

Without moving, the dog gazed at the boy, then turned and started down the path.

His feelings hurt, the boy muttered, "Dumb dog." He picked up a stone from the dirt and halfheartedly tossed it after the retreating dog.

"Bad boy. Bad boy." The words came in a low, muffled whisper just behind him.

Startled, the child whirled around. A man—tall and bulky looking in a winter parka—loomed over him. His face was completely concealed by a wool ski mask except for the unblinking eyes that stared intensely into

1

the boy's face. Fearful without quite knowing why, the child took a step backward. But before he could turn and run, the man's gloved hand snaked out and snatched the boy by the wrist.

"Bad boy." The horrible whisper came again. "Bad boys have to be punished." Then, in a quick movement, the man pulled the drawstring out of his parka's hood while he yanked the boy off the path and drew him next to a slim but sturdy tree. Pushing the child's back against the tree trunk, the man roughly jerked both small arms backward around the tree.

"Hey, let me go," the boy begged in a scared voice. "Please, mister."

Ignoring the child's pleas, the man began tying the two small mittened hands together at the wrists. "Sticks and stones will break your bones," he whispered. And, as he knotted and reknotted the nylon drawstring, he repeated the words in a singsong refrain. "Break your bones, break your bones, break your bones."

The man moved around to face the boy, and stared at him. He began to whisper again, and the child shrank back against the tree in fear, his eyes brimming with tears. "Please, mister." The words came out as a sob.

The man stared at the boy a moment longer. Then, without another word, he moved away and soon was lost from view in the silent wintry woods.

Between sobs and gulps the boy cried for help. His back hurt where his pack dug into it, and the cord was tight and painful around his wrists. He called as loud as he could. But as the afternoon light began to fade, he wondered if anyone would ever hear him.

CHAPTER 1

KATE AND PHIL walked out of the air-conditioned Chinese restaurant on upper Broadway, and braced themselves for the humid, fume-laden outdoor air. How could New York be so hot in September?

Even at ten o'clock on a Thursday evening the street swarmed with life. The neighborhood was a strange mixture of students and faculty from nearby Columbia University, elderly Jewish gentlemen in collarless shirts, winos and derelicts slumped in darkened shop doorways, and kids of every color and nationality noisily roller-skating and miraculously avoiding collision with the many weary shoppers pushing their laden wire carts. On one corner a tall black man with Rastifarian dreadlocks preached to a small crowd of onlookers. Farther along, three earnest-looking young women in jeans and T-shirts urged pedestrians to sign their petition to save the whales. A pair of uniformed policemen walked slowly past, and a Korean produce shop owner sprayed water over his neat open-air display of vegetables and fruit.

Usually, Kate reveled in this unceasing kaleidoscope of humanity. She liked to imagine the hundreds of separate dramas that were an unknowable part of these varied lives. Some nights she wondered what waited at home for that sad-eyed woman stepping off the bus, or what chain of circumstances had brought the turbaned old man and his two grandchildren chattering to one another in Hindi to the corner of 112th and Broadway. But tonight she wasn't interested. Tonight she just felt hot.

"Oh, come on, Kate, won't you change your mind?" Phil cajoled her for the third time. "I just got that film yesterday and I saved it to watch with you. My video-tape machine is all warmed up and ready to go."

Kate noted the petulant tone his voice had taken on. Replying more brusquely than she had planned, she said, "I imagine your whole apartment's all warmed up in this heat. Besides, I told you I had to get home early. I've got that appointment with my department chairman at the crack of dawn tomorrow."

"It's not my fault my place isn't air-conditioned, you know," Phil said stiffly. "And I have meetings of my own to go to."

"Well, good. Then we'd both better call it a night."

"Think what you're missing though," he insisted.

Kate gave him a rueful smile and brushed her red-blonde bangs off her forehead. "Yeah. Well, to be honest, Phil, I'm just not in the mood for another ancient horror film."

Phil stopped walking and looked at her with an insulted expression. "I thought you were interested in my work."

"I am interested," she said in exasperation. "But it's your thesis, not mine. I don't have to see every one of these films. Don't push me."

"I wasn't aware that I was pushing." Now he really was insulted.

They walked in silence the rest of the way to Riverside Drive, where Kate had miracuously found a parking spot earlier in the day. As Kate fished her keys out of her bag, Phil stood next to her with a long-suffering look on his face. Kate unlocked the car door and slid her legs under the steering wheel. Rolling down the window before she shut the door, she leaned out and said in a determinedly cheerful tone, "Good night, Phil, and thanks for dinner."

"Right," he said coldly. "Well, maybe we can get together over the weekend. That is, if you can find time for me in your busy schedule."

Kate smiled sweetly as she started the engine and put her aged VW in gear. "I'll let you know," she said as she edged out onto the street.

Driving north on Riverside toward the Henry Hudson Parkway and her apartment in Yonkers, Kate thought over the evening with Phil. Perhaps she hadn't been very nice to him. But, after all, he knew in advance that she had to go home early. When they'd talked about it, he was pleasantly agreeable, but from the moment they'd sat down to dinner he'd done nothing but nag her to come and watch his stupid film. Sometimes he was such a baby.

When she'd first met him, Kate had found his enthusiasm endearing, and his research for his thesis on the history of the horror film had seemed delightfully bizarre. And he certainly was an attractive guy. But after knowing him for six months, she'd begun to realize how self-centered he was. His enthusiasm was reserved for himself and his projects. When was the last time he'd asked her how the work was coming on her thesis about Jane Austen's portrayal of men?

He's not looking for a girlfriend, Kate thought to herself as she turned onto the Henry Hudson Parkway. What he wants is a doting mama.

Not for the first time, Kate reflected on her choice of men. Now Phil was falling into the pattern of unsatisfactory relationships she'd seemed to develop of late. Every man she'd dated in the last several years had been good-looking and charming enough at first, and none of them had been stupid. But each time she'd become disenchanted before too long. Even with Peter, whom she'd seriously considered marrying, things just hadn't worked out.

Kate slowed for the tollgate at the beginning of the Saw Mill River Parkway. She tossed her money into the coin basket and drove through. There was never much traffic on this last leg of her journey. As the little VW Rabbit chugged along the highway, Kate asked herself why she hadn't found someone who was right for her. Is there something about me that brings out the worst qualities in men I go out with? she wondered. Or maybe I attract people with problems.

Kate sighed. The Yonkers Avenue exit was coming up and she flipped on her turn signal, but her mind kept worrying at these questions. Was it possible that she expected too much? she thought with a start. Maybe she was looking for perfection and would always be disappointed. You've got to learn to overlook these faults and flaws, she lectured herself sternly. After all, she was far from perfect herself. But she knew that however much she tried to follow this advice, she wouldn't be able to do it.

She pulled into the parking lot of the old red brick apartment building and shut off the engine. Instead of hopping out of her car, Kate leaned back against the seat and stared into space. The fact of the matter was that she'd never met a man she truly cared about. Maybe when she did, these questions would resolve themselves. But would Mr. Right ever come along? Laughing at herself halfheartedly, Kate got out of her car and trudged across the pathetic strip of crabgrass to the heavy outer door of the building.

Kate picked up her mail and let herself into her tiny studio apartment. Shuffling through the envelopes she found she had a message from her congressman, a bill from Con Ed, and a brochure advertising Club Med. How had she gotten on their mailing list? Even if she had time for a vacation, she certainly couldn't afford it.

The glossy photos of sun-bronzed bodies happily splashing in the surf deepened her mood of dissatisfaction. And a glance at the drab furnishings of her cramped one-room apartment didn't help either. She knew she was lucky to have the place. Aunt Lil and Uncle Joe, who owned the building, let her have the apartment at a very low rent. And it wasn't as if they were hovering about either. They wintered in Florida and spent the rest of their time in their house on the other side of Yonkers. Kate was grateful for their kindness, but there was no denying that it was a cheerless place. The building, in fact the whole neighborhood, was old and getting older. And so were most of the residents. Sometimes Kate longed for neighbors her own age.

Snap out of it, Kate, she told herself. She tossed her mail on the Formica-topped table. She really should sit down and review the things she needed to discuss tomorrow morning with her advisor. Failing that, she should get herself right into bed so she'd at least be rested and alert. But she couldn't seem to settle down. Her mind kept wandering off on various tangents, and she was too keyed up to go to sleep. Finally, she poured herself a glass of wine and sat on the couch with that morning's newspaper. Normally she only glanced at the *Herald Statesman*, but tonight she found herself reading every word, even the sports and the weather. I guess this is one way to get out of that silly self-pitying mood I was in, she thought wryly as she moved on to the classifieds.

WANTED—Edgar's Lndg. Resp. adult. Care for bright 7-yr-old after school. Some eves. Lgt. cooking. No hskpg. Own transp. Refs. 678-1212

The ad caught her eye as she scanned through the want ads. When she finished the paper she went back to it. Edgar's Landing, she thought. That's only about fifteen minutes from here. It's a nice town. Kate found that she'd picked up a pen and was absentmindedly circling the ad. I'm not really looking for a job, she told herself. I've got my thesis to finish. But I never do get much done on it after about three in the afternoon anyway. I wonder how much this job pays.

Finally feeling sleepy, Kate opened up the couch and pulled the bed pillows out of the top of the closet. As she brushed her teeth, she thought again about the ad. It couldn't hurt to find out what the situation was. I'll call about it tomorrow, she decided.

On Saturday morning, as Kate stacked her breakfast dishes in the drainer, she reflected on her conversation with Mr. Cordell, the man who'd put the ad in the paper. It was a somewhat unusual setup. He lived alone with his seven-year-old niece, and needed someone to care for her, since he worked in the city every day. It certainly didn't sound like a very hard job, and the hourly pay seemed more than fair. Kate hadn't asked him exactly what he'd meant by "light cooking." She hoped it wouldn't be anything too elaborate—she could handle the *basic* needs of a seven-year-old girl.

What should she wear for her interview this morning? Her one good suit and high-heeled pumps probably wouldn't be quite appropriate for Saturday morning in Edgar's Landing. On the other hand, scruffy Levi's and her well-worn sweatshirt seemed a little too sloppy and unprofessional. What did she have that would strike a happy medium? I must be going crazy, she thought with a smile. I'm sounding like one of those "dress for success" articles in women's magazines. But still, first impressions did make a difference.

She finally decided on her brown corduroy skirt and a green cotton shirt. It wasn't exciting, but no one could really object to it. Green was always a good color for her because it emphasized her blue-green eyes.

Glancing at her watch, Kate quickly ran a comb through her cap of straight, shiny, red-gold hair, and dabbed on a little lipstick before dashing out the door. As she got into her car, she wished for the hundredth time that it weren't such a remarkably ugly shade of chartreuse. Oh, well, she thought, it runs perfectly well and when I'm inside it, I don't really have to look at the color.

Driving north along the Hudson, Kate rolled down the window and enjoyed the crisp, clean, fall air. This was the season she loved the best. The late heat wave seemed to have ended, and brilliant sunshine glinted on the slow-moving water of the river. As she passed through the small towns that lined its bank, she appreciated once again their different characters. These villages were not bedroom suburbs built to accommodate commuters fleeing the city. Some of the towns dated from before the Revolution, while others had sprung up in the nineteenth century around the industrial plants on the Hudson. The plants were long gone and barges no longer filled the river, but each town retained an appealing sense of its own identity. Kate had grown up on a river herself, and she always felt somehow cheered by the view of the flowing water and the cliffs on the other side.

A green and white sign proclaimed "Village of Edgar's Landing," and she drove through a street lined with small shops and Saturday morning crowds. Kate wondered idly who Edgar had been. He was probably a Revolutionary War hero of some sort, she decided, or maybe he'd owned a ferry service in the days before the bridges were built. Then she turned off the main street and drove up the hill, watching for Alder Drive on the right.

The street ran along the crest of the hill, and Kate pulled up in front of number 37. It was a big Victorian house set well back from the sidewalk and partially screened by huge evergreens and maples. This will look gorgeous in another couple of weeks when the maple leaves start to turn, Kate thought with pleasure. And what a fabulous house! It was painted gray with white trim. The huge front porch with its columns and ornamental railing, the louvered shutters outside the windows, and the fanciful gingerbread trim all looked like original features of a house that had been lovingly kept up. As she walked up the steps, Kate saw small stained-glass windows on either side of the front door. It's a fairy-tale house, she thought, like the ones in the old books I read as a child. What fun it must be to live here.

Before Kate could ring the bell, the door was opened.

"You must be Miss Jamison. I'm Adam Cordell." The man who extended his hand and shook Kate's in a firm clasp was tall with dark hair and cool gray eyes that gave her a measuring look. "Please come in."

Kate stepped into an entrance foyer the size of a small room. Through the arch to her left she could see a large, high-ceilinged living room comfortably furnished with a mixture of antique and modern pieces in warm earth tones. A massive staircase on the right led upward to a wide sunlit landing. Gleaming wood floors set off the woven Navajo rugs beneath her feet.

Adam Cordell ushered Kate into the living room. As she settled herself on the overstuffed couch, he sat in an upholstered armchair across from her.

"I think it will be easiest if I explain exactly what my situation is and what I am looking for," he told her. His manner was formal, almost aloof. "As I told you, Jessica is my niece. Her parents, my older brother and his wife, were both killed in an automobile crash a little over a year ago." He paused, but before Kate could make any sympathetic reply, he went on. "I am Jessica's guardian—in fact, I'm almost the only family she has. She came to live with me right after it happened, and she's doing pretty well, I think. I spend quite a lot of time with her on the weekends, but during the week I'm in the city, and she's much too young to be left alone.''

"She's seven, isn't she?" Kate asked.

"That's right," he replied. "She's in second grade here in Edgar's Landing. I've had someone to take care of her—a local woman named Mrs. Higgens. However, her husband has recently retired and they're going to move to Florida. That's why I'm looking for someone else.''

He stopped as if he expected a response. Not knowing what else to say, Kate nodded her head and murmured, "I see."

Adam Cordell leaned back in his chair. "What I need is a responsible person who will be here every day when Jessica gets home from school, between three and three-thirty, and who will stay until I get home. I'm usually here by six-thirty or so, but sometimes I have dinner meetings or I work late, and then I don't get home until a good deal later. I'm a graphic designer and I have my own firm in Manhattan. So the person I hire has to be flexible and willing to accommodate my schedule.''

As he spoke, Kate studied him. He really was a very handsome man. With his classic features, he could have stepped right out of an ad in *Gentleman's Quarterly*, except that the symmetry of his face was slightly marred by a crook in the bridge of his nose. He must have broken it at some time. But oddly, this small imperfection seemed to make him even more attractive.

Kate realized that he was waiting for her to say something. Casting about for a remark that wasn't completely inane, she finally said, "The advertisement mentioned light cooking. What does that involve?"

"Oh, that's just for Jessica. When I'm detained in the city, I expect the person who is caring for her to prepare her dinner. It needn't be anything fancy—just plain, wholesome food.''

He paused again, and once more Kate couldn't think

of anything to say. He really is hard to talk to, she thought, he's so formal and serious. But fortunately, before the silence stretched on too long, she heard footsteps running down the stairs.

"Ah, here's Jessica now," he said, and Kate saw him smile for the first time.

A pretty little girl rushed into the room and then stopped when she saw Kate. Like her uncle, Jessica had gray eyes, and her dark hair was pushed off her face with a plastic hairband. Hot on her heels and skidding on the bare wood floor was a big Irish setter. Tail wagging furiously, he galloped straight toward Kate and laid his large head in her lap.

"No, Red!"

The dog's tail drooped at the sharp sound of his master's voice. But Kate laughed and laid her hand on his head.

"It's all right," she said. "I love dogs. He's just being friendly." She stroked the animal's silky hair and scratched behind his feathery ears.

Adam Cordell put one arm around his niece and looked at Kate. "Miss Jamison, I'd like you to meet my niece, Jessica Cordell. Jessica, this is Miss Jamison."

The little girl smiled shyly. "How do you do?"

Kate smiled back at her. "Hello, Jessica, I'm happy to meet you."

Jessica's uncle said, "Jess, why don't you take Miss Jamison upstairs and show her your room?"

Jessica looked a little doubtful but said, "Okay." And the two of them went out of the room and up the stairs, trailed by Red, who had obviously decided that Kate was his special friend.

On the second floor, four bedrooms and a big old-fashioned bathroom opened off the center hallway. Jessica led Kate into a sunny room facing south.

"What a nice room," Kate said to the little girl as she looked around.

Against one wall was a set of bunk beds, the lower

one crowded with a collection of stuffed animals and dolls. Open and face down amidst the animals was a book Jessica must have been reading when Kate arrived.

"What are you reading, Jessica?" Kate asked.

"A riddle book," the girl answered softly. Then she glanced at Kate. "Want to hear one?"

"Sure."

"Let's see." Jessica thought for a moment. "Oh, I know! Why did the robber take a bath?"

Kate pondered and then shrugged helplessly. "I give up. Why did he?"

"Because he wanted to make a clean getaway." Jessica giggled as Kate smiled and shook her head.

"That was a good one." She gestured toward the bed. "Is this where you sleep? It doesn't look as though your toys have left much room for you."

"Oh, no," Jessica assured her. "I sleep in the top bunk—it's much more fun. Only Baby sleeps with me." She picked up a doll and held it out to Kate. The round plastic head with painted-on hair reminded Kate of her own dolls of years ago, and the soft cloth body was limp in her hands, clear evidence that this doll was well-loved.

"Baby used to have a dress with an apron, but it got too torn and dirty, so now she wears a nightie that was mine when I was a baby," Jessica told Kate seriously. "And one time her arm came off, I think when I was about four years old, but my mother sewed it back on again." She took the doll from Kate and pulled up its nightie to show the neat stitching. Then she hugged it close in her arms. "I love you, Baby," she whispered.

Kate's heart went out to the little girl, and when she noticed the silver-framed photograph on Jessica's dresser, she had to blink back sudden tears. The man in the picture bore a striking resemblance to Adam Cordell. He sat smiling on a park bench, one arm around a laughing blonde woman and the other around a younger Jessica, who sat on his lap. Kate reached out and gently stroked Jessica's hair. Then, looking at a drawing tacked to the wall, she asked, "Did you paint that picture in school?"

Jessica shook her head. "No, I made it upstairs in Uncle Adam's studio. He gave me an easel and he lets me paint with him sometimes. See, it's the trees you can see from the window up there."

"Yes, I see," Kate said. "And you put in some of the birds and squirrels in the trees. I think it's a super painting."

Jessica made a face. "It's okay, but I messed up the top part of it. I wish I could paint as good as Uncle Adam."

"Well, I'm sure he's been painting a lot longer than you have," Kate said consolingly. "He's had much more practice."

The girl smiled quickly, and then dropped down to hug Red, who lay sprawled in the exact center of the floor. She looked up at Kate. "I'm thirsty. Could we go get some juice?"

"I guess so," Kate said. "But let's go and ask your uncle."

As they started down the stairs, Jessica slid her hand confidingly into Kate's. Touched, Kate looked down at the small figure at her side. Then she glanced up and was startled to see Adam Cordell standing in the archway of the living room, watching them. Kate couldn't decipher his expression.

"Oh, Uncle Adam, is it okay if I have some juice?"

"Sure, Jess." He smiled, and Kate observed again how his face softened when he spoke to the little girl.

In the large kitchen Jessica gulped down her juice. Then her uncle said, "Jessica, will you please take Red outside in the back yard and throw his tennis ball for him a while? He's such a lazybones and he needs to run around."

"Okay, sure," she said cheerfully. "C'mon, Red, let's go!"

As the kitchen door closed, Kate said, "She's an awfully nice little girl, Mr. Cordell."

"I agree. I'm glad you like her." He gestured toward the kitchen table. "Please sit down. Do you have any questions about the job?"

"No," Kate said slowly. "Not at the moment anyway."

"Fine. I'd like to find out a little more about you," he told her in his serious voice. "First, how old are you?"

"I'm twenty-five," Kate replied.

He nodded. "And you said you're a student at Columbia?"

"Well, yes, I'm a graduate student. I'm working on my Ph.D. thesis."

"I see. Tell me, why did you apply for this job?"

Kate risked a small smile. "I need the money." Then she continued, "I'm trying hard to finish and get my degree, so I don't want any kind of full-time work. But I'm barely scraping by on my savings and I could use some income. And this kind of job would suit my needs. I like kids, and I think it would be fun to spend time with a child like Jessica."

"What about your classes?" he asked.

"Oh, I've finished all my class work. I only go in occasionally to meet with my advisor or use the library. I make my own schedule. And I find I do my best thinking in the mornings and early afternoons. After three o'clock I can't seem to concentrate on my research any more."

"That sounds good." He combed back his hair with his fingers in a surprisingly boyish gesture that contrasted oddly with his formal manner. Kate could hardly keep from smiling as the lock of dark hair immediately fell back again. "You see," he told her gravely, "it's important that I know that whoever takes care of Jessica will be here every day. I can't be worrying all the time about making last-minute arrangements. And it's important for Jessica to have some kind of continuity in her life. You do understand that the job entails staying late sometimes in the evening."

"Yes," Kate said, "you mentioned that. I don't see that as a problem."

"Well." He cleared his throat and gazed at her steadily. "I don't mean to pry into your personal life, Miss Jamison, but you're an attractive young woman. Won't your boyfriend object?"

Kate could feel the flush creeping up her neck and reddening her cheeks, and she fingered the medallion around her neck. But she kept her eyes on his as she replied, "No, Mr. Cordell, you don't have to worry about that."

"Oh." For a moment he looked a little uncertain. Then he went on. "In that case, if you want it, the job is yours."

"Thank you," Kate said with a smile. "I do want it. When would you like me to start?"

"As soon as possible," he replied. "Mrs. Higgens is anxious to get ready to move. Can you come on Monday?"

"Sure," Kate said. "That's fine with me."

"Good. I'll ask Mrs. Higgens to meet you here at two o'clock. That will give you time to learn where everything is before Jessica comes home. Mrs. Higgens can give you the keys and explain the household routine." He gave Kate one of his rare smiles. "It's not really very complicated." He stood up and moved toward the back door. "I'm sure Jessica will be delighted to know that it's settled."

When the little girl came inside, he said to her, "Jessica, we've been talking, and Miss Jamison is going to be taking care of you when Mrs. Higgens leaves."

Jessica gave Kate a big grin. "Great! When?"

Kate smiled at her. "I'll be here on Monday when you get home from school." She stood up and said to Adam Cordell, "Thanks very much."

The three of them walked to the front door and Jessica said, "'See you on Monday!"

Her uncle shook Kate's hand. "I think this will be a happy arrangement for all of us, Miss Jamison."

"I think so too," Kate told him. "But won't you and Jessica call me Kate? Miss Jamison always sounds like a little old lady in white gloves."

"Of course, if you prefer." He hesitated. "Then perhaps you should call me Adam."

Kate smiled slightly and called another good-bye to Jessica as she started toward her car. Driving down the hill, she felt a glow of pleased excitement. Jessica seemed like such a nice kid, it would be fun to take care of her. And the house was wonderful. She liked the dog too, but she wasn't quite so sure about Adam Cordell. Still, he must have approved of Kate—he hadn't even asked her for any references. But she'd never have known it from his manner. He was so distant and aloof. Oh, well, she thought, I won't be seeing much of him anyway.

For the rest of the way home Kate let herself imagine how she'd spend her first week's earnings. Maybe she would stop and take another look at those boots she'd seen last week.

Chapter 2

MRS. HIGGENS WAS a thin, older woman, her short salt-and-pepper hair tightly permed in curls that surrounded her long face with its thin lips and close-set brown eyes. When she opened the door to Kate she was wearing a pair of maroon pants and a white blouse with a pink cardigan sweater clutched closed with one hand. In her other hand was a pair of aquamarine, double-knit polyester pants.

"Oh, hi. You must be Kate," she said. "I was just hemming these pants." She indicated the blue ones over her arm. "It's my new pants suit for Florida. I hear everyone there dresses real well so I want to be ready. Well, don't just stand there. Come on in."

Kate followed her into the house, where Red greeted her with enthusiasm. She noticed that Mrs. Higgens carefully closed the front door and tested it to make sure it was latched and locked before proceeding. "Well, Mr. Cordell wanted me to be sure and show you all around and tell you about how things are done here and all. So why don't you put your bag down here on the couch and we can get started so we'll have a chance to sit down and have a nice cup of coffee before Jessica gets home.'' The woman folded the slacks over her arm and put them down beside her sewing things at one end of the couch in the living room. ''Let's see now. Where shall we start?'' The question was clearly rhetorical, for Kate had no chance to answer. ''I think we'll go upstairs and work our way down,'' Mrs. Higgens went on.

Kate followed the energetic woman up to the second floor, with Red tagging along behind. Mrs. Higgens led Kate to the open doorway of the large master bedroom at the front of the house. ''This here is Mr. Cordell's room. Not that I have need to go in it at all. But I must say he does keep it neat.'' She gave Kate a knowing smile. ''Real neat for a single man, I'd say. Though his wife may have taught him a thing or two before she left.''

Kate was a little astonished. ''His wife?'' she repeated.

''Oh, yes,'' Mrs. Higgens said with relish. ''Caused quite a bit of talk at the time. Of course, this is a small town, and some people just love to gossip.'' She watched Kate in eager anticipation.

''I hadn't realized that he'd been married,'' Kate said cautiously.

''He didn't mention it, huh? Well, I guess he wouldn't. It upset him pretty bad when she walked out. Must be more than two years ago now. Most people thought he'd sell the house. I know for a fact one or two were eager to buy it. But he didn't sell and it looks more and more like he's staying put.'' She crossed her arms over her cardigan, and went on. ''Seems like a pretty big house just for him and the little girl. Of course, he had that studio he'd fixed up on the third floor for his painting, and I guess he didn't want to leave that.'' She backed out of the doorway.

Hoping to turn the conversation in a different direction, Kate looked at the stairs leading up. ''So there's only Mr. Cordell's studio up there?'' she asked.

"That's right. Just one big room it is. I don't go up there and he doesn't like Jessica to mess with his things when he's not around."

Kate nodded and then turned toward the other front room. "And that's Jessica's room. I saw it the other day. Maybe you could show me where everything is kept."

Mrs. Higgens led the way in. "There's not much to tell. She's a good girl and she knows where all her clothes and stuff belong. Poor little thing, losing her parents that way. Still, she's mighty lucky her uncle could give her a home." She bent over the bed and picked up the doll that Jessica called Baby. "One thing I should tell you, though, Jessica can't go to sleep without this doll. She's getting a little old for dolls, but this one's real special to her."

They moved back out into the hallway, nearly tripping over the dog flopped on the floor. Mrs. Higgens pulled open a closet door to reveal shelves neatly stacked with folded sheets and towels and a variety of cleaning apparatus. "This is the linen closet," she said. "You won't be doing the laundry, of course—Rose Mullen comes two mornings a week to clean for him. She takes care of all that. But it's always good to know where things are, I always say."

She opened the door to one of the other two rooms off the upstairs hall. "This is the guest room. Not that he's had any guests that I know of. And this is his study," she said, opening the door to the other room. "Got it all fixed up like a library or something. Looks nice, doesn't it?"

Kate opened her mouth to reply, but Mrs. Higgens had already moved on. "Now this is the bathroom, of course. You'll find anything that Jessica might need in this cupboard above the radiator. And just remember she should use the mild shampoo, not this other stuff. And you've got to watch that she pulls the curtain all the way across when she takes a shower. If you don't the floor gets knee-deep in water. One time it leaked through the ceiling downstairs and Mr. Cordell got real upset."

"Okay, I'll remember," Kate said.

"Let's go downstairs," Mrs. Higgens suggested. "And maybe I'd better show you where things are in the basement. Not that you'll have any need to go down there, but it never hurts to be prepared, I always say."

They went down to the basement, where the woman showed Kate the furnace room, the water heater, and the laundry room. "This machine is real easy to run. Of course, when I first came to work for Mr. Cordell I told him I wouldn't be doing any housework. But between you and me, sometimes I run a few things through the washer for Jessica if she wants them special for the next day. After all, poor little kid. She's got no one else but her uncle." She opened up a cupboard door to reveal a set of circuit breakers. "Now this second one from the bottom is for the kitchen. Every now and then it gets overloaded and the whole kitchen goes out. But you just come down here and flip it back and everything goes on again. And now this meter here is the gas." Mrs. Higgens pointed to the round black box on the wall. "If the Con Ed man comes when you're here, you can let him come down here and read the meter. Just make sure it really is the Con Ed man." She flicked Kate a knowing smile. "I hate to say this, but even in a small town like this, you can't get careless. Letting someone inside who's got no business being here is just asking for trouble."

Returning to the first floor, Mrs. Higgens gave Kate a guided tour of the kitchen, making sure she knew where everything was. Thinking of her own meager supply of cooking utensils, Kate was surprised at the assortment here. "My goodness, it's certainly well-equipped," she said.

"Oh, yes indeed. Of course, the way I heard it, his wife took off with nothing but the clothes on her back and the money in their account. And I guess it's true. He'd sure never buy all this stuff for himself.'' She turned up the heat under the coffeepot and looked at her watch. ''Good. We've got time now for a cup of coffee and a nice chat before Jessica gets home. Anything I forgot to tell you?''

Kate was afraid Mrs. Higgens would reveal increasingly intimate details about Adam Cordell and his wife, so she searched around for a safe topic. ''What kinds of things does Jessica like to eat? Mr. Cordell told me that I might have to cook her dinner now and then.''

Mrs. Higgens sighed and shook her head. ''Well, she's kind of a finicky eater. She says she likes hamburgers and lamb chops, but then I make them and she hardly eats a bite. I really don't know what to tell you.'' Noticing that the coffee was hot, she poured a cup for herself and for Kate, and set them on the table. Waving Kate to sit down, she perched her own spare frame on one of the kitchen chairs and said, ''You know, when my Joe and I decided to move down to Florida and I had to give my notice here, I told Mr. Cordell that my sister Martha would be more than happy to take over. I don't think he ever called her, though. Anyway, now that I've gotten to know you, I feel better in my heart about leaving Jessica. A little girl needs a woman's touch.'' She smiled at Kate. ''Of course, I'm sure Mr. Cordell's fond of her, but it's hard to know how he feels about anything. And he's never very friendly.''

Mrs. Higgens glanced at her watch again. ''Jessica should be along any time now. I always feel a little jumpy until she's safe in the house.''

''Does she always walk home by herself?'' Kate asked.

Looking shocked, Mrs. Higgens replied, ''She never walks home alone.'' Then she saw Kate's look of surprise and confusion. ''Oh, I see. You meant, do I need to go to school to meet her. No, no. A bunch of the kids walk home together. But she has strict instructions. I tell her, 'Don't walk home alone. And don't walk through the woods.' " For a moment her small, close-set eyes looked fearful. "Some funny things go on in those woods by the school," she said in a low voice. "I don't suppose you heard about it, but last February there was a little boy and he didn't come home from school one afternoon. When they finally got worried and went out to search for him, they found him tied to a tree! He'd been crying his eyes out and the poor kid was just about frozen. All he could say was that some man in a mask had tied him up and kept talking about breaking his bones or some such. No one ever found out who it was or why he'd want to do such a terrible thing."

Kate felt a little shiver of fear. "Has anything else happened since then?" she asked.

"No, not that I know of," Mrs. Higgens answered. "Of course, Jessica comes home sometimes with stories about this one or that one chasing her, but that's something I meant to tell you about. She's got what they call an active imagination and you can't always believe her wild tales. Not that she's a liar, I wouldn't want you to think that. She's a good little girl, but she does sometimes like to make things up." She paused and then added, "Mr. Cordell talked to me about it. He says he discussed it with some psychiatrist or someone like that and it all has to do with what happened to her parents. I don't understand it myself, but anyway, when you pin her down she always tells the truth." She looked at her watch for the third time. "I think I'll just go and take a look outside and see if she's coming along. When she's a little late, I always start thinking about that guy in the mask."

Kate watched as Mrs. Higgens walked to the front door and out onto the porch. She felt a little overwhelmed. The older woman was obviously fond of Jessica and took her job seriously. But she certainly was a talker, and Kate could see that she'd be a bit wearing on a daily basis. No wonder Adam had been leery of getting on first-name terms with his new employee! Still, Mrs. Higgens had been really helpful in explaining things to Kate. And though it was inappropriate for her to gossip on about Adam's personal life to a virtual stranger, Kate couldn't help feeling that these revelations had given her a better handle on the Cordell household.

Just then the big Irish setter, who had been dozing peacefully on his rug in the corner of the kitchen, lumbered to his feet and moved to the front door, tail wagging madly. And Jessica came in, following by Mrs. Higgens.

"Hi, Kate!" she cried. "Oh, I'm so glad you're here. What can we do today?"

"Let's talk about that in a minute," Kate said with a smile. "I think Mrs. Higgens wants to say good-bye to you."

The older woman came into the kitchen, her sewing stuffed into a shopping bag. "Jessica, honey, come and give me a kiss good-bye." She bent down and held out her arms.

Obediently, Jessica put her arms around Mrs. Higgens' neck and hugged her.

"I'm going to miss you, Jessica," the woman said. "You be good now and do what Kate tells you. And I'll send you a postcard from Florida."

"Okay," Jessica said.

Mrs. Higgens turned to Kate. "Good-bye, dear. I wish you the best of luck. And I'm sure everything is going to work out just fine." She gathered up her pocketbook and shopping bag and departed, still clutching her cardigan around her narrow chest.

Mrs. Higgens proved to be right. In the first week, Kate found that she liked Jessica even more than she'd expected to. And Jessica obviously liked her, too. The child made it clear that she was pleased to be with Kate and looked forward to seeing her every day.

Each weekday, Kate arrived at the Cordell house by three o'clock. Red greeted her with delirious enthusiasm. Living alone in her tiny apartment, and before that at college, she'd forgotten how much fun it was to have a dog around. When the weather was warm enough she would take him out back and throw a ball for him.

Red wasn't really much of a watchdog since he loved everyone he met. But he barked to let her know when someone came up on the porch even before she heard the doorbell. Kate found this comforting, especially when she was upstairs in Jessica's room. It was a big house, and it had taken a bit of time before she knew where everything was.

The more Kate was there the more she appreciated the solidity and comfort of the big old house. The tall heavy wood doors with their wooden knobs, the beautifully designed moldings and staircases, and the imposing fieldstone fireplace surmounted by an antique wood-framed mirror all lent charm and dignity and a sense of permanence.

One day, impelled by curiosity, Kate ventured up to the third floor. It was one big room with dormer windows on three sides. A skylight had been cut into the roof, and sunlight drenched the room. Kate could see why Adam had made this his studio. It was almost bare —only easels and a couple of straight chairs stood in the center. Canvases leaned against the walls. Some of them were blank and others were either abandoned or in progress. Curious about what Adam's work looked like, Kate walked around the room, gazing at the paintings. The completed ones were done in somber tones. Faces, most of them female, swirled out of misty backgrounds, and the overall effect was moody and unhappy. Was this his way of expressing the emotional turmoil of his divorce and then his brother's death?

As Kate went back downstairs, she decided that she wouldn't mention to Adam that she'd been in the studio. He hadn't told her not to go up there, and certainly the door was left unlocked. But the paintings revealed too much pain—she wouldn't know how to talk about them.

Jessica got home every day between three-fifteen and three-thirty unless she had other plans. On Tuesdays she took tap dance lessons at the Unitarian Church; she and her girlfriend Louise walked there from school together. On Thursday afternoons her Brownie troop met at school until four o'clock. And, of course, Jessica had friends to play with, either at her house or at theirs. It took Kate a little while to learn the ins and outs of second-grade life, but by the second week she had a pretty good idea of Jessica's routine.

Kate discovered that she actually enjoyed taking care of the little girl. They had started a few of their own routines, like preparing Jessica's lunch for the next day at school. The little girl felt very grown up as she helped Kate make tuna salad, or wrapped a couple of cookies in plastic wrap. And Jessica happily chattered away whenever she was with Kate, telling her all about what happened at school and who was best friends with whom that day. Occasionally, her tales sounded a little farfetched. Once she fearfully told Kate that two boys had been fighting in the playground at recess.

"They had knives and everything, and I think one of them had a gun," she said to Kate. "There was lots of blood," she added, wide-eyed.

"How old were these boys?" Kate asked her.

"Oh, they're in my grade. But they aren't in my class."

"Boys in second grade don't have knives and guns," Kate told her gently. "And sometimes if a person gets hit on the nose, it bleeds a lot. Did you see them after school?" Jessica nodded, and Kate went on, "Well, then, I don't think that either of them got hurt very badly."

She wasn't sure she was doing the right thing by pointing out the unrealistic parts of Jessica's story without making an issue of them. But Jessica seemed to accept Kate's more rational explanations without protest.

Kate had seen very little of Adam. When he came home he was perfectly polite and pleasant. He'd always ask how the day had gone, but clearly didn't want to hear a detailed account. In fact, he seemed happy to leave more and more of Jessica's daily life in Kate's hands. When she told him that she'd noticed Jessica's sneakers seemed a little small on her, he replied with a sigh that he supposed he'd manage to get her new ones that Saturday.

"I'd be happy to take her into the village tomorrow and get some if you like," Kate said hesitantly.

"That would be awfully helpful. Here, let me give you some money." He paused and then added, "Thank you."

Over the weekend, Kate had a call from her friend Amy Stevens. The two of them had gone to English classes together at Columbia. Amy and her husband Mark had recently moved from their city apartment to a house in Greenwich, Connecticut. Amy's baby was due near the end of January, so they needed more space. But Kate suspected that Mark, a successful young stockbroker, would have ended up in a place like Greenwich sooner or later anyway.

"Oh, hi, Amy," Kate said. "It's good to hear from you. I've missed you." Even though neither of them attended classes anymore, Kate and Amy had seen each other fairly often before Amy had moved.

"Oh, gosh, I've missed you too. And I'm sorry I didn't call before now, but I've been really busy and tired," Amy told her. "However, I'm glad to report that we're finally sitting on chairs and using regular plates."

Kate laughed. "So, you're all settled in? How do you like it?"

"Oh, I love the house, and I've met a lot of nice people. But it's a lot different from living in Mark's apartment, and sometimes I get a little lonely. I imagine that will change once the baby's born. But, oh, Kate, I'm never going to finish my thesis," she wailed.

"Sure you are. It may take you a little longer, but you'll get it done. I know you. You've put so much time and effort into it already that you won't let yourself give up now."

"Well, I hope you're right. Anyway, what's new with you?"

"I've got a job. That's new."

"Really? What are you doing?"

Kate explained what her job was and ended by saying, "I'm kind of a glorified baby-sitter, but the hours are great and I'm making a little money."

"Oh, Kate, it sounds perfect. And what's the guy like?"

Kate paused and then said, "It's kind of hard to say. He's real good-looking, and he's got this graphic design business, so I guess he's pretty creative. But he's definitely not the warm and friendly type."

"Too bad," Amy said seriously. "But then it's not him you're taking care of anyway." Kate laughed, and Amy went on. "Listen, Kate, we're finally having our housewarming next Saturday. I really want you to come. And you can bring Phil."

"Mmmm. Of course I'll come—but probably not with Phil."

"Oh? Well, you can tell me all about it next weekend. In fact, why don't you plan to stay over Saturday night? I tell you, Kate, it's such a pleasure to be able to issue invitations like that, knowing there's an actual spare bedroom, and not just a sleeping bag on the floor. Anyway, then we'll have time to talk when all the party folks aren't around. So you'll definitely come?"

"I wouldn't miss it. Say hi to Mark for me, and I'll see you next Saturday, about four."

As Kate hung up the phone, she smiled to herself. It would be nice to see Amy. She's a good friend and I don't want to lose touch with her, Kate thought. Unlike some of the people in the university community, Amy would never feel that it was beneath Kate to take on a child-care job. That was the kind of thing Kate liked about her. Even though Amy's husband made quite a bit of money, and their life was very different from Kate's, Amy could always empathize with Kate and see things from her point of view.

As Kate got herself organized in her job, she discovered that it provided an unexpected bonus. The work on her thesis was going better than it ever had before. Somehow just knowing that she had to wrap up her research and writing by two-thirty every afternoon gave her a goal to shoot for. Her day was more structured, and she was working more efficiently. Sometimes she accomplished so much that she allowed herself the luxury of quitting early. The first day this happened she used the extra time to get her hair a much needed trim. But the next time she quit early she went straight to Edgar's Landing. She'd decided that she'd like to walk the route Jessica took home from school. That way if she ever needed to find the little girl between school and home, she'd know where to go.

It was the tail end of Indian summer, and Kate ambled along contentedly with Red, her eyes darting from time to time to the little stream that ran alongside the road. Someday it might be fun for her and Jessica to follow it to its source. As she continued up the road, skirting the woods, she could see why the children were tempted to take a shortcut through it. It was enticing. Quiet and thickly overgrown, this was a real woods that seemed untouched by civilization. I'll bet you can't even see the houses and the roads once you've walked in a few yards, Kate thought. And no one could see you either.

As Kate crested the hill, she saw the clean, modern lines of the one-story school building. It looked cheerful and serene with its playground full of equipment and the large expanse of grass for baseball and other sports. Kate plopped down on the grass beside Red to wait for Jessica. Then another thought crossed her mind. Maybe now would be a good time to let the school know that she was taking care of Jessica.

Tying Red's leash to a tree, Kate walked into the building and soon found the school office.

"Can I help you?" a motherly looking woman asked Kate.

Kate explained who she was and gave the woman her phone number. "It suddenly occurred to me that if Jessica ever gets sick at school and needs to come home early, you could call me. I'm a lot closer than her uncle, and I could pick her up and take her home. I'm usually around during the day."

"That's good to know. I'll put this in her file and in the nurse's file. But of course we'll need to have Mr. Cordell's authorization. He can just write a note for Jessica to bring to school."

"Fine, I'll tell him." Kate smiled and went outside, reminding herself to be sure and mention it to Adam that evening.

It was one of his late nights and he didn't get home until after Jessica was in bed. Kate told him she'd been up to the school and explained about the note.

"That was a good idea," he said. "I'll write it now so I won't forget in the morning."

Adam sat down at the kitchen table and took a pad of paper out of his briefcase. As he wrote, Kate thought how tired he looked. His gray eyes were shadowed, and his broad shoulders slumped wearily as he handed her the scrawled note.

"Will that do?"

Kate glanced at it. "I'm sure that's all they'll need." Then more hesitantly she said, "I made some chicken for Jessica and me tonight, and there's some left over, if you haven't eaten."

He looked at her in surprise. "Thank you, but I had

a sandwich at my desk earlier." He paused, and then added, "I don't expect you to prepare meals for me Only for Jessica, and of course for yourself when I'm late. Did anything else happen today that I should know about?"

"No, everything was fine as usual," Kate replied. "But I realized as I walked up to the school that the hillside is very heavily wooded. I don't know if you've been up there and seen the route Jessica takes to come home."

Adam nodded without speaking.

"Well, anyway," Kate went on, "it might be a good idea to remind her not to cut through the woods."

"Yes, I agree that she's a little too young for that," he said.

"Even for older children, I'm not sure it's safe," she persisted.

"What do you mean?" he asked sharply.

Flustered, Kate explained, "Mrs. Higgens told me about a little boy who was left tied to a tree in the woods last winter, and from what she said, I gathered that no one ever found out who did it. But if there's some man in a ski mask doing things like that to children, I think the kids ought to be extra careful."

"For God's sake." Adam's voice sounded annoyed. "I might have known she'd pass along some gossip like that. Mrs. Higgens is a nice woman but she is also something of an alarmist. I had to speak to her a couple of times about filling Jessica's head with scare stories of one kind and another. What she told you was true as far as it went. But my own feeling is that it was some kind of a prank. To a youngster, a teen-ager can look like a grown man, and while I don't approve of kids playing mean tricks on one another, I'm sure there was nothing more sinister about it. Jessica has had enough real problems in her life. I don't see any need to add to her fears."

After a moment Kate said quietly, "I understand."

"I do appreciate your concern," he said in a kinder tone. "And I know Jessica is very happy that you've come to work for us."

Recognizing the note of dismissal, Kate put on her jacket and said good night to Adam. On the way home she thought: He may well be right. It probably was just kids, and they don't realize how dangerous their pranks could be. And I can see his point about not frightening Jessica if it isn't necessary. But he sounded so cold, almost harsh, when he talked about it.

As she drove into the parking lot of her apartment building, she wondered if Adam behaved the same way toward other people, or if it was just her. If he'd been so unapproachable with his wife, Kate could understand why she'd left him. With an inward sigh, she thought, he's another one—attractive and intelligent but with no ability to relate to other people. Then she smiled. Well, at least she wasn't dating this one.

Chapter 3

Late afternoon sunlight slanted through the trees as a gentle breeze rustled the yellowing leaves on the wooded hillside. The road leading up toward the school was empty of traffic. The only sound that broke the quiet was the hollow clonk of a rock against a tree, followed by a muted splash as it fell into the stream beside the road. The sound was repeated at regular intervals.

A small wiry figure was standing at one side of the road, at a point where it became level. The girl, dressed in jeans and a blue sweatshirt, looked as if she were practicing to become a major-league pitcher. Her school bag lay on the ground beside her, along with a heap of stones and small rocks. She might have been eight or nine years old. Scowling with concentration, she picked up a rock, took careful aim, and threw it at the trunk of a large tree directly across the road. As it hit squarely, she grinned. "Got it! That makes two in a row!" Then she bent to pick up another stone.

Her attention was so completely focused on the task she had set herself that she didn't notice the big green car coming up the hill. It was still nearly fifty yards away when she made her next throw. Then she saw it and stood still, waiting for it to go by.

With a muffled roar, the car gathered speed. As it neared the girl, it swerved deliberately, crossed the oncoming lane, and headed directly for her. Startled, she had no time to react before it was upon her. With a sickening crunch, the big car hit the child head-on. The car didn't slow, and her small body flew into the air and slammed down onto the wide green hood before sliding off. It lay limp as a rag doll in the center of the road.

The driver now lifted his foot from the accelerator, letting the car slow to normal speed, and steered back across the road into his own lane. He glanced into his rearview mirror and then looked briefly toward the wooded hillside. A flash of red color caught his eye and he glimpsed a child standing immobilized among the trees. He stamped hard on the gas again and disappeared up the road.

The child in the red sweater stood frozen in shock for several long moments. Then she heard the sound of loud music, and a car came up the road, windows open and radio blaring. It jerked to a halt and someone yelled, "God! Look at that!" She saw two teen-age boys jump out and run toward the crumpled body in the road before she turned and fled through the trees.

Kate glanced at her watch and walked out onto the front porch. It was after four—Jessica should be coming along soon from her Brownie troop meeting up at school. She shaded her eyes against the rays of the autumn sun and absently ruffled Red's floppy ears.

"Let's go meet Jessica," she said to him. They went down the steps and out to the sidewalk, and Kate saw Jessica walking slowly toward home.

As she came nearer, Kate saw with concern that the child's face was pale and she looked droopy and tired. She greeted Kate with none of her usual bounce and enthusiasm.

"Are you okay, Jessica? Do you feel all right?"

"Yes," the little girl answered, but her voice didn't carry much conviction.

Kate took her hand, and when they got inside, she helped her take off her backpack and her red cardigan. Then she put her hand on the girl's forehead.

"You feel a little warm, Jessica. I think maybe it would be a good idea for you to take a nap."

"I don't like naps," Jessica told her fretfully.

"Well, you don't have to sleep then if you don't want to, but I'd like you to rest for a while."

The child allowed herself to be led up the stairs. While Kate hung up her Brownie uniform Jessica picked up Baby and clutched her tightly in her arms. Then she climbed onto the lower bunk and pushed some of the stuffed animals aside to make a nest for herself.

"I'm not going to sleep, so I don't have to be in my own bed," she said with a flash of her usual determination. "I can rest on this bed with Baby."

"Okay." Kate smiled at her and drew the curtains closed. "But I want you to really rest—no reading."

Jessica nodded and lay down, and Kate covered her with a faded patchwork quilt. Then Jessica asked softly, "Kate? Will you stay here with me while I rest?"

Touched by the child's trust in her, Kate replied, "I'll sit here in the chair for a while."

Ten minutes later she looked at Jessica and saw that she'd fallen asleep, one arm pillowing her head and the other holding Baby close beside her. Kate tiptoed out of the room and pulled the door to, leaving it open just a crack.

Downstairs Red moved ahead of her and stood in the kitchen doorway with an imploring look. Kate shook her head and laughed. "Oh, all right," she told him. "But if you keep this up, your dinner's going to be served at breakfast time." She went to the broom closet in the kitchen and lifted the top of the small plastic garbage can inside. Red quivered and ran in small circles of enthusiasm as Kate scooped dry dog food from the garbage can into his bowl. She set the bowl down beside his water dish, and Red eagerly began crunching up the kibble. "You certainly make me feel like I'm a good cook!" she said.

Undecided about how to use this unexpected free time, Kate looked around the kitchen. There was no point in starting dinner until she found out how Jessica felt when she got up from her nap. Some toast and a bowl of soup might be all she'd want.

Maybe I'll write to Mom, she thought. It's been quite a while. Kate's mother still lived in the small town on the St. Croix River in Minnesota where Kate had grown up. A widow now, she led a busy life, active in community and church affairs, but she always had time to keep up a voluminous correspondence with relatives and old friends. Even though Kate called her mother fairly frequently, she knew her mother secretly preferred chatty, newsy letters that she could select bits from and read to her friends.

Casting about for something to write on, Kate took a sheet of school paper from Jessica's backpack. Then she sat down at the kitchen table and began to write. Kate knew her mother would be happy to hear that the thesis was going so well. She smiled to herself as she remembered her mother going out and buying a complete set of Jane Austen's novels in paperback when she'd found out what the subject of Kate's thesis would be. She'd already been asking Kate what she wanted for Christmas this year, so Kate decided to put in a few ideas now. Her mother was not a last-minute person, and to her Christmas was just around the corner.

By the time Kate finished her letter, it was almost five-fifteen, and starting to get dark. I'd better go up and see how Jessica's doing, she thought. She must have really needed this nap. I wonder if I should wake her or let her sleep? She folded up the letter, put it in her purse, and went quietly up the stairs. The house was silent except for the clicking of Red's toenails as he followed her across the hall and into Jessica's room.

Not wanting to turn on a light and startle the child, Kate stepped softly over to the bed. In the shadowy darkness it was hard to distinguish a child's sleeping form from the lumpy shapes of stuffed animals scattered around on the bedspread. Bending closer, Kate realized with a start that Jessica wasn't there.

Kate stood up and called, "Jessica?" There was no answer. Crossing the hall, she pulled open the bathroom door, but Jessica wasn't there either. She walked back into Jessica's room and switched on the light. Now she could see that the quilt wasn't on the bed and neither was Baby. Puzzled, Kate wondered if Jessica could have decided to sleep in another bed. She walked into the guest room and into the master bedroom but saw no signs of the child. She wasn't alarmed yet, but when she opened the door to Adam's study and still did not see Jessica, Kate felt an irrational spasm of fear.

She stopped and thought a moment. Could the child be hiding as a joke? It wasn't like her, but it was certainly possible. Back in Jessica's room, Kate looked under the bed, in the kneehole of the desk, and inside the closet. Taking a step up the ladder, she looked into the top bunk. There simply weren't any other places for a little girl to hide. Annoyed, Kate stood in the center of the room and called out, "Jessica, if you're hiding, I want you to come out right now. This has gone on long enough." She waited for a long moment, but nothing stirred in the house. She repeated her tour of the whole floor, checking every hiding place and even looking in the linen closet, although there was hardly enough room for even a small child to crawl in. There was no sign at all of Jessica. The child seemed to have vanished.

Maybe she'd gone up to the third floor. The door at the bottom of the stairs was closed as usual. She opened it and called up the stairs. "Jessica, are you up there?" There was no response, but Kate switched on the light and went up anyway. The single bulb fixture gave little illumination, but even in that dim light Kate could see that there really was nowhere to hide. She saw only the large and small easels standing side by side, and a couple of kitchen chairs. The haunting faces on the canvases seemed to watch her from where they stood flat against the wall. There was a door at the far end of the studio opening onto a storage closet under the roof. Kate yanked it open and peered inside. It was jammed full of cartons and unused suitcases.

"Jessica! This isn't a game anymore!" Kate called as she went down the stairs to the second and then the first floor. She paused in the living room to listen for a telltale giggle. The only sound she heard was Red's snuffling as he stuck his nose into her hand.

"Where is she, Red?" Kate asked the dog. "Help me find Jessica." He looked puzzled but wagged his tail tentatively. Obviously something was wrong, but he didn't have a clue what to do about it.

Could Jessica have snuck downstairs while she was up on the third floor? Kate asked herself. She went from room to room, turning on lights and looking in every possible nook and cranny. Peering behind the couch, and thrusting aside the coats in the coat closet, she had to conclude that Jessica wasn't anywhere on the first floor.

Kate's heart pounded, and she breathed in short, shallow breaths. She stopped to think. There was only one other possibility—the basement. Jessica normally didn't like to go down there. It was too dark and spooky. Nevertheless, Kate opened the cellar door, flipped on the lights, and started down the stairs. Here there were lots of places Jessica could be hidden— behind the furnace, beneath the laundry table or old-fashioned laundry tubs, in the canning cupboard or the fruit cellar, or beside the ancient wicker rocker awaiting repairs. Kate got the flashlight from the laundry room and checked them all. No Jessica.

Returning to the first floor and still clutching the flashlight, Kate thought, Jessica couldn't have been running around the house hiding in different places ahead of me. I think I would have heard her. And I'm sure Red would have joined in her game. He'd have been following around after her everywhere she went. I've searched the whole house, but she couldn't have left. She had nothing on but her underwear. An image of Jessica, wrapped in her quilt out on the porch swing talking to Baby, leaped to Kate's mind.

"Stay here, Red," she commanded. Flashlight in hand, Kate went outside. As she had feared would be the case, Jessica was not calmly sitting on the porch swing. Going down the steps, Kate flashed her light into the shrubbery on both sides. The narrow, cool beam played over the grass and under the trees, but she saw nothing. Kate worked her way around to the back of the house and then moved on to the garage. But its door was securely locked, and there was no other way to get in. She finished her circle of the house, looking and calling Jessica's name. But even as she did, she knew it was an exercise in futility.

As she re-entered the house, Kate saw Red standing in the entry hall looking forlorn, his tail drooping. He started to whimper and Kate knelt down and hugged him, as much to give herself courage as to reassure him. She raised her head and once again called, "Jessica!" Her voice sounded perilously close to tears. "Please tell me where you are."

Kate got up and started pacing through the house. She'd searched absolutely everywhere. Jessica couldn't be here, yet she had to be. Kate went into the living room, through the dining room, through the kitchen, and back into the entrance hall. Red padded worriedly behind her. Kate's hands clenched and unclenched, and then she wrapped her arms around herself. She swept back the curtains, looked behind them, and then stared sightlessly out at the now inky black night. Where can she be, where can she be? The refrain kept running through her mind. She couldn't come up with an answer.

The front porch light was on, the back porch light was on, almost every light in the house was on. Kate stood at the kitchen door searching the night for a sign of a small figure outside. Abruptly she turned away. Jessica wasn't outside; she was somewhere here in the house. She had to be. I'll look some more, Kate thought half coherently. Striding to the stove, she yanked open the oven door and peered inside.

Suddenly she stopped and straightened up. "What are you doing, Kate?" she said aloud. "Pull yourself together." She glanced at the clock on top of the stove. Only ten to six, not much more than half an hour since she'd started searching. Yet she'd done everything she could think of.

I'll have to call Adam, she thought. Maybe he could think of something she'd overlooked. Don't sound hysterical, she warned herself. She dialed the number and took a deep breath as she listened to the ringing at the other end. What if he had gone to a late meeting or out to dinner?

"Yes?" Adam's voice sounded abrupt.

"Oh, Mr. Cordell, it's Kate. I'm sorry to bother you at the office but I'm terribly worried. I can't find Jessica."

"What do you mean?"

"Well, she was taking a nap and when I went up to look in on her, she was gone. I've looked everywhere I can think of. I wondered if she could be hiding from me. She doesn't usually play games like that," she rushed on, "but is there someplace special where she likes to hide?"

"There isn't any I know of. Could she have gone out-side?"

"I suppose she might have slipped out while I was upstairs looking for her. But she wasn't even dressed!"

Kate heard her voice rising. "I've looked outside, all around the house. Maybe I should ask the neighbors to help me search for her or call the police."

"No," he said sharply. "I'll come right home. Stay in the house until I get there." He hung up and so, after a moment, did Kate. She stood there, her hand on the phone. In a detached way she realized she'd called him Mr. Cordell and wondered why she'd done that.

It would be at least half an hour, maybe longer, before Adam got home. The silent house seemed to mock her. Kate gave herself a mental shake. I can't stand around here doing nothing while I wait for him. With desperate resolve she thought, I'll look through the house once more.

This time Kate shot home the bolts on both the front and back doors. Jessica could get them undone, but it would take her a few minutes. If she's in the house, she's not going to slip out without my knowing.

Kate decided to start with the basement and work her way up. She picked up the flashlight from where she'd left it on the kitchen counter, and marched down the stairs. Slowly and methodically she made her way from one end of the basement to the other. She opened every door and cupboard and searched them all the way to the back. She looked inside any box large enough to hold a curled-up child. Unused furniture was pulled away from the walls, a stack of storm windows and screens was shifted to reveal spider webs behind them. As she opened an old steamer trunk, she caught her breath. There was Jessica's quilt. But as she grasped it in her hand it proved to be just a pile of rags.

When she'd finished in the basement, she started on the first floor. But by the time she'd worked her way up to Adam's studio at the top of the house she was brushing away tears of frustration and fear. Jessica's got to be here, she thought. What will I do if she isn't?

The big room was just as empty as it had been before. There was no point in fooling herself. Not even a mouse could hide here. The only possible place was the storage cupboard at the far end. Wearily Kate opened its door. The space under the roof was still filled with cartons that were taped shut and suitcases covered with ages of dust. As she prepared to start shifting the piles of stuff, Kate said softly, almost hopelessly, "Oh, Jessica, please be here."

There was a slight scuffing sound and then a little voice quavered, "Kate?"

With a sob Kate cried, "Jessica!"

The little girl crawled out through an impossibly small space between the boxes, still clutching Baby and dragging her quilt behind her. Kate swept her up into a crushing embrace. "Oh, Jess, honey, I was so worried! What were you doing up here?"

Jessica looked at her with a solemn tear-stained face. "I had to get away. I heard noises."

"What noises, honey?"

"The bad men. They were coming to get me in my room. I had to hide so they couldn't find me. I was real scared."

Kate rocked the child in her arms. "I bet you were, honey, but it's okay now. No one's going to get you. Not while I'm here." She set Jessica down on the floor and took her hand. "Come on, sweetheart, let's go downstairs and have some cocoa and wait for Uncle Adam to get home."

CHAPTER 4

IN HER NIGHTIE and bathrobe, Jessica sat at the kitchen table watching Kate make French toast for her supper. Jessica was unusually quiet and she seemed content just to be with Kate in the cosy kitchen. As she put the plate down in front of Jessica and poured her some cocoa, Kate looked into Jessica's face. "You know there weren't really any bad men, don't you, Jessica? I was here all the time. It was really just a bad dream, or something in your imagination."

Jessica nodded slowly. "Yes, I guess it was."

When Jessica was finished eating, the two of them went into the living room. As they sat together on the couch to read a story, Kate listened for the sound of Adam's white Datsun pulling up in the driveway. When he arrived, Red barked a welcome and Kate jumped up to meet him at the door. "I found her—everything's fine," she said in an undertone as Jessica joined them.

Adam picked Jessica up in a bear hug and rested his cheek on her dark hair. "Is everything okay, Jess?" he asked her.

"Yes." She gave him a wan smile

"Were you scared?" His voice was gentle, and the little girl nodded.

As he put her back down he said, "Want to tell me what happened?" Jessica shook her head and he went on. "All right. But you know, Kate was really worried when she couldn't find you. And so was I. Next time you're scared try to remember that Kate is here. You don't have to hide."

They all moved into the living room, and Adam noticed the book lying open on the couch. He suggested that Kate and Jessica read a little longer and then it would be time for Jessica to go to bed. The little girl snuggled up against Kate on the couch while Adam took his chair opposite them. As Kate finished the next chapter in *The Wind in the Willows*, Jessica's eyes were drooping.

Kate closed the book and Adam got up to take Jessica's hand. "Say good night to Kate, Jess."

The little girl did as she was told and then added, "But you'll come up and kiss me good night after I'm in bed, won't you, Kate?"

Kate and Adam exchanged a glance and then Kate said, "Sure, honey. Run along now and I'll be up in a few minutes." Once Jessica and Adam were on the stairs, she leaned back and sighed. The last couple of hours had seemed like an eternity. She hoped she'd never have to go through that again.

When she'd given Jessica her good night kiss, and she and Adam were downstairs again, he said, "Can you stay a few moments and tell me what happened?"

Kate summoned up her energy. "Of course."

She sank back down on the couch and Adam gave her a sympathetic look. "Would you like a drink or a glass of wine or something? You look as if you could use one."

Kate smiled gratefully. "A glass of white wine would be wonderful." She started to get up.

"No, no. I'll get it," Adam told her. He returned with two glasses and handed one to Kate. Then he bent to light the fire that was laid in the big fireplace. When he'd settled himself once again in his chair, he asked, "Well, what happened?"

As completely yet concisely as she could, Kate told him what had taken place that afternoon, starting with Jessica's arrival home from school. She explained that she'd wanted Jessica to rest because the little girl had looked pale and feverish. When she got to the point of describing where she'd finally found Jessica, Adam shook his head in relief. "Thank God it wasn't anything worse than that," he said. "Although it all must have been quite harrowing for you. I'm awfully glad you were here and kept looking until you found her."

"It was pretty scary," Kate admitted. "The real problem is that I don't understand what triggered the whole thing. She was asleep when I left her room. Maybe she had a nightmare because she wasn't feeling very well. But she never cried out or made any sound at all. I'm sure I would have heard her if she had. She just crept out of her room and up the stairs."

Adam got up and poured them each another glass of wine. "I'm sorry this happened," he said. "I thought she was getting over some of the problems she had after her parents' death. Right after the crash she was terrified of being alone. Gradually that started getting better, but she still had a lot of fearful fantasies." He walked toward the window and then turned to face Kate. "I don't know much about children, so I had a talk with a friend of mine who's a psychiatrist. He said I shouldn't be too concerned about it. These kinds of fears apparently are a normal reaction to trauma, and Jessica's losing her parents so tragically certainly was traumatic. My friend told me that the most important thing was to make Jessica feel loved and secure. Eventually she'll stop having fantasies like these, he thinks. But I guess it's going to take longer than I'd imagined."

Kate looked up at the tall, handsome man standing

across from her, his face full of concern. He cares a lot about Jessica, she thought. Quietly she said to him, "Thank you for telling me."

Walking back toward the window again, Adam said over his shoulder, "Well, it's only right that you should know. Jessica has already formed quite an obvious attachment to you, and I'd like you to know that I appreciate all the care and attention you give her." His voice had again taken on its customary coolness. "I don't want you to blame yourself for what happened today. You did the right thing, and that's as much as anyone can expect."

Clearly, he had nothing further to say, so Kate got up and took her wineglass to the kitchen. While she was putting on her sweater and picking up her bag she thought, when he's talking about Jessica, he really sounds almost human. Too bad he isn't that way talking about anything else. Saying, "Good night. See you tomorrow," she left.

The next morning Adam called Kate. "I'm sorry to phone you so early, but I wanted you to know that Jessica seems fine now. She wants to go to school, so you can just come at your usual time."

Kate barely had a chance to say, "All right," before he'd hung up.

She worked all through the morning and then made herself a sandwich for lunch. While she ate, she read that day's *Herald Statesman*. In the second section, a short article with an Edgar's Landing dateline caught her eye.

Police have no leads yet in yesterday's tragic hit-and-run death of Rosemary Donegan, nine years old, a fourth-grade student at the local elementary school. Chief Caruso of the Edgar's Landing force said this was the first such fatality in more than twelve years. "We're proud of our safety record in this town," he said. When asked if he expected to apprehend the hit-and-run driver, he replied, "You bet I do." Anyone with information is asked to call the Edgar's Landing police department.

What a terrible thing to happen, Kate thought with a shudder. I wonder where it happened? Poor little kid, and her poor family.

Finishing her work around two o'clock, Kate decided to stop at the Edgar's Landing market on her way up to the house. More and more, she had taken over the grocery shopping, and Adam left money for her each week to buy whatever she and Jessica wanted to eat. Jessica had been asking her to get a frozen pizza she especially liked, and Kate thought this would be a good time to have it, after the troubled afternoon the girl had had yesterday.

She stood in the express checkout lane with the pizza and a few other items. When she reached the checker, the older woman greeted her with recognition.

"Hi, how are you today? That's a real good brand of pizza—it's the only one my husband will eat." She rang up the total and began putting the things in a bag while Kate got out her money. "Did you hear about the hit-and-run yesterday? Isn't it just awful? I felt so bad when I heard. I knew Rosemary, I had her in my Sunday school class a couple of years ago. I don't know what I'm going to say to her mother at the wake. I told my husband, 'They've just got to do something about these crazy teen-agers driving so fast all the time.' "

Kate nodded as she handed over a ten-dollar bill. "Where did it happen?" she asked.

"Oh, it was on that road that goes up to the school," the woman replied. "That's what's so sad—it wasn't even on one of the busy streets."

Kate nodded in agreement. Pocketing her change, she thought, I wonder what I should say to Jessica about it.

She's sure to have heard all about the accident in school today. Maybe I'd better let her bring it up and take it from there.

While she waited for Jessica to come home from school, Kate realized that her job was giving her a new appreciation of the complexities of parenthood. Taking care of a child meant dealing with a lot of things that had never crossed her mind before. It occurred to her that her own mother and father had no doubt gone through similarly difficult situations that Kate had been blithely unaware of.

But when Jessica arrived home, she didn't say a word about Rosemary Donegan. She was in good spirits and asked Kate if they could go down to the park and play on the big swings. Kate snapped on Red's leash, and the three of them set off, scuffing through the fallen leaves.

"How was school today, Jessica?" Kate asked. It was her usual question, but she waited for the answer with some trepidation.

"Fine," the girl replied. "I got all my problems right in math and we got to have gym outside and we played freeze tag."

"That sounds like fun," Kate told her. She cautioned herself, Jessica will talk about it when she's ready. Don't push.

At the park, Kate stood near the fence with Red and watched Jessica pump higher and higher. She could remember that exhilarating feeling, almost like flying, your toes looking as though they could touch the trees. It was good to see the little girl enjoying this purely physical pleasure, especially in light of everything Adam had said last night. Jessica had been through so much emotional distress. She needed a chance for childish, unthinking fun. Kate felt a glow of satisfaction when she thought about the warm relationship that had already been established between her and Jessica. The child had told Adam how much she liked her, and Kate knew herself that it was true.

The swing began to slow, flying lower and lower. A woman and two children were walking toward them beside the road, outside the park fence. The boy looked up and called, "Hi, Jessica."

"Hi, Tommy," she replied, still swinging.

Then the younger child stepped out into the roadway. Before she'd taken more than a step or two, her mother yelled at her, "Jennifer! Get out of the street!" The little girl hurriedly returned to her mother's side, but the woman went on, "How many times do I have to tell you? That's how that little girl got killed yesterday—being out in the street. Do you want that to happen to you?"

Kate quickly turned to look at Jessica, but the girl on the swing seemed oblivious. She must have heard what the woman said, but clearly she was trying to pretend she hadn't. I guess she just can't cope with it, Kate concluded. Her own parents were killed in a car accident, and maybe this is too similar for her to deal with.

When they went home, Jessica went upstairs to do her homework while Kate got supper started. She heard Red give a sharp bark, and almost immediately afterward the doorbell rang. "Good boy, Red," she told him as she went to the front door.

On the front porch stood a young man, smiling. He was thin and not very tall, with lank, dirty-looking hair that straggled over his forehead. Kate had never seen him before. Pushing open the outer storm door a little way, she said to him, "Yes?" When he just kept smiling at her, she added, "Can I help you?"

"Is this Mr. Cordell's house?" he asked.

"Yes, it is," she replied, puzzled by his manner.

"Is he here?"

"No," Kate answered, "he's not home right now."

"I'm a friend of his," the young man told her, still smiling in that odd way.

"Oh," Kate said. "I'll tell him you stopped by—what's your name?" As she spoke, she thought he didn't really look like someone who would be a friend of Adam's. His army surplus fatigue jacket looked too big for his scrawny frame, and his grubby jeans and sneakers somehow didn't fit in with Adam's own casual elegance.

"I'm Walter," he said. "I'm a painter too, like Mr. Cordell. Can I come in?" His hand was already on the door handle, and he pulled it toward him and took a step forward. Taken by surprise, Kate grabbed the handle on her side and pulled hard, shutting the door with a bang. "No, I'm sorry," she said as it closed, "but I'll tell him you were here."

He stood there for a few seconds, staring at her through the glass and still smiling his fixed smile. Then he turned and went down the porch steps.

Kate closed the inner door and put the chain on it. What a peculiar guy, she thought with a shiver. He really gave me the creeps. And I sure didn't like the way he tried to pull the door open. As she turned back toward the kitchen, she wasn't certain whether she felt more annoyed or scared.

That evening as she was getting ready to leave, Kate said to Adam, "A strange thing happened this afternoon. Some guy came to the door and tried to come inside. He said his name was Walter and that he's a friend of yours." Noticing Adam's blank look, she went on, "He looks like he's in his early twenties and he's kind of blondish and a little scruffy looking—he said he's a painter, and I wondered if maybe he was a student of yours."

Adam shook his head. "I never taught painting. I have no idea who he is. He didn't tell you his last name?"

"No," Kate said, and Adam shrugged.

"Well, if it's important, he'll get in touch."

As she left, Kate thought, I didn't really believe that Walter person was Adam's friend. But if Adam doesn't even know who he is, I'm certainly glad I didn't let him into the house. She felt a little shudder of disquiet—it had been an unsettling incident.

Saturday afternoon, Kate set off in her chartreuse Rabbit for Greenwich. She'd looked in the paper that morning, but there had been no more news about the hit-and-run accident in Edgar's Landing. She wondered if it was best to simply go along with Jessica's need to deny that the child had been killed. Perhaps she should ask Adam about it at some point.

Less than an hour later, she found her friend's stone and shingle two-story house. It reminded Kate of houses she had seen in the middle west—solid and comfortable but unpretentious. As she got out of the car, Amy came out to meet her. "Oh, Kate, I'm so glad you're here!" Amy threw her arms around Kate and the two women embraced.

Kate gave Amy's protruding belly a pat. "I see that Mark or Amy junior is growing. You're a lot bigger than the last time I saw you."

Amy laughed. "Oh, yeah. I'll probably be even bigger before I'm through." She grabbed Kate by the arm. "Come on in and see the house."

They trooped into the living room together, and Kate admired the way Amy had arranged the furniture from her old apartment into this much larger space. "It all takes on a new look here," she said.

Amy gave Kate a complete tour, including the three bedrooms and bath upstairs, and the knotty-pine paneled rec room in the basement. When they were back in the kitchen, Kate said, "It's a great house, Amy. It feels so comfortable."

"Yeah. I think we're going to really like it. Of course, Mark thinks of this as a 'first house.' He figures that in a few years we'll be trading up. And did I tell you that next summer he plans to build a deck off the back?"

Silently Kate said to herself, Mark ought to see my apartment if he thinks this is a starter. But aloud she said to Amy, "Sounds like a good idea. Then the baby can be out there in the warm weather."

"That's what I thought." They heard a car drive up and then Mark's voice.

"Open up, honey, my hands are full."

When Amy had opened the door, he staggered in, laden with a case of bottled beer. "Hi, sweetheart! Hi, Kate! What do you think of our palatial estate?" He dumped the beer on the counter and went back for more.

When he returned, Kate said, "It's great, Mark. I love it."

"Good," he said with a grin. "It's a start at least on what the rising young stockbroker deserves."

Soon the kitchen was filled with party preparations, and Kate helped Mark put the leaf in the dining-room table. Then she and Amy set up the buffet. While Amy tasted the chili and made last-minute adjustments to it, Kate put out the bowls of grated cheese and chopped onions, and made sure there were lots of napkins.

"I didn't bother with hors d'oeuvres," Amy said. "You know how all those starving student types eat. And Joanna said she's bringing some tortillas from the city—I haven't found out where to buy them up here yet. Oh, Kate," she flung her arms around her friend impulsively. "I'm so glad to see you!"

A trickle of guests began to arrive, and it soon became a flood. The house filled with laughter and talk. The crowd was a mixture of young couples Mark and Amy had met in Greenwich and their friends from the city. Kate had a good time, but she was as exhausted as Amy when the last guests finally departed. They flopped on the couch and kicked off their shoes.

"Nice party, Amy," Kate said, wiggling her toes. "And you've met a lot of nice people here. I'm sure you'll find good friends before long."

"Yeah." Amy sighed contentedly. "It was a good party, but I'm wiped out."

      •   •   •

By nine o'clock the next morning, Mark had left to play golf, and the two women were lounging lazily over the Sunday *Times*. "So, Kate, how's the job going? I want to hear all about it," Amy said.

"Well, Jessica, the girl I take care of, is a real sweetie. I like her a lot and I'm actually having fun doing stuff with her. Good practice for motherhood if that day ever comes, don't you think?" Kate laughed, and Amy did too. "But wait till I tell you—she's had a really tragic life." Kate told Amy what she knew about Jessica's parents' death and her coming to live with Adam. "It's amazing that she's as normal and nice as she is. Of course, she's got some problems, but who wouldn't?"

"What kind of problems?" Amy wanted to know.

Kate described what had happened on Thursday, when Jessica had hidden in the storage closet and Kate hadn't been able to find her.

"Good God!" Amy said. "You must have been out of your mind with worry." She looked down at her bulging belly. "Hey, in there, don't listen to this."

Kate smiled. "I was frantic," she admitted. "And Adam was pretty worried too when I called him. But after it was all over, he seemed to think it wasn't very surprising. He said he'd talked to some psychiatrist who said Jessica might have this kind of reaction because of her parents' dying. I don't know—I think she's a pretty resilient child, and she's coping pretty well with everything. She's never done anything like this with me before. I suppose she might do it again, but somehow it's out of character. She's told me exaggerated tales, but she always 'fesses up when I call her on them."

"Well, she probably just needs some time," Amy said. "It's only been a year since they died, right?" When Kate nodded, she went on, "And she's still young. I'm sure she'll settle down, and I'm sure having you around is real good for her. But tell me about Adam. I notice you're on first-name terms."

"Don't get your hopes up, Amy." Kate laughed.

"This is not going to turn into a paperback romance —and don't look like you don't know what I'm talking about. I know you read them—there's a whole pile of them in the room I slept in."

Amy looked sheepish. "Oh, well, Kate. I could tell you they belong to my aunt—"

"But I wouldn't believe you! Anyway, about Adam. I have nothing to complain about. He's perfectly polite and pleasant, but he's the coldest fish I've ever met."

"But how can he resist you?" Amy's eyes twinkled. "There you are every day in his house, and him a single man."

"I don't know." Kate shook her head in mock despair. "But I told you he was married before, and I'll bet his wife had reason to leave. Seriously, Amy, he's gorgeous to look at, but I don't think I really want to get to know him any better."

"That's really a shame." Amy looked at her friend. "I want you to find somebody and be as happy as I am with Mark."

"So do I," Kate said. "But believe me, Adam Cordell is not the one."

By Sunday afternoon, Kate and Amy had caught up on everything in each other's lives. Kate said reluctantly, "I'd better be going home. I've got a job and a thesis to think about tomorrow."

"It was wonderful to have you here. Come back soon," Amy said.

"I will. I had a great time and I love your house."

Kate kissed her friend good-bye and drove off westward to Yonkers. On the way, she reflected that Amy seemed to be enjoying her new life. Kate smiled—she was happy for Amy, and she looked forward to seeing the baby when it arrived.

On Monday there was nothing in the news about the hit-and-run case, and Kate was just as happy that other events had captured the public interest. But that afternoon, as they worked on a jigsaw puzzle, Jessica calmly announced, "I saw the car that hit Rosemary."

Kate looked at her in astonishment. "What do you mean, honey?"

"I saw it," the little girl repeated solemnly. "Rosemary was throwing stones at a tree, and the car came up and hit her on purpose."

"Where were you when you saw this?" Kate wasn't sure if this was one of Jessica's fantasies or not.

Jessica looked down at the puzzle pieces. "I was in the woods." She wouldn't meet Kate's eyes. "I didn't want to tell you that I'd taken the shortcut. Camilla didn't walk home with me after Brownies, so I was walking by myself."

"Jessica, you know you're not allowed to do that." At least it was something Kate could safely say to her.

"I know. I'm sorry. But Camilla's mom came to pick her up and go somewhere," Jessica rushed on, "and I was playing with Wendy behind the bushes, and then she had to go home, but she lives the other way so I had to go by myself."

"I see," Kate said. "Even so, you shouldn't have been cutting through the woods." She put her hand on Jessica's. "Did you really see the car hit Rosemary? Or have you just been thinking about how it might have happened?"

"No. I really truly saw it. I saw Rosemary throwing the stones to hit the tree. And then this big car came up the hill and all of a sudden it went real fast and went across the road and right into her. She wasn't even in the road or anything," Jessica told Kate earnestly. "And then it drove away. And then another car came, and some people got out. And I ran away and came home." She stopped, and then said softly, "I was scared."

Kate reached out and drew the girl toward her. With Jessica on her lap, she said, "I'm sure you were. I would have been scared, too." She stroked the child's hair gently away from her face. "Did you tell your Uncle Adam about it?"

Jessica shook her head. "No. I only told you."

"I think we ought to tell him when he comes home then," Kate said.

Soon after six o'clock, Red barked excitedly, and Adam arrived as Kate was fixing some scrambled eggs for Jessica. "Let me add some for you too. And you can sit down and hear what Jessica saw the other day," Kate said.

Adam gave her a questioning look but sat down at the table and asked, "Well, what did you see, Jess?"

With a little prompting from Kate, Jessica began her story once again. By the time the three had steaming plates of food in front of them, the child had told Adam pretty much what she'd already confided to Kate. He suggested, gently at first and then more strongly, that this was a story just like the bad men in the house the week before. But Jessica insisted that it was really true. Kate could see that Adam didn't believe Jessica, that he thought it was another of her fantasies, but that he was shaken by the child's determination. Wishing she could think of something useful or helpful to add, Kate ate her food and listened as the two of them ran through the story yet again. Finally, when they had finished, Adam said to Jessica, "Why don't you go and play in your room for a little while. I've got to talk to Kate."

Once they were alone, Adam said without preamble, "Do you believe this tale?"

Since Kate had heard Jessica's story earlier and had had time to absorb it, she was able to say, "Yes, I think I do. When she tells an exaggerated version of the truth, she's usually willing to admit it when I press her about it. Even last Thursday when she was so frightened, she agreed with me that the bad men hadn't been real. And now I'm beginning to believe that seeing this terrible thing happen is what caused her to look and act so strange when she came home. Perhaps this is what made her hide in the closet.''

Adam stared at Kate for a moment. Then abruptly he stood up and began clearing the plates from the table. "I don't know," he said. "It's pretty incredible. If it happened the way she says, she's the only witness to a crime that was deliberate, not an accident. That's a distressing thought." He paced from the sink to the stove and back again. "But I have to admit," he said at last, "I think you're right."

They discussed it a little while longer, and finally Adam decided that he would have to inform the police. His hand on the phone, he said to Kate, "I'll see if they have someone who can come up tonight. I want to be here when they talk to her."

Adam ended his phone conversation with the police and told Kate that they were sending someone up right away. "Would it be an imposition for you to stay? I think Jessica might feel better if you were here too."

Kate told Adam that it would be no problem for her, and a few moments later Red let them know that a car had pulled into the driveway.

Detective Roper was a kind-faced man in his late fifties. Adam ushered him into the house and began to explain what Jessica had told them, but the officer held up a hand. "I'd like to speak to the little girl and hear what she has to say directly, if you don't mind, sir."

Adam called Jessica down from her room and introduced Detective Roper. "He just wants to hear what you told us about the accident that happened last week, Jess."

Jessica looked at the detective and waited for him to begin. Finally Roper said pleasantly, "I understand you saw a car hit Rosemary on Thursday. Is that right?"

"Yes," Jessica said reluctantly.

"What exactly did you see?" Roper asked her.

The little girl was silent for a long moment. At last she

whispered, "I don't want to talk about it any more."

"I guess something like that would be pretty frightening," the older man said softly. "Were you scared?"

"Yeah," Jessica admitted.

"What was Rosemary doing when you saw her?"

Jessica looked down at the floor. "I don't know."

"Was she playing in the street?"

"I don't know," Jessica answered again, still looking at the floor.

"Jessica, if you saw what happened, I'd like to hear about it. Do you think the driver of the car knew he hit Rosemary?"

She refused to look at him. "I don't know," she repeated, her voice an almost inaudible whisper.

"Is there anything about what happened that you'd like to tell me?" the detective asked gently.

Jessica shook her head. In the silence that followed, Roper looked at Adam and shrugged. Then Jessica whispered, "Uncle Adam, can I go play in my room?"

"Sure, Jess. Go ahead. I'll be up in a few minutes, honey." After the girl left the room Adam turned to the policeman. "I tell you she rattled off every detail before, once to Kate here and again to me." He looked to Kate for confirmation.

Detective Roper smiled sadly. "Kids are like that sometimes. Don't worry about it. She'll tell us when she's ready. Or she won't. It's one of those things." He turned to Kate. "Did she say anything specific about the car or the driver?"

"No. She was quite definite that Rosemary had been throwing stones across the road at a tree and that the car had accelerated and swerved to hit her. Jessica made a point of saying that Rosemary wasn't on the edge of the road but well off it, and that the driver clearly meant to run her down. But the only thing she said about the car was that it was big."

"That's kind of too bad, because we think we have the car. The Manhattan police towed it after it had been sitting for a couple of days, and they're running some tests on it now. It was stolen from up here in Edgar's Landing. So it would have been nice if she'd told you the color or any other details."

"I'm sorry," Kate said.

"That's okay. But if she should mention anything else, you might just give us a buzz." He looked at his watch and asked apologetically, "Could I possibly use your phone? I'd like to call and tell my wife I'm heading home."

Adam took him to the phone in the kitchen. As Roper dialed and listened to the ringing at the other end, he went on, "You know, kids are funny. I've got four of my own, and they still surprise me with what they come up with. 'Course mine are . . ." Into the phone he said, "Oh, Richie. Hi. It's Dad. Is Mom around? Oh, okay. Well, tell her I've just finished checking out a tip on that hit-and-run and I'll be home soon. I'm down here at the Cordell house on Alder so it won't take more than a couple of minutes." He paused, listening. "Yeah. Well, we can talk about it when I get home." He listened again. "Okay, Richie. Like I said, we'll talk about it."

He hung up and Adam said, "I think I know your son Richie. He's about twenty, isn't he?"

"More like twenty-two now."

There was a pause. Then Adam said, "I'm sorry to have dragged you up here for what turned out to be nothing at all."

"No, no, it was no trouble," Roper assured him. "It's on my way home as a matter of fact—I live just over on Brook Lane." He smiled once again at Adam and Kate. "You did the right thing by calling us, Mr. Cordell. Don't feel bad that it didn't work out. Like I said, kids are funny. But be sure to give us a call if your little girl says anything more."

After Adam showed Detective Roper to the door, he came back in and poured wine for both Kate and himself without asking if she'd like any. "I don't know what to think," he said with a worried look. "To listen to her with Detective Roper you'd think Jessica made the whole thing up. But earlier I was convinced that she hadn't." He frowned and sat wearily in his armchair. "God, I hope this doesn't mean that she's regressing and starting to go through another bad time. I really don't want to send her to a psychiatrist, but if these fantasies continue, I don't know what else I can do."

"Oh, I don't think you should decide to do that just yet," Kate protested. "Of course, you're closer to her than I am, but it seems to me that she's doing pretty well handling problems that would be hard for an older person. If she really did see the accident—well, that's enough to shake anyone up."

"If she did see it, it wasn't an accident," Adam said somberly.

"All the more reason!" Kate responded. "I think she needs her life to be as regular and normal as possible now. If things get worse, I agree that she'll need professional help. But won't you wait to see how it goes?"

He smiled at her—a genuinely warm smile that lit up his normally stern face. "You're a persuasive champion, Kate. I hope Jessica realizes how lucky she is to have you on her side."

CHAPTER 5

THE NEXT DAY, Kate let herself into the Cordell house at three o'clock. She took Red outside and tossed the ball for him a few times. Jessica would be going straight to her tap dance class with her little friend Louise, who lived near the church where the classes were held. Kate glanced at the gray overcast sky and thought that maybe she'd drive down today and pick up Jessica at four-thirty. The long walk home from the Unitarian church was fun when the weather was warm, but now that the days were shorter, it wasn't so appealing.

She went back inside and turned on the lights in the kitchen. Since she had time today, she'd decided to make a big pot of spaghetti sauce. She and Jessica would have some tonight, and she could put the rest in the freezer for another time. Kate smiled to herself as she began chopping the onions. Having this big, well-equipped kitchen to work in and all the empty space in the freezer was turning her into quite a little home-maker, she thought with amusement. And she'd found she enjoyed cooking for someone besides herself. It was gratifying that Jessica seemed to like almost everything Kate fixed for her and was even willing to try new and unfamiliar foods. Kate was careful to label everything she put in the freezer, but she couldn't help noticing that some of the containers were back in the cupboard, clean and empty, the next time she looked. She suspected that Adam was helping himself, even though he never mentioned it. He's a strange one, she thought; I really can't figure him out.

Once the onions were sautéed, she dumped them into the big cast-iron enameled pot and put the meat in the skillet to brown. As she broke it up with a wooden spoon, she wondered how Jessica was doing. That whole business last night was confusing and a little upsetting for me, she realized. I still think that Jessica saw the other girl get hit, but maybe it didn't happen quite the way she told me. She could have been exaggerating, or remembering it with a kind of overlay from her parents' death. After all, they died in a car crash and she must have a fear of the damage cars can do to people. I wish I understood more about how her mind works.

Kate opened three large cans of tomatoes, added them to the onions, adjusted the heat, and began stirring the contents of the pot. She kept trying to resolve her feelings about the events of the previous evening. The fact that Jessica had told Adam exactly the same story she'd told Kate, and hadn't budged even when he'd doubted her, seemed good evidence that she'd been telling the truth. And really, it was hard to blame her for not wanting to tell it all again to a third person, one she didn't even know. It must have been a frightening, threatening experience in lots of ways—it was surprising that she'd been able to tell anyone.

The sauce was almost finished except for the seasoning. Kate looked in the cupboard and found basil and oregano as well as a little jar of minced garlic. Adding a bit of this and a little of that, she gave the sauce a final stir and put the lid on the pot. She was still preoccupied with the hit-and-run. I wonder if the police have gotten any closer to finding the driver, she thought. I hope they'll find out who did it. Of course, it was unreasonable to expect that anyone who was driving a stolen car would stop at the scene of an accident. And as it had turned out, it wouldn't have done much good—the little girl was already dead. Nevertheless, she thought angrily, there's no excuse for driving off like that. She could have been alive. I suppose anyone can have an accident, although people ought to know that children are walking home from school in the afternoon. But to leave a child injured or dead is unforgivable.

She was slightly surprised to find herself so vehement. She realized that her relationship with Jessica had made her protective and concerned about anything that meant danger to a child.

The phone rang, and she picked it up. "Cordell residence."

"Miss Jamison? This is Janet Black—Louise's mother?"

"Oh, hi," Kate said. "What's up?" She looked at her watch. It was almost three-thirty, and the girls should be just starting dance class. Had it been canceled for some reason?

"I wanted to let you know. The girls are both here at our house. They're kind of upset—they had a little scare while they were walking to dance class and they came here instead."

"What happened?" Kate asked quickly

"Well, I'm not sure it was really anything. But Jessica says a man stopped his car and tried to pick them up. As I say, it's hard to tell if it was anything to be alarmed about. But I thought I ought to call you."

"Oh, yes, thanks. I'm glad you did." Kate paused and Mrs. Black went on, "I'm going to walk the two of them to class now, and I think I'll just stay there and watch. I don't want them to worry about this."

"That's nice of you," Kate told her. "I'll drive down

to the church in a little while, and then when class is over I can bring Jessica home. That will probably work out best."

"Fine, then, I'll see you there."

Hanging up the phone, Kate thought, Now what? I guess for Jessica, any frightening incident has a lot of aftereffects. This sounds like the bad men coming to get her all over again. I'll have to try hard to reassure her until she gets over this. Mrs. Black had made it sound as if Louise hadn't said anything about the man, only Jessica. How long would Jess keep perceiving everything in terms of her own secret fears?

Turning off the stove, Kate gathered up her jacket and car keys and started toward the door. The phone rang again and she turned back to answer it. "Cordell residence."

For a moment there was silence, but before Kate could say anything more, a soft voice began to whisper. "What are little girls made of? What are little girls made of?" There was a brief pause, and then the whisper resumed slowly, "Nothing that's nice, nothing that's nice. That's what little girls are made of."

Kate waited and then said sharply, "Who is this?" But the person on the other end of the phone was silent, just listening over the open line between them.

Kate hung up the phone, gave Red a good-bye pat, and went out to her car. I guess kids always do stuff like that, she thought. I remember when Prince Albert in the can was the best joke around. But I hope this one doesn't make these joke phone calls into a habit. There was something unpleasant about the twisted nursery rhyme—it was more nasty than funny, and she'd just as soon not hear any more like it.

Kate drove down to the church and went inside to the community room where fourteen serious-faced little girls were counting aloud as they practiced a new routine. The clicking of their shiny black tap shoes echoed off the bare floor. The kids might not have been completely synchronized, but they were definitely enthusiastic. Kate gave Jessica a little wave and then walked over to sit with Louise's mother.

"Hi," she said. "How's everything? Are Louise and Jessica still feeling upset?

Mrs. Black shook her head. "No, I don't think so, they seem fine now. They'll have forgotten all about it by tomorrow. But I must tell you, I was a little upset myself. I didn't want to make too much of it in front of the girls, but you know, I don't like the idea of some guy stopping his car to talk to them and then following them along the street."

"What?" Kate asked in surprise.

"Oh, yes. What they told me was a little confused—they're only seven, after all. But both of them say there was some guy in a car who pulled over to the curb and stopped and was talking to them. Jessica says he told them to get in the car and kind of beckoned to them. Louise doesn't seem to know what he was saying at all. They didn't answer and just kept on walking, and he apparently followed along real slowly, just keeping up with them in the car. That's when they got scared and ran to our house."

"Good Lord! I'm not surprised they were scared—I would have been myself. That's really creepy. Who was this guy?"

Mrs. Black shook her head. "I have no idea. They can't even seem to remember what color his car was. You know how it is—one says it was green, the other says no, it was black, and then they both think maybe it was brown." She glanced toward the line of little girls and then back at Kate. "There's really no way to find out who it was, and even if we could, what could we say?"

"I guess you're right," Kate replied. "I'm glad they were close to your house, though, and that they had the presence of mind to just run there.''

"Oh, yes, that's what I said. I told them they did exactly the right thing.'' The woman sighed. "It's always a problem with little girls. You don't want them to grow up afraid of their own shadows, but on the other hand, you can't let them go around trusting everyone they run into. It's just a fact of life. I can remember my own mother telling me exactly the same things I tell Louise. And she was right. Even in a small town like this, you just never know what strange ideas people might have.''

The girls were now clustered around the tap teacher, and it looked as if class was almost over. Kate stood up. "Thanks again for calling me and explaining what happened,'' she said. "I'm sure I'll hear about it from Jessica on the way home.''

Mrs. Black smiled. "I'm sure you will,'' she agreed. "Jessica's got a good little imagination and she's always got some kind of dramatic story to tell. So I wanted to make sure you heard about it from me first.''

Jessica was very quiet on the way home, and Kate didn't want to ask her about the man in the car. When they got to the house, Jessica went straight upstairs. In a couple of minutes Kate followed her, Jessica's dance bag in her hand. She walked into Jessica's room and found the girl huddled on the lower bunk, Baby clutched fiercely in her arms. Jessica looked up, and Kate was distressed to see tears sliding down her cheeks.

"Jessica, honey, what's the matter?'' She sat on the bed and cuddled the little girl on her lap.

"I'm afraid, Kate,'' Jessica wailed softly. "The bad man in the car was going to take me away and I could never come back. I'd never see you and Uncle Adam ever anymore!'' She flung her arms around Kate and held on tightly.

"Tell me what happened, Jess.''

Jessica sniffled a bit. "Me and Louise were walking to tap class when a man stopped and talked to us.''

"He was in a car?" Kate asked.

Jessica nodded. "Yeah, and he leaned over and said, 'Get in the car, Jessica, I'll give you a ride home.' "

"Are you sure he said your name?"

"Uh-huh."

"Well, maybe he was someone you know. Was he somebody's dad or maybe one of your friends' brothers? Maybe you've met him but you didn't remember?"

Jessica shook her head vigorously. "No, I didn't know him at all. And he sounded mean. So me and Louise kept on walking, but then he kept following us in the car and it was too scary, so we ran to Louise's house."

"That was a good thing to do," Kate told her. "You shouldn't ever get in a car with someone you don't know really well. So that was smart of you girls."

"But I was so scared," Jessica said. "I don't want a bad man to come and get me. What if a bad man came and killed me?"

"Oh, Jessica, honey, that's not going to happen." Kate hugged the small body close. "And I'm very proud of you. Even though you were scared, you acted so grown-up." She reached for a Kleenex to wipe Jessica's face, and then gave her another quick squeeze. "Now, do you have any homework to do?" When Jessica said she didn't, Kate told her, "We're having spaghetti for dinner and I have to go and start the water for the noodles. Would you like to watch some TV?"

" 'Wonder Woman'?" Jessica asked eagerly.

Kate looked at her watch and then smiled. "Sure, why not?"

Downstairs in the living room Kate turned on the TV set and left the girl happily mesmerized by Wonder Woman's exploits. She went into the kitchen, and while she put on water to boil and fed the dog, she considered what Jessica had told her.

The more she thought about it, the stranger today's

incident seemed. It just didn't sound like the sort of
thing a little girl, let alone two of them, could make up.
And Jessica was very definite that it was no one she
knew. Kate paused in the middle of setting the table as
an unpleasant possibility struck her. Could it have been
the hit-and-run driver? If Jessica had seen him, perhaps
he had seen her watching. And now that she thought
about it, the girl had been wearing the same red cardigan today she'd had on last Thursday. She wore it
almost every day; maybe that's how he recognized her.
But that didn't explain how he'd known her name.

Confused and worried, Kate called Jessica to dinner.
As they sat at the table, Kate asked her, "Jessica, do
you think the man in the car today was the same person
who ran over Rosemary?"

Jessica stared at her for a moment. Then she said, "I
don't know. I don't think so; it wasn't the same car."

"It wasn't? You're sure?"

"Yeah. That other one was big. The one today was
sort of regular." The child took another bite and said,
"Kate, did Rosemary go to heaven?"

Kate didn't know what to say. She had no idea what
kind of religious training Jessica had had or what she'd
been told about her parents' death. As she cautiously
felt her way toward an answer on this delicate subject,
another part of Kate's mind continued along its previous train of thought. Jessica's statement that the two
cars weren't the same seemed to confirm Kate's suspicion that the man today was in fact the hit-and-run
driver. The police had already located the hit-and-run
car. Of course the man was driving a different one now.
But Jessica hadn't heard the policeman tell them about
the stolen car being found. It all fit together.

After dessert, the two of them cleared the table and
put the dishes in the dishwasher. "Jess?" Kate asked.
"Do you think you'd be willing to talk to that nice policeman who was here last night and tell him what happened today? It really isn't nice for people to do stuff

like that and scare people. And I'd like you to talk to the policeman so maybe he can find that man and tell him not to do it anymore. Okay?''

"I guess so," Jessica replied slowly.

"Good girl," Kate told her. She dialed the Edgar's Landing police number and asked for Detective Roper. When he came on the line, she explained to him that Jessica had had a scary experience that day. While it wasn't directly related to the hit-and-run, Jessica was willing to talk to him, and Kate thought he ought to hear about it.

Detective Roper arrived about ten minutes later. Kate ushered him in, and noticed that Jessica had gone upstairs to fetch Baby. As she came down again, Kate said, "You remember Detective Roper, honey. I'd like you to just tell him what happened today when you and Louise were walking to tap class."

In contrast to the previous night, Jessica started right in on her story without hesitation. Detective Roper was a good listener, and after Jessica finished her recitation he began cautiously asking a few questions.

Red barked. "Good boy," Kate told him and went to intercept Adam. As he stepped into the entry way he asked, "Whose car's out there? Is somebody here?"

"Yes. It's Detective Roper, the one who was here last night. He's talking to Jessica."

"Oh?" Adam raised his eyebrows in surprise. "So she decided she wanted to tell him her story about the hit-and-run?"

Kate shook her head. "No. Something else happened today." Quickly she told him about the incident.

Adam frowned. "And you thought it necessary to call the police about this?" His voice was cold and disapproving.

Flushing, Kate said hastily, "Well, maybe I should have waited until you got home . . ."

"I think so. This sounds just like all of Jessica's other fantasies and your calling the police only validates it and encourages her to continue this behaviour.''

Adam strode into the living room, leaving Kate to trail behind him. Jessica's face lit up. "Oh, hi, Uncle Adam.''

Detective Roper stood up and held out his hand. "Good evening, Mr. Cordell. I've been having a nice talk with Jessica.''

"Hello," he said to the policeman. Then he gave Jessica a hug and told her it was getting a little late. "Why don't you run up and put on your nightgown and brush your teeth and everything. That way we'll have time for part of your book before bed.''

Jessica scampered up the stairs, leaving the three adults standing together in the living room. "She's a nice kid," Detective Roper said to both of them. "And I got a pretty complete picture of what happened today.''

"Well, from what I can gather it really wasn't anything to bother the police force with," Adam said, not looking at Kate.

Roper smiled. "Well, I'm not sure it had anything to do with our hit-and-run. Although I can see how you might have thought so." He nodded in Kate's direction. "But that doesn't matter. It's always good for us to know about unpleasant incidents. Gives us something to refer to if it happens again. I know that people are hesitant to call the police for things like this," he went on, "but we want to know. Even in a town like this you can't tell what kind of people are hanging around and it helps us do our job when everyone tells us what's going on and keeps us informed.''

"Well, I guess I can see what you mean," Adam said in a more friendly tone than he'd used earlier.

Roper nodded. "Oh, listen, I could tell you stories. I mean, I've lived here close to forty years. It's always been a nice town and it still is, but I can remember when nobody locked their front door. Not that way anymore. I've raised four kids myself—three girls and a boy—and

I know how it feels to worry. 'Course my daughters are all grown and out of the house. Two of them married, and the other one is living with some guy." He shrugged. "And my youngest, Richie. I guess you'd say he's still trying to find himself. Oh, yeah. I know what it's like to raise kids. But it's always better to be safe than sorry." He headed toward the front door. "Not likely we'll really find this creep who's picking on little girls, but we can certainly keep our eyes open. And don't you hesitate to call if anything else strange pops up. 'Night.''

CHAPTER 6

AFTER DETECTIVE ROPER left, Adam went to tuck Jessica in and read to her. He seemed to assume that Kate would wait and have a drink and a chat with him after the little girl was in bed. It had become part of the routine without either of them discussing it.

Kate sat in the living room and wondered if Adam would still be angry when he came down. Had she exceeded her authority by calling the police herself? She could hear the murmur of voices floating down the open stairway as Adam continued with the adventures of Rat and Mole. The phone rang. Not wanting Adam to have to interrupt the story, Kate went to answer it.

"Hello. Cordell residence," she said.

There was silence at the other end, and then the click of someone hanging up.

Well, that's annoying, she thought as she hung up herself. They could at least have been polite enough to say, "Sorry, wrong number."

When the chapter was finished and Kate had gone up to give Jessica her good night kiss, she and Adam walked down the stairs together. "What can I give you to drink?" he asked her. "I'm fixing myself a Scotch."

Kate told him that wine was fine. It was a cool evening and Adam lit the fire. It blazed cheerily as they settled once again in the living room with their glasses.

Before Kate could say anything about the events that had transpired, Adam told her, "I think I owe you an apology. I shouldn't have been so quick to criticize. Obviously Roper thought your calling was entirely appropriate. And, I guess, upon reflection, I do too. It's just that I was worried about what effect it would have on Jessica." He gave her a crooked smile. "Anyway, I'm sorry."

Kate was surprised and relieved at his apologetic tone. "Well, I probably should have waited until you got home, but I didn't know what time that would be, and it seemed pretty important." Adam nodded understandingly and Kate thought, he's really attractive when he's relaxed and in a good mood. "But now it all just seems inconclusive."

Adam looked thoughtful. "I can understand why you're confused," he said. "It is confusing. Jessica doesn't make up these stories on purpose. She's not trying to lie to you, Kate, or to fool you. I believe *she* thinks her stories are true." He took a sip of his drink. "That's where your problem is. When she tells you these fantasies with her big gray eyes all wide and innocent, you say to yourself, 'She must be telling the truth.'"

"But the man in the car was real," Kate protested. "Jessica didn't make him up, Louise saw him too."

Adam smiled at her. "Of course he was real. But I feel certain that he just wanted to ask them where Elm Street is or something like that. Jessica's fears are so close to the surface and her need for reassurance from us is so great that she makes ordinary events into frightening ones. That way she gets the adults she's dependent upon to tell her once more that she's protected and secure."

"That makes a certain amount of sense," Kate said

slowly. "And it explains what happened last Thursday. There weren't any bad men in the house. But today was a different kind of situation. First of all, the man was there and both Jessica and Louise were really frightened. But more important, it isn't the kind of incident that a child would find frightening. She didn't tell me he was brandishing knives or a gun or something like that. She just said that he told her to get in the car and then followed them when they kept on walking." Kate picked up her glass. "It seems far more likely to me that it was the hit-and-run driver. He must have seen her watching him and somehow found out who she was!"

"Whoa," Adam said with a little laugh. "Let me get us a refill before I tell you why I don't agree." He returned a few minutes later with a tray bearing their drinks and a plate of cheese and some pathetic-looking crackers.

"Oh, gosh, let me fix you something," Kate said when she saw the food. "I forgot you haven't eaten."

Adam handed her a glass. "No, no. This is fine. But next time you go to the store, do you think you could get some more crackers—I had to scrape the bottom of the barrel for these. I know I told you that you didn't need to get things for me, but if it wouldn't be too much trouble . . ."

Kate grinned. "Of course not. And if there's anything else you want, just make a list."

"Thanks. Maybe I will." He took a bite of cracker and cheese. "Well, anyway, the reason I don't think this man today is the hit-and-run driver is that if you buy Jessica's story about the hit-and-run—and I think I do —then she was up in the woods looking down on what happened. He probably had no idea she was there, and even if he saw her he must have realized that she was too far away to see him clearly. But in addition, supposing he does think she can identify him. Would he pull up beside her in broad daylight in the middle of town? What if she started screaming, 'There he is! That's the hit-and-run driver!''? It just doesn't make sense either way you look at it.''

"But look at it this way," Kate persisted. "If he's not the hit-and-run driver, who is he? The man didn't just ask directions. He called Jessica by name and told her to get into the car. It almost sounds like a kidnapping attempt. But that seems pretty unlikely. After all, she's not the Rockefeller heiress or anything like that.''

Kate watched Adam as he swallowed more of his drink. He jiggled the ice in his glass and then took another sip. "Well," he said finally, "that's not exactly the case. Certainly she's no Rockefeller, but when she grows up she's going to be a very wealthy young lady.''

Kate looked at him in surprise. Adam went on, "My own family isn't particularly well-to-do, but my brother Don's wife—Jessica's mother—came from a rich family in Texas. When she and Don died, quite a lot of money was left to Jessica. But that's only part of the story. Mary Ellen, that's Don's wife, had had a pretty sheltered and traditional upbringing. She was terrified of having to support herself and Jessica if anything ever happened to Don." He held up his hand at Kate's look of protest. "I know it sounds strange, given her family's wealth. I mean, she wouldn't have ever had to go out and get a job or anything. But that's how she felt. So she bought an enormous insurance policy on Don's life. Of course, I'm sure she never dreamed that anything would really happen. Still, when they were killed in that crash, it meant that Jessica inherited a great deal of money. Jessica will never have to work a day in her life if she doesn't want to.''

Not knowing what to say, Kate just stared at him. She was having trouble taking it all in. Jessica certainly didn't want for anything, but she didn't live like a child who had inherited a huge fortune. Her life in Edgar's Landing wasn't Kate's idea of living in the lap of luxury.

Almost as if he'd guessed her thoughts, Adam continued. "Of course, Jessica doesn't have the money now, and she isn't really aware of how much of it there will be. It's in trust and she won't be able to start spending any of it until she's twenty-five. But naturally it pays for her upbringing. As her guardian I tell the trustees what she needs."

Wow, Kate thought, this is beginning to sound more and more like the rich orphan girl in *The Secret Garden* or something. I guess people like this really do exist. "You mean the trust pays for her food and clothes and stuff like that?"

Adam nodded. "They send me a quarterly check to take care of all the day-to-day expenses. And if there's something special she needs, like summer camp or braces for her teeth, I just let them know and they pay for it out of her funds." He grinned at Kate. "Sometimes when things aren't going too well at the office I think I should tell them that what she really needs is a rich uncle."

Kate smiled back at him. "I can imagine," she said with a chuckle.

"But seriously," Adam told her, "I think it's important for Jessica to have a normal upbringing. I don't want her to be a pampered, indulged brat, or to think of herself as different from her friends. I'm trying to bring her up the way both Don and Mary Ellen would have wanted. After all, I'm the only family she has except for her grandfather in Texas. So I would appreciate it if you wouldn't discuss her inheritance with Jessica or with anyone else who might mention it to her. She's still much too young to have to cope with it."

"I agree," Kate said. "And I certainly won't say anything about it." Suddenly she realized that they'd been sitting and talking for quite a while. Adam probably had things to do, and he was looking a little tired. So, saying she'd see him tomorrow, she told him good night and left.

Back at her apartment, Kate set up her ironing board

and then looked in the TV section for a show to watch. There was nothing very interesting, but she flipped on the set anyway, and got out her laundry basket.

She couldn't get over her amazement at Adam's revelations. Who would believe that Jessica was such a rich kid? Of course, Jessica didn't know that herself. Kate was flattered that Adam had confided in her what was obviously pretty much of a secret. She was surprised at how outgoing he'd been, and pleased at how much he trusted her. What a strange and sad story. Poor Don and Mary Ellen hadn't had a chance to see their little girl grow up. And no matter how much money Jessica had, it didn't make up for losing her parents. At least she had Adam. And Kate was beginning to see that he could be a warm and friendly person. Usually he treated her simply as an employee. And, of course, that was what she was. But tonight he'd gone out of his way to explain things to her, and he'd actually seemed to enjoy talking to her. He'd even made that little joke about wanting to have Jessica's money for himself. That was the first time she could remember ever hearing him make a joke of any kind.

Kate finished another blouse and put it on a hanger. It must have been a terrible shock for Adam. Not only did his brother die suddenly, but there he was, taking on the responsibility for a six-year-old. Kate thought, it couldn't have been easy. He didn't have any children of his own, and it happened not long after he and his wife split up. Being on your own and raising a young child must be pretty hard. But she admired Adam's attitude about Jessica's inheritance. She agreed with his philosophy. No matter how much money Jessica would eventually have, surely it was better for her to grow up in a normal environment and learn to be independent and self-reliant. She'd have a chance to develop herself and her talents without relying on the family fortune to define her value as a person.

The phone rang and she picked it up. "Oh, hi, Phil,"

she said. "Hang on a minute while I turn down the TV."

When she returned, he said in an aggrieved voice, "I haven't seen much of you lately. What have you been doing?"

"I've been working," Kate replied a little more tartly than she'd intended.

"I guess your new career as a baby-sitter is keeping you pretty busy, huh?"

Irritated, but determined not to let him know that, Kate said sweetly, "Yes. Between that and writing my thesis, I haven't had much spare time."

"Well, you had time to go up to Connecticut over the weekend." He paused and when Kate didn't reply, went on, "Well, anyway, I called to tell you that Bob and Elaine are having a party Friday night. I thought we could catch a bite to eat first and then go over to their place."

"Oh, thanks, Phil, but I don't think so. I won't know how late I'll have to work until that day, and besides . . ."

He broke in with, "And besides, I'm sure that a handsome, successful graphic designer with his own house in the suburbs has a lot more to offer than I do."

"It's not like that at all," she said. Then she thought angrily, I don't owe him an explanation of how I spend my time or who I spend it with. He's got no claim on me. "But you can think whatever you like, Phil," she finished coolly.

"Kate, are you trying to tell me something?"

Kate paused. Now that he'd asked the question, she realized that she didn't have any desire to see Phil any more. She took a deep breath. "Yes, I guess I am. I don't think this relationship is very good for either of us, and I'd like to call a halt while we're still friends."

"If that's the way you feel," Phil said in an injured tone. He paused a moment to give Kate a chance to reconsider. When she didn't speak, he went on, "Fine,

Kate. Well, have a nice life,'' and hung up.

Kate put down the phone and said to herself, what a baby. Is that any way for a grown person to behave? I was right to tell him I wouldn't see him anymore.

She'd realized while they talked that she'd barely thought about Phil, and hadn't missed seeing him at all in the past couple of weeks. And she'd forgotten how whiny and childish Phil could be. That remark about Adam was a perfect example. What he'd implied certainly wasn't true, but Kate had to admit that Phil suffered in contrast to her employer. Whatever his faults, at least he was a mature adult who took responsibility for his own life, and who was capable of loving and caring for another person. She couldn't imagine Phil taking in a six-year-old without letting her know what a burden she was.

Kate sighed. She wasn't sorry that she'd said goodbye to Phil, but it was too bad that now she couldn't very well go to the party on Friday night. She'd have to let her other friends know that she was available and interested in meeting new men.

The next day, Wednesday, Jessica seemed perfectly cheerful, and she made no further mention of the man in the car. She walked down the hill from school with her friends, and when she got home, she asked Kate if she could get her bicycle out of the garage. Kate agreed, and she took Red outside where the two of them watched as Jessica careened up and down the sidewalk. When they went in again, Jessica did her homework while Kate made supper. When it was almost ready, she called, ''Jess! Please come and set the table, honey.''

As they moved around the kitchen, Jessica nudged Red affectionately with her knee. ''Get out of the way, silly!'' Then she told Kate, ''I don't really like those cookies I had in my lunch today. Could we get a different kind?''

''Sure.'' Kate smiled at her. ''Or we could make some.''

"Right now?"

"Well, no. But we could do it tomorrow, after Brownies. What kind would you like to make—peanut butter or chocolate chip?"

"Hmm." Jessica considered the question. "I guess chocolate chip this time."

"Good, I like that kind myself. I'll pick you up from Brownies so we'll have plenty of time for our baking."

As they sat down to eat, Kate thought, That worked out well. I wanted to go and pick Jessica up tomorrow anyway, but it's nice that I didn't have to make a big deal about it. She was sure the girl had not forgotten yesterday's incident, but she didn't seem to be having any problems as she'd had before. I guess she'll work it out at her own pace, Kate concluded.

The next afternoon, Kate drove up to the school and was waiting when the troop meeting ended. Jessica jumped into the car. "Kate, do we have a shopping bag at home?"

"I imagine there's one somewhere around. Why?"

"Well, I need to bring one to Brownies next week," Jessica told her importantly. "We're going to decorate them for our trick-or-treat bags. Kate, is it almost Halloween?"

"Yes, it's less than two weeks away. We'd better start thinking about your costume. Do you know what you want to be?"

"Oh, I can't decide. Last year I was a witch—Mrs. Higgens bought me a hat and a mask. So I don't want to be a witch again. Do you think I could be a jack-o-lantern?"

Kate laughed. "I think that would be pretty hard to do. But you could be a black cat." She glanced at Jessica's undecided face. "Think about it, honey, we still have some time for you to make up your mind."

When they got home, Jessica was eager to get going on the cookies. Kate couldn't find any aprons, so she tied a dish towel around her waist and one around the little girl's. Then they set to work mashing the butter and sugar together. While Kate measured the flour, Jessica cracked the eggs with fierce concentration.

"Oh, Kate, some shell got in it!"

"That's okay, Jess, just fish it out with a spoon."

By the time the flour was added, the dough was too stiff for Jessica to stir. But she poured the chocolate chips and watched anxiously as Kate mixed them in.

"I like lots of chips, and so does Uncle Adam," she said with satisfaction. "These are going to be good!"

"Of course they are," Kate told her with a grin. "Now get two spoons because this is all ready."

Jessica began to spoon little heaps of cookie dough onto the cookie sheet, concentrating on making them neat and evenly spaced. Red began to bark noisily in the living room. "I'll go see what's bothering him," Kate told Jessica. "You're doing a great job with those."

Walking into the living room, Kate thought, I'll bet it's that same squirrel that loves to tease poor Red. She smiled to herself—the squirrel seemed to know that the dog was unable to reach it, and it took delight in sitting on the porch rail and flicking its tail at him. "What's up, Red?" she called cheerfully as she entered the room.

A shadow moved across the front window, and Kate saw with a shock that a man was standing outside on the porch, peering into the room. He noticed her and stepped back, smiling.

Kate's heart was pounding even as she realized that it was the same young man who'd come by before—Walter. She went to the front door, angry and still shaken. He had no business scaring her like that—it wasn't as if he'd rung the doorbell and gotten no answer. He was just peeking inside, and if it hadn't been for Red, Kate wouldn't have known he was there at all. She didn't like the exposed feeling it gave her, and she didn't like being frightened.

Keeping her hand on the door handle, she looked out at the young man, who had moved to the door. He said,

"Hi. I'm Mr. Cordell's friend. I want to come in."

"He's not here," Kate said firmly.

"I want to come in," he repeated. "I'll wait for him." He reached for the door handle.

His constant smile was unnerving. Kate said, "I'm sorry, you can't do that." Remembering what Adam had said, she asked, "What's your name?"

"Walter."

"Walter what?" she persisted.

He didn't reply, but just stood there, staring at her, his mouth still smiling. After a moment Kate shut the door and then watched until he turned and went down the steps.

Ugh, Kate thought. I've got to think of something to say next time that will keep him from coming back. Then she thought she'd better talk to Adam about him again. What if Jessica opened the door? This guy would walk right in. Kate was sure he was harmless, but it was hard enough to get him off the porch—she'd never be able to dislodge him once he came inside. And there was something creepy about him. Why did he only come around when Adam wasn't home?

She went back into the kitchen. "Who was that?" Jessica asked.

"Some guy I don't know," Kate told her. Then she looked at the cookie sheet. "Boy, these look just perfect. Let's get them into the oven."

Jessica opened the oven door and Kate slid the cookies in, then set the timer. By the time the second cookie sheet was ready to be put in, the first batch was nearly done. Kate spread waxed paper on the counter, and while she shifted the hot cookies onto it, Jessica licked the last morsels from the mixing bowl. She turned to Kate and Kate burst out laughing.

"Oh, Jessica! You could be a clown for Halloween!" The little girl's face was smudged with flour and sticky with cookie dough. "Come and look in the mirror—you'll see what I mean."

In the bathroom, Jessica giggled at her reflection; then Kate helped her clean up. As Jessica dried her face and handed Kate the towel, she said impulsively, "I love you, Kate. Do you think we could pretend sometimes that you're my mother?"

Touched, Kate felt a lump in her throat. She knelt and hugged the girl to her. "I love you too, Jess. Of course we can pretend that if you want to. But, honey, you do know it's just pretend." She looked into the child's face and Jessica stared back at her solemnly.

"I know, Kate."

Kate hugged her again and then stood up. "Let's go see how those cookies taste. That's the best part of being the cook—you get to try things before everyone else."

The phone rang, and as she went to answer it Kate said, "Pick out a good one for me, too. Cordell residence."

There was a silence. Then a whispering voice began. "Ding, dong, bell, Pussy's in the well. Who put her in? I'll never tell." It stopped for a moment and then went on, sounding quieter and somehow more menacing. "Who pulled her out? Nobody." The voice trailed off, but Kate was sure the line was still open.

She hung up the phone and stood next to it, trembling. This was the second time someone had called, with the same kind of twisted version of a nursery rhyme. The whispering voice was masculine, she felt certain, but she couldn't tell if the speaker were young or old. Was it just someone with a sick sense of humor? Somehow Kate didn't believe that. But then what could these calls mean? As she looked across the kitchen at Jessica pondering which two cookies were most full of chocolate chips, she felt a shiver of apprehension.

CHAPTER 7

ADAM CAME HOME that evening as Kate and Jessica were eating dinner. He ruffled Red's ears and then walked into the kitchen, where he stood sniffing appreciatively. "Mm, it certainly smells good in here. Did somebody bake cookies today?"

"Yes!" Jessica exclaimed delightedly. "We made your favorite kind—chocolate chip!"

"Oh, boy, isn't that nice!" he said to her. "I think I'd better have one now and make sure they're okay."

"You can have just one," she told him as he reached into the cookie jar. "You didn't have dinner yet, did you?" When he shook his head, she went on seriously, "You have to eat your dinner before you have any more. Right, Kate?"

"Right, honey, that's the rule." Kate smiled.

Jessica seemed to be taking her housewifely role very seriously. "You have to wash your hands before you sit down to eat, Uncle Adam. And I'll set a place for you."

She hopped up to carry out her promise, and Adam gave Kate a questioning glance. "Don't worry, there's plenty," she told him, gesturing toward the stove. "The chicken is in the oven keeping warm and there's rice and broccoli in those pans on top of the stove."

After he'd washed his hands and filled a plate, he sat down and asked Jessica, "Have a good day today, sweetheart?"

He listened with interest as she related the day's doings at school and at Brownies. Watching them, Kate noticed again how much Jessica looked like Adam. She was going to be quite a beauty when she grew up. And they even had some of the same engaging mannerisms, Kate thought as Jessica brushed an unruly lock of hair out of her eyes.

When Jessica paused for breath, Adam asked her, "And what's your plan for tomorrow? Do you know yet?"

"Oh, I'm going to go bike riding with Carla," she said. "Is that okay, Kate?" she added.

"I think so," Kate replied. "But who's Carla?"

"Oh, she's in my Brownie troop and she asked me today if I could come over tomorrow with my bike. She lives near the park."

"Well, I think we should ask your Uncle Adam if you can bike over there by yourself," Kate told her.

"It's fine," Adam said to Kate. "She's done it before." He looked at Jessica. "You're going to come home and get your bike and meet Carla at her house, isn't that right?" She nodded and Adam turned to Kate. "It's no problem. She knows the way and she won't have to cross any busy streets to get there."

"Good," Kate said. "That sounds like fun."

When everyone was finished, Adam said, "Well, I didn't do any of the cooking so I guess it's my job to clear the table. Jessica, will you get the dessert ready?"

Kate helped Jessica arrange the cookies on a plate and put it in the center of the table. She poured a glass of milk for Jessica and then asked Adam if he'd like some coffee.

"Thanks," he said, "that would be nice."

When they were seated again, he looked at his plate, where Jessica had placed three carefully chosen cookies.

"Jess, these look terrific. There's only one thing wrong."

"What?" She looked worried.

"I think they need some ice cream to go with them. How about you?"

"Oh, yeah." Jessica beamed. "Can I do it?"

"Sure, why not?"

She got the carton out of the freezer, and then looked in the drawer for the scoop. "Should I put it in these blue bowls?" she asked.

"Sure, that's fine," he answered. "You're getting to be pretty good in the kitchen, honey."

"Kate lets me help a lot," she told him.

While she carefully scooped neat mounds of ice cream into the bowls, Adam said to Kate, "Since Jessica's going to Carla's tomorrow, I wonder if I could ask you to look through her winter clothes? They're all still up in the cedar closet from last winter. I'm sure she's outgrown most of them, but I just haven't gotten around to making a list of what she'll need this year. Would you mind?"

"Of course not," Kate said. "Maybe I should put away her shorts and her other summer things at the same time."

"I'd appreciate it." Jessica served the ice cream, and he smiled at her. Then he went on, "Kate, there's one other thing I'd like to ask. Red is due for a bath—he really needs one. I meant to take him last Saturday, but I didn't have time. Do you suppose you could run him up to Ardsley to the groomer's tomorrow afternoon before Jessica comes home? I expect to be home early tomorrow, and I can pick him up after I get here."

"I don't think that's any problem," Kate said after a moment. "I'll just come a bit early."

"Thanks very much." He smiled at her and then said to Jessica, "These are just about the best cookies I've ever eaten. You'd better not make them too often, or I'll get fat."

Not wanting to scare Jessica, Kate waited until the girl was in the tub before telling Adam about Walter's reappearance that day. "He kept saying that he wanted to come in and wait for you," she said. "And I'm sure he would have walked right in if I hadn't held onto the door. He was really insistent, and I have to admit I was frightened."

Adam frowned. "I don't like the sound of that. I guess you'd better keep the door on the chain when you're here—though I feel you're actually quite safe with Red around. Did you get his name this time?"

Kate shook her head. "I asked again, but he still didn't tell me his last name."

"Well, I don't believe it's anyone I know," Adam said. "If it happens again, be sure to tell me, and I'll take some steps to find out who this fellow is. But in the meantime I hope you won't worry about it too much. He probably won't try it again."

I hope not, Kate thought. Aloud she said hesitantly, "There's one other thing I wanted to tell you about. I've gotten two very strange phone calls here." She told him about the whispering voice that recited familiar nursery rhymes whose words had been changed to give them a sinister cast. "I was wondering if this person had ever called while you were home," she wound up.

Adam shook his head. "No. I know that kind of thing is annoying, but it's probably just kids. The best way to handle it is to hang up without saying anything at all. They'll soon get tired of their game."

Before Kate could reply, Jessica called from upstairs to say she was finished with her bath, and Kate let herself out the front door as Adam went up to read Jessica her story. Starting up her little car, Kate thought, I wish I could believe those phone calls are from kids fooling around. But I don't. If only Adam had actually heard one, he'd know there's something really weird and sick about them. But it's so hard to explain that to him without sounding like a scaredy-cat. I'll just have to hope it doesn't happen anymore.

At two-thirty the next day, Kate was driving up to Ardsley, with Red taking up most of the back seat of her chartreuse Rabbit. She stopped for a light and he stood up, resting his heavy chin on her shoulder. "Get down, Red, you can't help with driving."

He gave her ear a lick and a man who was crossing the street grinned. "Nice dog!" he called.

"Thanks," Kate replied. "No, Red, get down, I can't see anything in the mirror."

She found the groomer's shop and took Red inside, where he greeted Joe with enthusiasm. She introduced herself, and Joe said, "Oh, yeah, Mr. Cordell called me. Me and Red are old friends, aren't we, fella?" He scratched the dog under the chin, and Red closed his eyes in doggy pleasure. "We'll get this boy all prettied up. He never gives me any trouble," Joe told her. "And Mr. Cordell said he'd be stopping by to pick him up later, right?"

Kate nodded and turned to go. "Nice to meet you, Joe. And be a good boy, Red. I'll see you on Monday."

When she got to the house, Kate opened the heavy garage door so Jessica would be able to get out her bike. Then she went upstairs to the guest room, where she dragged out the big box of Jessica's winter clothes from the cedar closet. Leaving it in the middle of the floor, she went back down to wait for the little girl.

"Hi, Kate!" Jessica wriggled out of her backpack. "I have to put on my jeans," she went on, turning her back so that Kate could pull down the zipper of her plaid jumper. "Then if I fall off my bike, I won't skin my knees."

She dashed up the stairs, and Kate grinned to herself, remembering many skinned knees of her own. When Jessica returned in jeans and a turtleneck, Kate asked, "Will you be warm enough? Maybe you should wear your sweatshirt."

"Okay." The girl got the hooded yellow garment out of the closet and pulled it on.

"I've opened the garage so you can get out your bicycle,'' Kate told her. "But now, Jessica, I want you to be careful going to Carla's house. Look both ways when you cross the streets. And be sure to call me when you get there. Can you remember that?"

Jessica nodded and then gave Kate a hug. " 'Bye, Kate. See you later." She went out the kitchen door, and Kate started back upstairs.

She decided it would be easiest to dump all the clothes out on the floor and sort them into piles. The blue parka and matching ski pants looked as though they might still fit, so she put them aside for Jessica to try on. But many of the other items looked as if they had barely fit well last year, and certainly wouldn't now. And although there were a lot of things, few of them seemed to go together. Perhaps Mrs. Higgens hadn't considered color coordination very important for a child's wardrobe.

Kate held up a bright pink crew-neck sweater that might have fit a small four-year-old. Jessica would certainly need a new one. She'd looked terrific in her yellow sweatshirt—it set off her dark hair and gray eyes. Maybe Kate would try to find a sweater in that color if, as she suspected would be the case, she ended up doing the shopping for Jessica's winter things. Then she found a pair of gloves with faces knitted into each finger. They looked well worn, but she wouldn't throw them out— they were probably Jessica's favorites.

Corduroy pants, wool skirts, tights, knee socks— there was a mountain of stuff. Kate sat back and reflected that it was amazing how much gear a child needed. And most of what was here wouldn't fit Jessica now. It hadn't occurred to her that children outgrew all their things at once. The child would need a lot of new clothes, just about everything from underwear to a new coat. But, Kate thought, it will be kind of fun to take her shopping and help her pick things out.

She glanced at her watch and frowned. Jessica should have gotten to Carla's house by now. But she hadn't called. Maybe she forgot, Kate thought; kids often do.

Going down to the kitchen, she looked for the piece of paper with Carla's phone number on it. As she dialed, she realized that she'd been unconsciously listening for the padding of Red's feet behind her as she moved through the house.

"Hello?"

"Hi, is that Carla? This is Kate Jamison, Jessica's baby-sitter. Can I talk to Jessica, please?"

"She's not here." The little girl's voice sounded forlorn. "I thought she was coming right away. Is she mad at me or something?"

"No, no, she's on her way. But I thought she'd be there by now. Well, be sure and have her call me as soon as she arrives, okay?"

Kate stood with her hand on the phone. What was taking Jessica so long? Perhaps she had fallen off her bike. Or maybe she'd stopped to talk to another friend along the way. But, though she tried to repress it, an image of the man who'd asked Jessica to get into his car crept into her mind. I'm sure she wouldn't have gotten into anyone's car willingly, Kate thought, but last time she was with a friend. This time she was by herself.

Quickly Kate resolved to walk along the route Jessica would have followed on her bike. If Jessica had taken a spill, Kate would find her, and if she'd just dawdled on her way, Kate would catch up with her at Carla's house. She refused to consider any more sinister possibilities.

Kate snatched up her sweater and the ring of keys she'd left on the kitchen table. Going out the door, she pulled it shut behind her and then tested to make sure the latch had caught. As she walked down the back porch steps toward the driveway, she could see that the garage door was closed. She took another couple of steps and then stopped. That's funny, she thought. I opened it for Jessica, and I know she can't reach high enough to pull it shut. She looked at it again, and this time she could see thin wisps of smoke curling out from under the door.

Dear God, something's burning inside the garage! And then a cold hand of fear clutched at her heart. What if Jessica's in there, she thought wildly. I've got to get her out!

Racing to the garage, she tugged at the handle of the heavy door. It didn't budge. She yanked upward again and then realized that the handle was pointing down. It was locked! She searched frantically for the garage key on the ring in her hand and with shaking fingers tried to insert it in the keyhole. It was stiff, but at last it turned and she wrenched at the handle once more.

The door flew up, and dense smoke billowed out through the opening. Waving a hand in front of her face, Kate shouted, "Jessica! Where are you?"

There was no answer, and there seemed to be more smoke in the garage than before. Kate coughed. Her sweater still hung loosely around her shoulders, and she pulled it off and held it up to her face, covering her nose and mouth. She took a step into the small structure. Trying to peer through the smoke, she yelled again. "Jessica!" She moved a little farther inside and tripped, falling flat on her face and banging her shin painfully on some sharp metal object. She looked at it—it was Jessica's bicycle, lying on its side as if dropped hastily.

More certain than ever that the child must be here, Kate got to her hands and knees and crawled forward. She thought she could see a glimpse of bright yellow near the back wall. As she moved toward it, Kate could just make out the shape of the little girl's body, curled up on the floor under a picnic bench.

Floundering to her feet, Kate stumbled to the back of the garage and lifted the wooden bench away from the girl. Kneeling down, she scooped Jessica up in her arms and then struggled to stand up. She turned toward the door and was horrified to see a smoldering pile of newspapers burst into flame. Her head bent, Kate lurched through the hot blackness and staggered out onto the driveway. Behind her she heard a muffled explosion.

She carried the child in her arms down to the end of the driveway and lowered her to the grass. Turning once more, she saw the flames licking up beside the garage doorway and heard the crackling of the old painted wood as it burned.

CHAPTER 8

KATE HEARD SIRENS wailing in the distance. She realized that a neighbor must have called the fire department. Even as she thought about it, the white-haired woman who lived across the street came out of her house and scurried over to Kate. "Is the little girl all right?" she asked anxiously.

By this time Jessica was sitting up. Pale and confused looking, she clung to Kate. The neighbor patted Jessica on the head and said, "It was really the boys, the ones raking my leaves, who saw what was happening. They came and rang the doorbell and said they thought I'd better call the fire department. And that's just what I did." Before Kate could thank her, the woman gasped and said, "Oh, my goodness. Look at that!" The heat of the fire had broken the windows at the side of the garage, and flames were shooting out and licking at the roof. "I hope it doesn't spread to the house," the neighbor told Kate fearfully.

Just then the fire truck wheeled around the corner from the main street and pulled up in front of the driveway. The men jumped off the truck, some still buckling up their slickers, and began unreeling hoses. One of them called to Kate, "Anyone inside there?"

"No, not now," Kate told him.

"Okay, ma'am. You folks better stay where you are. Don't get any closer."

The fire chief's car arrived a moment later. A burly, middle-aged man got out and came over to where Kate, Jessica, and the neighbor were gathered. "Are you Mrs. Cordell?" he asked Kate.

"No, I work for Mr. Cordell. I take care of his niece Jessica," she said, indicating the child still clinging to her but now watching the activities of the firemen.

"Were you here when the fire started?"

"I was inside the house," Kate said. "And when I came out I saw smoke. Then I realized that Jessica must be trapped inside the garage, so I got it open and carried her out."

The fire chief looked at Jessica in concern. "How do you feel now, honey?" he asked kindly. "Are you okay?"

Jessica nodded, wide-eyed. "Yeah, I guess so."

"Well, she looks all right to me," the chief told Kate, "but I can call the ambulance if you want."

Jessica clutched convulsively at Kate's arm and Kate could see the terror in the child's eyes. She probably associates ambulances with her parents' death, Kate thought. "I'd rather you didn't, if that's okay. But I would like to go and call her own doctor and see what he advises. And I'd better call and let Mr. Cordell know what's going on."

The chief nodded in agreement and then glanced toward the garage to see what progress his men were making with the fire. Kate patted her pockets for the keys to the house and suddenly remembered where they were. "Oh, gosh, I can't get in the house," she said. "I left the keys in the garage door lock when I opened it up."

The lady from across the street spoke up. "Just come over and use my phone, dear."

"Thanks," Kate said to her. Then she turned to

Jessica. "You stay right here, Jess. I'll be back in a few minutes." She gave the child's shoulder a reassuring squeeze, but Jessica looked a little panicked.

The fire chief smiled at Jessica. "You can stay with me, can't you, honey? Tell you what. You can come and sit in my car while I call in and tell the boys we don't need the hook-and-ladder. How's that?"

Giving him a tremulous smile, Jessica said, "Okay."

As they crossed the street, the neighbor said, "I'm Helen Baker, dear. And I don't know your name." Kate told her, and Mrs. Baker went on. "My husband is going to be so upset that he missed all the excitement. He left not half an hour ago to take the radio down to get it fixed. And, of course, he used to be a volunteer fireman here himself. He still goes to all the meetings." By now they were in the house. "Well, here's the phone, dear," Mrs. Baker said to Kate. "Just go ahead and make your calls."

The list of emergency numbers was still locked in Adam's house, but Kate remembered the doctor's name. She looked it up in the local directory next to the phone and soon was speaking to his answering service. Kate explained the problem and the woman at the other end was sympathetic. "Don't worry, I'll track him down," she told Kate. "I'm sure he's still at the hospital doing rounds, and I can catch him there before he leaves. I'll just tell him to stop by."

"Thanks very much," Kate said gratefully. Then she dialed Adam's office number. His secretary answered, and Kate said, "Hi, this is Kate Jamison. Is Mr. Cordell there?"

"Oh, hi. No, he hasn't been here since about noon. And I don't think he's planning on coming back to the office today."

"Oh. Well, do you know where I can reach him? It's kind of important," Kate told her.

"Well, no I don't. Are you calling from the house?" The secretary sounded puzzled.

"Sort of. Yeah."

"Gee, that's funny. I thought that's where he said he was going. Well, if he calls in, I'll tell him to be sure and get in touch with you."

"Oh, okay. Thanks," Kate said before she hung up. Then she headed toward Mrs. Baker's front door. I hope he gets here soon, she thought, so we can get into the house. But it's too bad I couldn't reach him. It will be quite a shock to drive up and see the fire trucks.

She went outside. On the sidewalk in front of Mrs. Baker's house was a group of onlookers. The firemen had obviously told them all to stay on that side of the street, and Mrs. Baker now had quite an audience for her account of what had happened. The fire appeared to be out, but the firemen were still moving around the garage and the driveway. Kate hurried across the street to the fire chief's car. The chief motioned for her to join him and Jessica in the front seat.

"Now, I need to know more exactly how this happened," he said to Kate.

"I really don't know," she said. Then she explained as much as she knew of the events from the time Jessica got home until she'd carried her out of the garage.

The chief nodded, and then turned his attention to the little girl. "Well, now, Jessica. Can you tell me what went on after you left the house to go get your bike?"

Jessica still looked shaken, but she talked readily enough. "Well, I went into the garage . . ."

"Was the door opened?" he interrupted gently.

"Yeah, I can't open it by myself." She took a breath and started again. "Well, I went in and at first I couldn't find my bike. Usually it's right by the door. But then I saw it in the back, sort of behind the lawn mower, and it was real hard to get it out. I had to move Uncle Adam's bike first and the pedal got caught in my wheel. Then I started to go out, but the door was closed, and I can't open it by myself. I tried and tried, but it never opened. So then I tried to open the window and I couldn't get that open either." She looked up at Kate and went on. "I called for you, Kate. A whole bunch of times. But I guess you couldn't hear me." Jessica's voice faltered and her eyes filled with tears. "And then I saw some smoke and I got real scared and I ran and hid as far away as I could."

"Where was the smoke, Jessica?" the chief asked.

"By the door."

"Now, Jessica," he went on. "Did you have any matches in the garage?"

Surprised and puzzled, Jessica said, "No."

"That's out of the question!" Kate was indignant but tried not to show it.

"Mmm. Well, all right, Ms. Jamison. Can you tell me what was in the garage that might have caused the fire?"

Kate shrugged. "I've never been in it farther than the doorway, but it was cluttered with all the usual stuff people keep in garages. You know, the lawn mower, the picnic table, the bikes, and a lot of gardening stuff. I really don't know what else, but it was pretty full. Mr. Cordell never puts his car in it because there's no room."

A station wagon came along and parked in front of the chief's car. Dr. Phelps, a tall, gray-haired man, climbed out and looked around. Kate got out of the chief's car with Jessica. The doctor spotted them and hurried over. "My goodness, Jessica, never a dull moment," he said jovially. "Let's take a look at you. How are you feeling?"

"Fine," Jessica responded.

"Good. Now you come on over here and we'll pretend that the back of my car is the table in my office." He lowered the tailgate and lifted Jessica up onto it. He pulled out his bag, and as he examined her, he kept up a steady stream of joking chatter, interrupted with requests that she take a deep breath and so on.

When he'd finished, he turned to Kate. "She seems

fine to me. A little shaken, but that's to be expected. I think a night's rest and a relaxed day tomorrow will be all she needs.'' He patted Jessica on the head and helped her down from the tailgate. ''I can't find a thing wrong with you, young lady. If all my patients were as healthy as you, I'd be out of business. But I want you to take it easy tomorrow. Can you do that?'' Jessica nodded and the doctor said to Kate, ''I think the best thing now is for her to get inside and go to bed, or at least rest on the couch or something. If she doesn't feel like eating tonight, don't force her, and of course let me know if she develops any sort of symptoms or if there's anything you're worried about.''

''Fine,'' Kate said. ''I'm glad she's okay. But I have a small problem. The house is locked and I can't get it.''

Dr. Phelps glanced at the house and then looked at Kate in surprise. ''An old house like that? Just ask that policeman to open a window for you. My wife does it all the time—it's no problem.'' Before Kate could respond, Dr. Phelps motioned to the patrolman who was talking to the fire chief. Kate hadn't even noticed his arrival. When he walked over to them, the doctor told him what had happened.

''Okay,'' the cop said to Kate. ''But do you know if any of the locks on the porch windows don't catch quite right? That's usually the easiest way to get in.''

''No. No, I don't,'' Kate told him, somewhat amazed at his matter-of-fact approach to breaking into the house. She watched as he went along the porch, looking carefully at the windows, and then chose one of them to tackle. He pulled some sort of tool out of his pocket and wedged it under the window frame and a moment later he was raising the window and climbing carefully through it. He came around and opened the front door. Coming back down the steps, he told Kate, ''Okay, you're all set. But if I could make a suggestion, it would be a good idea to get better locking devices for those windows.''

"Yes, well, thanks a lot," Kate said. She was starting to feel a little overwhelmed herself with all that had gone on. She managed to thank Dr. Phelps before he drove off, and then told the fire chief that she was taking Jessica inside. The little girl looked quite pale as Kate helped her into her nightgown and bathrobe and then settled her on the couch in the living room. She thought it might be a good idea to make a pot of coffee and had just put the water on to boil when there was a knock at the front door. It was Detective Roper, and she asked him in. He followed her to the kitchen.

"I was at the station when I heard about the fire up here, so I thought I'd just drop by and see what it was all about." He shook his head. "You folks have sure had more than your share of trouble lately. The little girl's okay?"

"Yes," Kate told him, "the doctor thinks she's fine and just needs some rest."

"That's good," Roper said. "But what exactly happened?"

Wearily Kate went through the story once again, explaining what she had done and what Jessica had said.

"Oh, my gosh," she said suddenly. "I never called Carla again. Poor kid—she's probably still waiting and wondering what's happened to Jessica. Excuse me a moment—I'd better do it now before I forget again."

When she got off the phone, Detective Roper began to ask her for more details. He seemed particularly interested in how the garage door had closed when Jessica was inside. "Is it one of those old ones that's loose on its track? Or maybe you didn't push it up all the way when you opened it?"

"I'm quite sure I did," Kate replied. "It would have come down right away if I hadn't."

She poured each of them a cup of coffee, and then went to check on Jessica. The little girl was fast asleep on the couch with Baby. With all the coming and going, Kate felt Jessica would be better off in her own room.

Picking her up in her arms, she carried her upstairs and placed her in the lower bunk. She covered Jessica with the quilt and kissed her forehead gently. Pulling the door partly closed, she returned downstairs.

"Maybe you ought to sit down, Ms. Jamison." Roper sounded sympathetic. "This has been pretty hard on you too. It's not every day you have to carry a child out of a burning building, thank the Lord. I believe that litle girl probably owes you her life."

Kate gave him a smile, grateful for his concern. She sank down on one of the kitchen chairs and picked up her coffee cup. But before she could take a sip, she heard the slam of a car door. Excited voices were raised outside.

"That must be Mr. Cordell," she told Roper. She went to the front door and opened it just as he ran up the steps.

"Where's Jessica? Is she all right?" he demanded.

"She's fine. She's asleep upstairs."

"Thank God for that. When I drove up and saw the fire truck, and then I saw the garage . . . How did it happen?"

Feeling a little like a broken record, Kate told him what she'd just finished telling Detective Roper. While she was talking, Chief Slezak tapped at the door and came inside. He lifted a hand to Detective Roper and then listened in silence to the end of Kate's story. When she finished, he turned to Adam.

"Mr. Cordell? I'm Jim Slezak." He put out his hand and Adam shook it.

"Chief Slezak, nice to meet you. Although I'd rather it had been under different circumstances. This is quite a shock."

"I'm sure it is. Now, there are a few things I'd like to ask you. Can you give me an idea of what you kept in the garage?"

"Well, let me think." In the pause Kate heard the phone ring and she went to answer it. If this is another of those hang-up prank calls, I'll tell the kid exactly what I think of him, she thought. This has gone far enough. But when she picked up the receiver, it was Joe, the dog groomer.

"Ms. Jamison? I was just wondering when Mr. Cordell was planning to pick up Red here. It's almost five-thirty and . . ."

"Oh, I'm so sorry, I forgot all about him. We've had a lot of excitement here. There was a fire in the garage and . . ."

Joe broke in, his voice full of concern. "Oh, dear. Everything under control now?"

"Yes," Kate said, "the fire is out but the fire chief is still here and the police and everything. I'm afraid I just didn't think about Red."

"Oh, listen, I can understand that. How about if I just drop him off at the house after I close up here? It's no problem."

"Oh, would you? That would really be a big help," Kate said. "You know how to get here?"

"Sure, 37 Alder Drive. I'll be there in a little while."

Kate hung up. Is it really only five-thirty? she thought. It feels like midnight at least. I'd better just check on Jessica and make sure she's still asleep.

When she saw the child's sleeping form still huddled under the quilt, Kate realized suddenly that she felt relieved. I guess I was really worried that the fire would trigger another of her episodes of nightmare and fear. It wouldn't be surprising, she thought. She's been through an awful lot lately, and most of it has been pretty scary.

Leaving the girl's room, she caught a glimpse of the piles of clothing still strewn on the guest-room floor. Oh, dear, I'd forgotten all about that. It seems like such a long time ago. I'll ask Adam to just leave it alone until Monday—I'll deal with it then.

She went back down the stairs and heard Adam explaining to Chief Slezak that he'd put a bucket of ashes from the fireplace inside the garage that morning. He'd planned to use them in the garden that weekend. "But I'm sure they were cold," he said.

Chief Slezak shook his head. "You'd be surprised how long ashes like that can retain some heat, even if you don't see any glowing embers," he said. "And it's never a good idea to put them inside a closed structure. It's always better to leave them outdoors where there's nothing combustible around. It sounds to me as though fumes from the gasoline can for your lawn mower may have traveled along the floor and been ignited by the ashes. I've known it to happen before. Naturally, we'll run a complete investigation, and we may find that it was something in the wiring, or some other cause we haven't thought of yet. Anyway," he concluded, "in the future, I don't think it's a good idea to store your gasoline and fireplace ashes in the same location, Mr. Cordell."

The doorbell rang, and Kate hurried down the last few steps to answer it. Joe was standing at the front door, Red's leash in his hand. The dog was prancing about on the front porch, obviously thinking he was the center of everyone's attention with his newly bathed coat. "Here he is, Ms. Jamison," Joe said. "Wow, that garage looks like it's totaled. Some fire you had here."

"Yes, it was pretty exciting while it lasted. Thanks, Joe. Hang on a minute, I want to pay you."

Kate returned a moment later with the money. "Thanks again. Red looks gorgeous. And I'm sorry we were so much of a bother."

"Don't worry about a thing. I was happy to do it. See you next time."

As Kate brought Red inside, she could tell that the men's conversation was about finished. "Well, good night, Mr. Cordell. We'll let you know what we find out," Chief Slezak said to Adam. Then he and Detective Roper moved toward the front door where Kate was standing. "Good night, Ms. Jamison. That was quick thinking on your part today. It gives me the shivers when I hear about people running into burning buildings to save someone or something. It's best to leave it to trained professionals—that's our job," he said with apparent pride. Then he smiled at Kate. "But in this case you certainly did the right thing. I'm glad you didn't wait for us to get here."

Kate returned his smile. "Thanks, but I was awfully happy to hear those sirens."

Adam joined them. "Well, I really feel pretty stupid. But thanks again. I can't tell you how much I appreciate everything you've done."

"That's what we're here for. I'm glad things turned out as well as they did. Good night again, folks." He stopped as he was going out the door. Touching Kate's arm, he said, "Be sure and get some rest yourself."

Detective Roper was right behind him. "Good night, Mr. Cordell. I'll stay in touch." He too gave Kate a smile. "Keep taking care of that little girl," he told her. Then he and the fire chief went out.

As they went down the steps, Kate heard Roper say to the chief, "Jim, the one thing that bothers me is that damn garage door. I just don't see how it could have come down by itself."

Kate turned back toward the living room and saw Adam coming from the kitchen. He had two glasses in his hands, and he held one out to her. "I think we both could use a drink," he said. And as Kate took her glass, he went on, "I can't believe how stupid I was. Any ten-year-old would know better. And when I think what almost happened. Thank God you were here and had the good sense to act. If it hadn't been for you, I don't know what would have happened to Jessica. I feel so guilty."

Kate could hardly take in what he was saying. She felt as though she were hearing it through a fog. Glancing up, she caught her reflection in the oak-framed mirror above the fireplace. Her sea-green eyes looked huge in her pale face, and the brilliant color of her hair was a strange contrast to her dazed and weary look. She saw the figure in the mirror sway slightly and the dark handsome man beside her catch hold of her arm.

"Oh, Kate. Here I've been doing nothing but talk about how I feel and you're the one I should be worried about. Come and sit down. You look exhausted." He eased her onto the couch and tucked an afghan over her.

As Kate leaned back against the warmth of his strong arm, she realized hazily that this was the first time since they'd met that Adam had touched her.

CHAPTER 9

KATE SLEPT LATE on Saturday, exhausted from the ordeal of the day before. She had a leisurely breakfast at home, but since it was a beautiful October day Kate didn't want to spend it in her apartment. Boring chores like going to the Laundromat had no appeal, and she just wasn't in the mood to concentrate on her thesis.

As she dawdled over her coffee, Kate found herself reliving yesterday's events. What if she hadn't gone downstairs to call Carla's house? What if she'd simply waited instead of going outside to look for Jess? She shuddered as she wondered how long the little girl could have survived in the smoke-filled garage. It was amazing that she'd seemed to have suffered no ill effects from what she'd gone through. At least not physically. But the poor little kid. Even though Kate knew that the fire was a freak accident that could have happened anywhere, it was almost as if Jessica were the victim of some kind of evil forces.

Kate shook herself mentally. Of course that wasn't true. It was just bad luck that it had happened to Jessica. In her mind's eye, Kate saw Adam's stricken face as he walked into the house. He'd felt so guilty, and her heart had gone out to him. Obviously, he blamed himself, and there was nothing she could say to make him feel any better.

Now that I think of it, I wasn't in any shape to say much of anything, she realized. I guess I must have been suffering from some sort of delayed shock that hit me when things calmed down and the worst was over. And Adam had been so sympathetic, even though he was preoccupied with his own reaction to the near tragedy.

She could still feel the strength of his arm around her as he'd helped her onto the couch. How warm and secure it had been sitting close beside him while he pulled the afghan up around her. For a moment Kate allowed herself to fantasize that their relationship had changed and become more than just employer-employee.

"Don't be ridiculous," she suddenly said out loud. "You don't even like him." Kate got up and poured herself another cup of coffee and picked up the newspaper. You were all shaken up and needed someone to be nice to you, she thought silently, and for once he managed to be human. That's all it amounted to.

Paging through the paper's weekend entertainment section, Kate stopped at the museum listings. The Brooklyn Museum had a show of Walker Evans photographs that she'd really like to see. I think I'll just drive out there today, she said to herself. It'll be fun, and maybe I'll call Bob and Elaine to see if they want to go too.

When she got Elaine on the phone, Kate said, "How was your party last night?"

"It was fun. I'm still throwing out empty beer bottles. Too bad you couldn't make it."

Kate heard the unspoken question in her voice. "Yeah, I would have liked to. But it would have been a little awkward since I knew Phil was going," she said.

"That's what I kind of guessed," Elaine said. "You're not seeing him anymore?"

"No, I'm not."

"Well, I know it's none of my business, but I never did think the two of you were such a terrific match."

Kate laughed. "Well, I guess you were right."

"I'm glad to hear you don't sound upset about it. Have you found somebody else, or are you looking?"

"No, I haven't found anybody else," Kate said lightly. "And, of course, if you come across any fabulous, unattached men, please keep me in mind. But the reason I called, Elaine, is that I'm playing hooky today and I thought I'd go out and see that Walker Evans show at the Brooklyn Museum. You interested?"

"Oh, gosh, yeah. That would be fun. You driving, I hope?"

"Yep. I'll be glad to pick you up. Is it just going to be us or do you think Bob would like to go, too?"

"Well, I'm sure Bob would love to, but here's the deal. My ex-brother-in-law Keith is staying here with us for the weekend. In fact, he's the reason we had the party last night. You'll notice that I said ex. My sister has made a total fool of herself. I may have told you, she got involved with some guy who runs a commune or something just outside Carrington—Keith teaches at Stuart Academy there. Anyway, there they are in this tiny town up in the Berkshires and she's filed for divorce and poor Keith is sick of everybody he runs into asking him about it. And I figured, there's no reason we can't be friends. He's an awfully nice guy. So I suggested he come down here and get away from it all."

"Well," Kate started, but Elaine swept on.

"Would it be okay if he came along? I mean, he's not anyone you'd be interested in, I don't think. And besides he's not ready to start looking yet, as you can well imagine. But he's smart and interesting and all, so it wouldn't be like dragging somebody's dumb relative along or anything."

"It's fine with me, Elaine," Kate told her. "When shall I pick you up?"

"Maybe in about an hour? Oh, hang on a second,

Bob and Keith just walked in. They went out to pick up some bagels." Kate overheard a muffled conversation and then Elaine got back on the phone. "Okay. They both want to go. So how about if we meet you downstairs in front of the building at noon? That way you won't have to park."

"Great. See you then," Kate said and hung up the phone.

As she got ready to go, Kate smiled to herself. Elaine was never at a loss for words; Kate always remembered not to call her when she was in a rush. But Elaine was a good friend, and she certainly couldn't ever be called unenthusiastic.

The exhibit was terrific, and afterward they stopped in the museum gift shop. "I love this place," Elaine said as they admired a display of baskets in the shop. "They always have such unusual things. Bob, don't you think this basket would be great for my mom and dad for Christmas? Or maybe this one would be better. What do you think?" She held up first one and then another until Bob finally nodded. "Oh, great," Elaine went on. "I always wonder what to get them and it's so nice to have it all decided so early." She called to Bob again. "How do you like this one for our place? It would be great to put mail in. What do you say?"

While Bob helped Elaine make her choices, Kate wandered around, looking at all the strange and fascinating ethnic items the gift shop had to offer—carved Eskimo tools made of bone, Greek wine skins, Indian wall hangings covered with tiny mirrors, and Navajo pottery. *When I have a place to live in that I like better than that dingy apartment I have now, I'll come back here to get some things to furnish it,* she promised herself. Then she saw a display of shadow puppets from Indonesia. Their fanciful shapes, some fierce, some smiling, intrigued her. *I bet Jessica would love to see these,* she thought. Kate noticed that there were a number of miniature puppets slightly simpler in design. They're not very expensive, she noticed. Maybe Jessica would enjoy playing with it and figuring out how to make it cast shadows. She bought one of the more whimsical puppets and stuck it in her bag.

Kate and her friends decided to go to Sheepshead Bay where they could stop at one of the nearby seafood restaurants after they'd strolled around looking at the fishing boats.

Keith turned out to be a perfectly pleasant companion. Kate thought he was cute with his shock of curly blond hair and bright blue eyes. And he was really a lot of fun to be with. It turned out that he taught English at Stuart Academy, and he wanted to know all about Kate's thesis on Jane Austen.

"I think you've chosen a hard topic," he said with a laugh. "Austen was really a closet feminist, wasn't she? And after the reader has met Elizabeth Bennett, it's all over. No man could possibly be worthy of her!"

Kate laughed too. "I've loved that character since the first time I read *Pride and Prejudice* when I was in high school," she told him. "I can read it over and over and never get tired of it—I guess that's a good thing, since that's what I have to do for my thesis."

"But do you think there are still men like Darcy?" he asked her, obviously interested in the idea. He must be a good teacher, Kate thought. Keith went on, "You know, that tall, dark, handsome man who's cold and aloof and critical of everyone else. Or was he just a product of eighteenth century English aristocracy? Or maybe he was drawn from her embittered imagination. After all, Austen herself never married, did she?"

"Jane Austen wasn't embittered," Kate protested. "Ironic, even caustic at times. I'll go that far. Listen to me," she said with a smile. "I have to defend my subject!"

They drove back into Manhattan and Kate was persuaded to come up to Bob and Elaine's for a night cap. Luck was with them and she found a parking space right outside their building.

"That's an omen, Kate," Bob told her. "If you pass up a parking place on the upper west side, it's seven years bad luck, you know. You'll have to come up. Just for a little while."

They sprawled on the comfortable furniture that had seen better days, and soon got involved in a half-serious argument over whether Mayor Koch had been good for New York City or not. Finally Kate stood up and said, "I've really got to get home while I can still keep my eyes open. Thanks a lot, you all—this has been a terrific day."

"Well, thanks yourself for calling this morning!" Elaine exclaimed. "It worked out just perfectly."

"Yeah, it was a big treat for us poor city dwellers to go for a ride in a car," Bob told Kate with a grin.

"Oh, Bob!" Elaine made a face at him.

Keith went down in the elevator with her and walked her out to the car. "Good night, Kate, I'm awfully happy to have met you. I had a wonderful time today. And good luck with Jane and the fellows. I hope you'll let me know what new insights you come up with."

As she drove toward the West Side Highway, Kate thought that it really had been a lot of fun. She was pleasantly surprised somehow. *Has it been that long since I've just had a good time without complications?* she wondered.

Keith was awfully nice. No wonder Elaine thought her sister was a fool. He was intelligent, considerate, good-looking, and he even had a sense of humor. What more could any woman ask? It was easy to see how someone could fall in love with him.

And yet he doesn't make me feel all shivery, Kate thought. *I didn't feel that exciting connection. I'd like to be his friend but not his lover. I just didn't respond that way, even though in spite of what Elaine told me,* he was definitely sending out signals.

Oh, dear, what's wrong with me? Am I just too particular and picky, like Dad used to tell me? Or is it just that I haven't found my Mr. Darcy?

Kate worked through most of Sunday. Inspired by her conversation with Keith—it was a treat to meet somebody who actually understood what she was doing —she accomplished a lot and felt that her thesis was taking shape nicely.

Late in the afternoon she called her mother in Minnesota. It was a while since she had spoken to her, and her mother wanted to know all about Kate's thesis and her job.

"They're both doing fine, Mom," Kate told her. She couldn't tell her mother about the fire or any of the other disturbing things that had been happening. It would only upset her to no purpose. So she concentrated on safer topics. "I went to see a show of Walker Evans photographs with some friends yesterday. You would have really enjoyed it. And then we went out to dinner, and one of the guys was very interested in what I'm doing on Jane Austen and we had a nice long conversation about it. It was just what I needed. I've been full of enthusiasm today and got a lot of work done."

"That's nice, dear. And who was this young man? Anyone special?"

"No, I don't think so, Mom, he was just a nice person and I enjoyed talking to him."

"Well, good. I got your letter and I answered it, a little late I'm afraid. I've been so busy with my garden group tours. Did I tell you we're taking people up along the river to see the autumn color? It's quite spectacular this year. And of course I'm arranging the schedule for the winter lecture series at church—it's surprising how many people promise to do things and then back out at the last minute."

"Mother, you tell me that every year, but I think you secretly like to be the one who saves the day."

"Oh, Kate." Her mother laughed. "Maybe you're right, but everyone likes to be appreciated, you know. Well, I won't keep you talking, I know this is costing you a fortune, but it was good to hear from you, dear."

After Kate had said her good-byes and hung up, she thought she ought to call Amy and thank her for last weekend. She'd meant to do that much earlier in the week. When she got hold of Amy, she told her how much fun she'd had.

"Oh, good," Amy said. "I hope that means you'll come back soon. How's the job going?"

As soon as she spoke, Kate realized that she was longing to talk to someone about what had been going on. And Amy was the perfect person. She could give Kate a little perspective on the whole thing without getting hysterical and upset. "A lot has happened since last Sunday, Amy." She went through the sequence of events, starting with the hit-and-run accident and her own suspicion that Jessica's seeing it had set off her strange behavior the week before. Then she told her about the man who had tried to pick up Jessica in his car and about the fire on Friday. "So you can imagine it's been quite a week."

"My God, Kate. It almost sounds like someone is after this kid."

"Well," Kate said slowly, "in a way I think that might be true. I think the man in the car was really the hit-and-run driver. If he knows it was Jessica who saw the accident, he might want to make sure she keeps quiet about it."

"Kate, you're giving me the shivers. Are you thinking that this guy set fire to the garage too?"

"I don't know, I hadn't really thought of that. But it could be." Kate took a deep breath. "You know, Amy, at this point I'm not sure I can tell what's real and what's in my imagination. And I haven't even told you —on top of everything else there's this weird guy who keeps coming around to the house. He claims to be a friend of Adam's, but he arrives in the middle of the afternoon when anyone would know that Adam is at work. And he keeps trying to come inside . . ."

"What!"

"Well, he's not exactly breaking down the door or anything, but he says he wants to come in and grabs at the doorknob as if he's planning to just make himself at home. And one time I caught him peering in through the windows."

"No kidding! Do you think he could be the hit-and-run driver? Jesus, Kate, you'd better be careful!"

Kate paused, digesting this new idea. "That hadn't even occurred to me. I've just been thinking that he's kind of lonely and pathetic—I tell you, Amy, he doesn't really look dangerous. But he is pretty weird."

"See what I mean?"

"Well, yeah. But the other thing is that I've been getting these bizarre phone calls at the house."

"Like what? You mean an obscene caller?"

"No, not like that. It's someone whispering—I think it's a boy or a man. And he says these nursery rhymes. But they're all wrong. Like he changes them so they sound nasty and scary."

"How many of these have you gotten?" Amy asked.

"Well, only a couple. And then there was this hang-up only they didn't hang up until I'd been on the phone listening a while. It's getting so I hate to answer the phone over there."

"Have you told the police about all this?" Amy demanded. "And what about Adam? What does he think?"

"He thinks I'm overreacting, I guess. Actually, I haven't told him all this stuff. When I think about it, I don't really know what he thinks, but if he thought Jessica was in danger, he would have said so."

"Yeah, I think that's right," Amy told her. "And from what you said, he's not likely to be very willing to confide in you even if he does think some strange stuff is going on. Kate, I hate to say this, but I'd be scared to be in that house with nobody around but the kid."

"Well, the dog is there," Kate reassured her. "He's friendly but he's also large. And I can't believe anyone would try anything with him around."

"That makes me feel better," Amy said, "but I still think it's scary. I'll call you later in the week and make sure nothing else has happened. Bye, Kate, take care."

"Thanks, Amy, I will. Bye."

Kate sat down to do a little more work. But, as she retyped her cryptic scribbles into readable notes, she found it hard to concentrate. It had been good to talk to Amy. But as she went on typing, she suddenly remembered that the fire had started when Red was not in the house. Could someone have been watching? Did someone see me drive off with Red and come back without him? And is that why the fire happened on that day? Kate, be reasonable, she told herself. The firemen decided the fire was an accident. Nobody set it on purpose. But her mind raced on. Then how did the door of the garage get closed and locked? I don't believe that could have happened by itself. The firemen had no reason to think it wasn't an accident, so maybe they didn't look hard enough. And what about the man who tried to pick Jessica up? Red wasn't around then either, he was home with me. The silent argument went around and around in her brain until she was ready for bed.

On Monday, Jessica was cheerful and full of energy. She loved her little puppet and began to make up stories for it. Carla came over after school and they rigged up a screen to put on a shadow play while Kate finished sorting though Jessica's winter clothes. At five o'clock, Kate, Red, and Jessica walked Carla home, and when they returned Adam's car was in the driveway.

"Look, Kate! Uncle Adam's home early," Jessica said. "He'll be able to have dinner with us."

They went inside. "Gosh, I wondered where you two girls were," Adam told them with a smile. He squatted down as Jessica flew into his arms.

Kate stood watching them, feeling a little flustered. Maybe I ought to go home now, she thought. After all, my job's really over when Adam gets here. I don't want to hang around when he doesn't want me to. On the other hand, it's a bit awkward. Jessica obviously assumes that I'll stay on and we'll all have dinner together.

"We're having hamburgers tonight," the little girl confided to Adam. "And for dessert we're going to make baked apples. I never had those before. Kate says I can help her make them."

"That sounds good, sweetheart. But did you think that there might not be enough for all of us? After all, Kate didn't plan on my being home early."

Maybe I'll just help Jessica get the apples ready and stick them in the oven, Kate thought. Then I can get out of their way. To Adam she said, "Well, there's plenty, but maybe you'd rather . . ."

Adam cut into her sentence. "Fine. I've got a couple of phone calls to make, so I'll be up in my study. Just give me a call when you're ready."

Kate and Jessica went into the kitchen and started on the baked apples. After she'd cored them Kate let Jessica fill the holes with raisins and brown sugar and cinnamon while she got the rest of the dinner ready. The apples would take about an hour to bake, so she and Jessica would have time for a quick game or two of Old Maid before she started the hamburgers.

At the table, Jessica chattered animatedly to both of them until Adam gently reminded her that there was dinner to be eaten before the dessert came on. She certainly seems happy, Kate thought. The little girl had practically pranced around the table while she was setting it and she'd fussed over everything, making sure it was just right. And it's not just because her Uncle Adam is here, Kate realized. Jessica was dividing her conversation between both of them as if they were equally important to her. To see her now, cheerful and excited, no one would ever guess that this child had survived the tragic destruction of her family.

Suddenly Kate saw how the three of them would look to an outsider, sitting around the table having dinner together and talking over each one's day. Just like Mama Bear, Papa Bear, and Baby Bear. Of course, Kate thought, that was what Jessica was trying to do. She was re-creating a family to replace the one she'd lost. Kate remembered when Jessica had asked if it was okay to pretend Kate was her mom. Had it been a mistake to say yes? She really didn't think so, and she had reminded Jessica that it would only be pretend. But maybe she should talk to Adam about it at some point.

Soon the table was cleared and Jessica proudly placed a bowl with a baked apple in it beside each of their plates. "Am I supposed to eat the skin?" she asked Kate.

"It's up to you. Some people like to scrape out the soft part and just eat that and leave the skin. But I like the skin, so I eat the whole thing."

"Then I'll eat my skin too," Jessica decided. She took a bite and then another. "Boy, this is good. It's like apple pie without the pie part. I like it a lot."

"Me, too," Adam said. "I don't think I've had one of these since I was a kid. I'd forgotten how tasty they are." He smiled at Kate and then turned to the girl. "Now, Jess, I have a surprise for you. How would you like it if we went on a little vacation next weekend? I thought I'd take next Monday off and we'll go to this place in the Catskills called Mohonk Mountain House. It's a great big hotel and they have lots of fun things to do there."

"Like what?" Jessica asked.

"Oh, they have boats, and you can walk in the woods and climb on the rocks, and I'm pretty sure they have horses."

Jessica's eyes opened wide. "Horses!" she breathed. "And I can go riding?"

"I don't see why not."

"Oh, boy!" Jessica exclaimed. She turned to Kate. "Won't it be fun? Do you know how to ride, Kate?"

"I used to, but I haven't done it for a long time."

"It's okay. I'll show you how," Jessica promised. "And then we can go for a ride together in the woods, right, Uncle Adam?"

Kate's face flushed as she suddenly realized that Jessica expected her to go along. "Oh, I . . ." she started.

At the same time Adam said, "Jessica, I think . . ."

They both stopped. Adam gestured for Kate to finish what she was saying, and more embarrassed than ever, she said, "Jessica, I don't think your Uncle Adam meant for me to go along. This is supposed to be a vacation for just the two of you."

"But I want you to come," Jessica said earnestly. "Uncle Adam, Kate's invited too, isn't she?"

"Well, honey, Kate probably has other things to do next weekend."

Jessica turned to Kate. "Do you?"

"Well," Kate started. She really felt on the spot.

"Oh, say you'll go," Jessica implored. "You can stay in my room with me. It'll be like a sleepover only we'll be in a hotel. And Uncle Adam said there are lots of fun things to do, so I know you'll have a good time." When Kate didn't respond, Jessica's eyes filled with tears. "Please, Kate."

Kate glanced helplessly at Adam and he said to the little girl, "Well, Jessica, Kate and I will have to talk about it. And we'll see. But right now, it's time for a bath and bed for you, young lady." He put his napkin on the table and stood up. "I'll be down in a few minutes," he said to Kate. "Jess, I'll race you to the top of the stairs."

Between bath and story time and good night kisses, it was more than a few minutes before Kate and Adam were alone in the living room. Kate was feeling awkward about the Mohonk trip and was relieved when Adam began talking about another topic altogether. "By the way," he told her, "that Walter fellow came by this weekend." He poured both of them drinks at the little cart in the corner and handed Kate hers. "I finally figured out who he is. I was a judge for the local art show a while ago, and he's one of those people who comes and chats to anyone in a position of authority. He told me that he's a painter and would like me to look at some of his work."

Adam settled himself in the chair across from her and smiled. "I'm not sure he has any work to show. I really didn't know what to think of him." Taking a sip of his drink, Adam went on, "Anyway, he came around on Saturday and I had a brief chat with him. I told him not to bother you during the week when I'm not here. I think that should take care of things."

"Thanks," Kate said. "He did make me a little nervous." For a moment she was tempted to tell Adam about her conversation with Amy and her friend's suggestion that Walter might be the hit-and-run driver. Then she rejected the idea. She wasn't sure she believed it herself, and she was certain that Adam would think she was being paranoid. Instead, Kate moved onto a safer topic.

"I finally finished going through Jessica's winter things today," she said to him. "And I've made a list of what I think she'll need." She held out the sheet of paper covered with handwriting. "I know it seems like an awful lot. In fact, it is an awful lot," she said with a little laugh as he concentrated on the list. "But almost nothing she has now fits her. She must have had a growth spurt over the summer."

"I guess she has grown quite a bit. It's the kind of thing I don't really notice as much as I suppose I should.

I'm not surprised that she needs a whole new wardrobe. And it was very good of you to do all this work, writing every item and size down. Thanks a lot." Adam pushed back the lock of hair that had fallen over his eyes and sighed. "I guess I'd better plan a couple of Saturdays to take her shopping."

"Well, I'd be happy to do some of it with her myself if you'd like," Kate told him.

Adam kept his eyes on the list. "I wouldn't want to impose on you like that."

"It wouldn't be an imposition at all," Kate assured him. "In fact I think it would be fun."

"Well, if you really wouldn't mind." He gave her a little smile. "You've probably already guessed that shopping isn't my favorite activity. And I'm sure you'd do a better job than I would. I do want Jessica to look nice . . ." he trailed off.

"Of course. She's such a pretty little girl. And I must say she looked wonderful today. I was a little worried after everything that happened on Friday that she'd be still upset, but she seems in great spirits."

Adam nodded. "Yes, I was concerned myself about the effect the fire would have on her. And, of course, I felt terribly responsible. But she's perked up. I spent all of Saturday and Sunday with her, just being around and doing quiet sorts of things. I hope it helped."

"I'm sure it did. You have a wonderful rapport with her, and she loves you a lot. Her eyes just light up when she sees you," Kate told him.

"Well, thanks. It's a big responsibility, but I feel more comfortable about her since you started taking care of her," Adam said. "She's very fond of you, you know." Adam stopped speaking, and there was an awkward pause which lengthened until at last he went on. "That's why she wanted you to come with us this weekend. I could see that you were embarrassed and I want to assure you that I don't expect you to give up your weekends to Jessica."

Kate said slowly, "I *was* a bit embarrassed. I didn't want you to think I assumed I was included. After all, it's a chance for you and Jessica to spend time alone together."

"Oh, I can spend lots of weekends with her by myself. It's just that I know you have your own life and it doesn't seem right to take up your weekend as well. Besides, I imagine you have plans, don't you?"

"Well, not exactly," Kate said, not knowing how else to respond.

Adam kept fiddling with the clothing list in his hand. "Well, if you've got the time, I'd appreciate your coming, but please don't feel you have to. It's supposed to be a nice old place, but perhaps you would be bored. It seems an awful lot to ask."

"I can't imagine I'd be bored, and I'm sure it's a terrific place. But, well, it also sounds a bit expensive . . ."

Adam leapt in. "No, no. Of course I'd pay for it. After all this whole weekend is for Jessica." He paused and looked at her. "You really wouldn't mind?"

"I'd love to go," Kate said with a smile.

For the rest of the week Jessica couldn't stop talking about their forthcoming trip. She was so happy and excited about it that Kate was glad that she'd agreed to go along. It obviously meant a great deal to the child. Adam had eagerly accepted her offer to take Jessica shopping, and they spent a pleasant afternoon at Macy's in White Plains buying school clothes. Kate found a buttercup-yellow crew-neck sweater—exactly what she'd pictured—and the little girl wanted to wear it home.

"You can take it on the trip to Mohonk, Jess. You'll probably need a warm sweater up there," Kate told her with a smile.

But the anonymous phone calls resumed on Tuesday. Kate picked up the phone on the ninth ring. Whoever it was, he was persistent. "Cordell residence," she said cautiously.

She heard the familiar pause and then the creepy whispers. "Lady bug, lady bug, Fly away home. Your house is on fire, and your children are gone. Going, going, gone." By the end, the voice had dropped to a satisfied murmur and Kate stood transfixed in horror as she listened.

Then she slammed down the phone. What was the matter with her? Why didn't she just hang up as soon as she heard that haunting whisper? She hugged herself, thankful that Jessica was upstairs doing her homework. At least the child hadn't witnessed her listening helplessly to some crank rattling off mixed-up nursery rhymes. Suddenly, Kate knew why she stayed on the phone. She had a morbid curiosity about what the caller would say, how he would switch around or add onto one of these harmless jingles. It was like sticking your tongue into the spot where a tooth had come out just to see if it hurt. And it did. There was something very wrong with the person who made these calls.

The next call came on Thursday while Jessica was at Brownies. Kate waited while the phone rang and rang. Finally it stopped only to start up again a moment later. It was as if someone were watching the house and knew she was home.

"Cordell residence," Kate said, and held her breath.

For a moment she thought she had a hang-up but suddenly the soft whispering began. "There was a little girl and she had a little curl. Right in the middle of her forehead." He stopped and Kate heard the heavy intake of a deep breath. I should hang up the phone right now, she thought, but she found herself clutching the receiver, waiting for him to go on. "When she was good, she was very very good. But when she was bad, she was in big trouble. Ha. Ha. Ha." The unreal, disjointed laugh trailed off, and Kate found herself listening to a broken connection.

By this time Kate was thoroughly unnerved. She decided to call Detective Roper at the police station and ask his advice. When she'd told him about the calls, he asked several questions.

"Did the caller say anything rude or obscene?"

"No," Kate said, "that's partly why the calls scare me. Whoever it is just recites these nursery rhymes, except he changes the words so they sound a little sick. Then he doesn't say another word."

Detective Roper sighed. "Well, Ms. Jamison, I'm sorry to tell you this but there just isn't a whole lot you can do about it. You can call the phone company, but they can't trace these calls, and I doubt that they'll have anything helpful to suggest. I know it's real annoying, but my guess is that it's just kids, and they'll get bored with it after a while. Of course, if they go on, Mr. Cordell can have the phone number changed, but that's a big pain to go through."

"Isn't there anything I can do?" Kate asked him. "How about blowing a loud whistle into the phone? I've heard that's supposed to discourage prank callers."

"Well." Roper sounded doubtful. "I wouldn't recommend it myself. It might discourage them if they're just kids fooling around. But if it's a weirdo, and there's always that possibility, you can't predict how he'd react. He might get really upset, and if he knows where you live . . . I don't think it's a good idea. Your best bet is to just ignore it."

"But what if it's the hit-and-run driver?" Kate was aware that her voice was a bit shrill.

"Now, Ms. Jamison, I don't think that's something you need to worry about. Nobody but you and Mr. Cordell and us here in the police station know that the little girl said she saw the accident. And even at that, she hasn't said she could recognize the driver again. We'll catch that guy sooner or later, but in the meantime I don't think she's in any danger at all. I don't see how she could be. Still, I'll make it a point to drive by the house whenever I'm up that way and make sure there's nothing going on. But on these phone calls, you're doing the right thing. Just don't say anything at all besides hello. These people get their kicks by making you scared or angry, and anything you say to them just makes them keep on doing it."

"Well, thanks," Kate said. "I'm sure you're right."

"Call me any time," he told her.

On Friday evening as Kate was leaving, Adam asked her if she could be at the house by nine o'clock the next morning. That way they could get a reasonably early start and drop Red off at the kennel on their way to the Catskills.

"Fine, I'll see you then," Kate said.

Jessica ran to the door and gave Kate a big hug. "We're going to have so much fun!" she cried. "See you tomorrow, Kate!"

When Kate got home, she thought she'd better get her things packed and ready for the morning. Adam had told her that Mohonk was old-fashioned enough to have a dress code for dinner—no blue jeans, and jackets were required for men. She'd better take a skirt and sweater and perhaps a dress for Saturday night.

Suddenly she thought, I'd better call Amy and tell her I'm going out of town. I wouldn't want her to try to reach me and imagine that I'd been caught by the mad kidnapper or something. She dialed Amy's number and spoke briefly to Mark before Amy got on the line.

"Hi, it's me. I just wanted to let you know that I'll be away this weekend. I didn't want you to call and get worried."

"Oh, where are you going?"

"I'm going up to Mohonk—you know, that place in the Catskills—with Jessica and Adam."

Amy whistled. "And you told me he was a cold fish. Kate, I think you'd better come clean. This is your old friend Amy, remember—"

Kate laughed and was glad that Amy couldn't see her

blush. "No, no, Amy, it's not like that at all. It's just that Jessica assumed that I was going with them and he didn't want to disappoint her."

"Well, whoever wanted you along, it sounds like a lot of fun. But now, Kate, nothing else weird has happened this week, has it?"

"No, not really," Kate said, "except that I've had more of those phone calls. But I talked to that policeman who came up to the house before, and he didn't think there was anything to worry about."

"Well, I hope he's right. I'm glad you talked to him. You'll be back on Sunday, right?"

"No, not until Monday evening."

"Well, listen, why don't we have lunch on Wednesday? Can you do that? I'm going to be in the city in the morning, and I could drive up to Yonkers, or we could meet near Columbia, or whatever."

"Yonkers isn't really much of a lunch place," Kate told her with a laugh. "But I could meet you anywhere around school—I have to go in to the library sometime soon anyway. How about if we meet there and go have a nice lunch someplace nearby?"

"Sounds great," Amy said, "and I'll be expecting to hear all about your glamorous weekend."

CHAPTER 10

By NINE-THIRTY ON Saturday morning the three of them
were in Adam's car and on their way. As Kate looked at
the sunlight filtering through the tall trees along the Saw
Mill River Parkway, she thought with amusement of all
the gear crammed into the back of the little car. Who
would have thought that two adults and a child would
need so much stuff for a mere three days in the country?
She gave a little sigh of contentment. It was a glorious
autumn day, crisp and clear, and if the weather kept up
like this they could hardly help having a wonderful time.
All her feelings of awkwardness and embarrassment
seemed to have slipped away, and she felt ready to relax
and enjoy this unexpected holiday.

The little white Datsun followed the signs to the New
York Thruway and soon they were speeding across the
Tappan Zee Bridge. There was little traffic, and they
had clear views up and down the majestic Hudson
River.

"Look, Jessica, you can see all the way to the George
Washington Bridge," Kate said, twisting around in her
seat to point south down the river.

Jessica gave a perfunctory look in that direction.
"Yeah," she said, "but look over on your side. There's

a lighthouse! And look at all those boats!''

"Those big flat ones are called barges, honey," Adam said with a glance out the passenger window. "They don't have any engines—they have to be pushed by tugboats to go anywhere. There used to be lots of them carrying all kinds of things up and down the river in the old days."

Jessica peered out the window. "I'd like to ride on a tugboat," she said. "I used to have a book about one —I think its name was Scuffy."

Jessica chattered on, obviously pleased and excited to be setting off on a journey. As the thruway turned north again, the landscape was dotted with flaming color. Kate and Jessica admired a particularly gorgeous maple whose branches were enveloped in a cloud of brilliant orange-red. The two of them giggled as they spotted a whole group of trees whose autumn colors seemed to be coming out in splotches. Patches of red dotted the still-green foliage, and Jessica decided that this grove of trees must have the chicken pox. But after another half hour, the little girl was getting restless.

"When are we going to be there, Uncle Adam?" she asked plaintively.

"I can't tell you exactly," he said, "but it won't be too much longer."

Kate thought, it's hard to remember that what seems like a short time to an adult can feel very long to a child. This is beautiful country we're passing through, but it's still just trees and hills. There are hardly even any signs to read. She could recall many car trips with her mother and father when they had been exclaiming over the scenery and she had been impatiently waiting to arrive at their destination. What had she done to make the miles go faster?

Turning to look at Jessica, she said, "I've got an idea. Why don't we play Grandmother's Trunk?"

"What's that?"

"It's a great game for riding in the car—I'll tell you how to play."

She and Jessica started off with an apple and a bobcat, and Adam insisted on taking his turn with a clarinet. By the time they'd gone twice through the alphabet, they were on the ramp for Exit 18 at New Paltz.

Adam looked at his watch. "I thought we'd stop in town for lunch," he said, "but it's still a bit early. So we'll explore and see if there's anything interesting to look at."

It was a typical college town, the main street lined with bars and restaurants and shops selling things such as leather goods and art posters and books and records. But in about a quarter of a mile there was a historical marker on the right, and beyond it an ancient graveyard. Adam pulled off the road and they all got out.

The cemetery was lovingly maintained and Kate was struck by the pathos of many of the worn gravestones. These people had died so young, especially the women. Then she saw two gravestones side by side, each bearing the same name. She read the names and the dates more closely and then called to Adam.

"Look at this. Isn't it sad? These people had one little girl named Harriet Ann, and she died when she was only a year old. Then, less than a year later, they had another daughter and they named her Harriet Ann also. And look, she was only three when she died—see this stone. It says 'the second daughter.' Think how they must have felt. What a hard life it was for them—it's almost impossible to imagine it now."

"Yes," Adam said soberly, "it makes you realize how lucky we are to live in the age of modern medicine." He glanced at Jessica who was stalking a red squirrel. "Not so many children now die of disease."

Kate shuddered, and the phrase "someone walking over my grave" popped into her head. She was glad that

Jessica skipped up just then, a bunch of brightly colored leaves in her hands. "Look, Kate," she exclaimed. "Aren't these neat? Can I take them home?"

"Sure you can, Jess," Kate replied, "but you know, the colors never last as well as you want them to. That's one of the fun things about seeing the leaves turn in the fall. Every year you're surprised all over again by how bright and beautiful the colors are."

Adam ruffled Jessica's hair. "Ready for some lunch now, Jessica?" When she nodded eagerly, he went on, "Let's see what New Paltz has to offer."

They drove back into the town and chose one of the many hamburger pubs that seemed well patronized by students. Forty-five minutes later they emerged and Adam said cheerily, "That was just what I wanted." He grinned at Jessica. "A good start to the trip, don't you think, Jess? Beautiful weather, interesting historic sights to see, and a tasty lunch. Now on to Mohonk!"

In the car, he handed Kate the typed directions to the hotel. She hardly needed them since the way was clearly marked, and they wound their way up the narrow country road until they came to the gatehouse of the old resort.

"I guess you can't just wander through here without permission," Kate said as she looked over the posted rules and regulations for hotel guests and day visitors. "They seem pretty serious about their privacy." She gestured toward the substantial building manned by two uniformed employees. Before Adam could reply, the car in front of them moved off up the hill, and one of the guards came over to Adam's window.

"Are you staying at the hotel, sir?"

"Yes, we are."

"Name, please?" Adam told him, and the man referred to his clipboard. Satisfied, he made a check mark on his list. Then he stepped back and wrote down the license plate number on a tag which he presented to Adam. "Just give this to the bellman and he'll attach it to your keys when he parks your car. Have you been here before?''

"No."

"Well, enjoy your stay, and welcome to the nineteenth century."

As he let in the clutch, Adam smiled at Kate and Jessica. "Well, ladies, this should be interesting."

The little white car climbed up the winding road through stands of tall trees displaying their autumn magnificence. Discreet but firmly worded signs instructed walkers to stay on the marked paths.

"Look at that!" Jessica pointed to a small open-sided wooden structure perched on a rocky overhang not far from the road. It had a look vaguely reminiscent of a mountain hut in a Japanese landscape. "What is it, Kate?" Jessica wanted to know.

"It's a place for hikers to rest and look at the view," Kate told her. "See, it's got benches inside."

"Oh, neat!" Jessica said. "And if it rained, you could stay inside it and keep dry."

"Well," Kate said with a laugh, "I don't think you'd stay very dry in that one. You can see the sunlight coming through the spaces in the roof."

"Well, it's neat anyway," Jessica said firmly.

The road led out of the trees, and they saw a vast expanse of carefully tended green lawn. To the left was the longest grape arbor Kate had ever seen, and behind it the grass stretched back to a steep hillside clothed in fall foliage. "Oh, Jessica, look at the grape arbor—it's like a long tunnel. These gardens must be gorgeous in the middle of summer."

But Jessica was more interested in the funny-looking stone house on their right, which she decided would be a perfect place to play Sleeping Beauty or Rapunzel.

And then they rounded a bend, and there, sprawled in front of them, was Mohonk Mountain House. Kate gasped. "What an amazing place!"

It was huge, imposing in height, and stretching its

massive wings from the center entrance. Victorian influences were evident in the numerous turrets and towers and gabled windows, and nearly every room had a balcony equipped with two sturdy, old-fashioned green wooden lawn chairs. Kate thought, you couldn't say it's pretty, but it's definitely memorable, even awe inspiring.

"Welcome to Mohonk House." The bellboy greeted them politely. Adam walked to the check-in desk while Kate and Jessica gazed around the small lobby, which was dominated by a central staircase with lovely wood banisters. Hallways marched off in almost every direction, and there was a profusion of lounges and oddly shaped seating areas.

Adam returned and said, "The rooms won't be ready until four, so we may as well look around." He squatted down and zipped up Jessica's jacket. "Ready for some exploring, Jess?"

A moment later, armed with a sheet showing the paths and trails, the three of them moved into a lounge whose doors led onto a large veranda.

The back of the hotel overlooked a lake and the wooded mountain rising just behind it. A wide path led past the nearby boat dock and appeared to continue into the woods at the far side of the lake.

As Jessica bounded joyously ahead, Adam took an expansive breath. "Mountain air—nothing like it," he informed Kate. "I think this place is going to be just great."

The setting was certainly beautiful. Sunlight glinted off the calm waters of the lake, and a slight breeze ruffled the changing leaves. An elderly couple strolled toward them and smiled a silent hello. There was an air of peace and tranquility.

As Adam and Kate rounded the bend and entered the woods, they saw Jessica reading a wooden sign at the edge of the path. "What's a labyrinth?" the girl asked when they got closer.

"It's like a maze," Kate explained while she and Adam read the sign Jessica had been looking at. It pointed the way to a path called the Labyrinth and informed walkers that this rugged route required sturdy shoes and should not be attempted by those uninterested in strenuous exercise. Looking where the arrow pointed, Kate saw the reason for the sign. A wide swath of broken rock angled up from the lake path they were on. The blocks of stone were huge and sharp edged, and looked as if some giant had tumbled this jumbled heap down the side of the mountain. From where Kate stood, the "path" seemed no more than an indication of where to start climbing the sheer slabs and crawling through the dark crevices between them.

"Boy, those rocks are big," Jessica said, a mixture of fear and longing in her voice.

Adam laughed. "They sure are. And that climb looks like it would be fun. But not today, honey. We have to get ourselves settled in and I think that trail might take quite a while. Let's keep on going around the lake and see what we discover." He touched the child's hair and gave her a smile, but as they moved on along the lake path, Jessica looked wistfully over her shoulder at the rocks of the Labyrinth.

The lake shore path was wide and fairly level, closely following the water's edge. Boughs of fir and maple arched over their heads, and at frequent intervals they came upon a side excursion to yet another gazebo perched on rocks jutting out into the lake.

The hillside that sloped sharply upward from the path was strewn with boulders, and the rocky terrain had numerous outcroppings and overhangs. Jessica had decided to make her way around the lake without setting foot on the path. As she scampered across the rocks she called down to Adam and Kate, "Look at me! Look at me!"

"I see you, Jess," Adam called back. "You're turning into a regular little mountain goat."

Kate looked across at his upturned head with its distinctive profile. How different he looks and sounds when he's relaxed, she thought. It's almost as if he becomes another person.

The path ran alongside a small crescent of sand, and skirted the base of the granite cliffs now rising near the water's edge. Then it ended, and Kate and Adam were forced to retrace their steps back to a set of wooden stairs that took them up to the top of the cliffs.

Jessica was there ahead of them, exploring the numerous narrow side trails that ran nearer to the edge of the rocks. "Kate, Uncle Adam, come on over here," she called from a gazebo perched out over a long sheer drop.

The two adults made their way over a skimpy wooden bridge and across the smooth rock surface to the structure at the edge of Pine Bluff. "Isn't this neat?" Jessica went on as they came closer. "It's like a little house in the air. Let's pretend we're sailors up at the very top of the highest mast on the ship."

The view from the gazebo was spectacular. The hotel loomed up from the lake beyond the curve of the cliffs, casting its convoluted shadow across the water. Slanting afternoon sunlight sparkled on the surface of the lake and warmed the wooded rocky slopes behind it. Perched on the mountain's highest point, a tall stone tower stood lonely sentinel.

"That must be Sky Top," Kate said, pointing up at the mountain crest. "Remember, Jess, we passed a sign for the path to Sky Top just when we started into the woods." Skimming the information on the back of her map, she went on, "Sure. That must be it. It says that the Tower is at the top of Sky Top Path, and that on a clear day you can see six states from the observation deck."

"Oh, wow!" Jessica was impressed.

And so was Adam. "That's something I want to see.

How about if we make that our plan for tomorrow morning?'' he suggested.

"Oh, goodie," Jessica said. "Come on, let's go."

Adam and Kate followed her energetic figure and soon came to a set of wooden bridges which led across to the porch of the hotel.

Many wooden rocking chairs sat facing out over the railing of the big three-sided porch. When they'd started on their walk it had been virtually empty, but now a number of people were sitting about sipping tea. The three of them went inside and found a long table filled with empty cups and saucers. A smiling young lady dispensed tea from a fat china pot.

"Well, this is a nice welcome," Kate said.

The girl looked in their direction. "Can I give you some tea?" she asked.

"I'd love some," Kate said gratefully. "But, Jess, what about you, honey?"

"I'll have tea, too," Jessica told her in a grown-up tone.

"Make one of those just half full," Kate said as the girl poured cups for the three of them. "We'll have milk and sugar in ours, Jessica."

Tea and cookies in hand, they moved toward an empty corner of the lounge. "Can't we go outside?" Jessica asked. When Adam nodded, she led the way through the wood and glass doors to the porch, where they settled themselves in rockers overlooking the boat dock.

Not far away sat another threesome that included a little girl who looked about Jessica's age. The girl got some money from her dad and scooted around the corner of the porch. A moment later she returned with a handful of brown pellets and began tossing them over the wide balustrade and into the lake below. "What's she doing?" Jessica whispered to Kate, her eyes on the other girl.

"I don't know," Kate answered. "Why don't you go and ask her?"

Jessica sidled over to watch the other little girl, and soon the two of them were huddled together in conversation while they peered over the wide ledge. A minute or two later Jessica skipped back to where Adam and Kate were sitting. "I need a nickel, Uncle Adam," she announced.

"Oh, you do, huh? And what do you plan to do with that vast sum?" Adam countered with a grin.

"I need to buy fish food." As Adam dug into his pocket, she went on, "You can see the fish down there in the water. There's a whole bunch of them, and some of them are really big. When you drop the fish food in the water, they all try to get it!"

"Sounds great, Jess." Adam held out a nickel to the little girl. "But don't lean too far over the edge, okay? I don't want to have to go fishing for you."

Kate went inside to get more tea for herself and Adam, and when she came out she saw him sitting on the balustrade watching the fish. She walked over to join him.

"Jessica, throw some over there where all those little guys are," Adam suggested, pointing to a group of smaller fish. "That's the way. Look at them gobble up that food!"

Kate and Adam watched the girls feed the fish for a while longer, and then Kate glanced at her watch. It was almost five-thirty. "I think I'd better go up and unpack Jessica's and my stuff pretty soon," she told Adam. "And I'd like to take a shower before dinner."

"Fine. Here's your key. We'll stay here for a while and then I think we'll go and investigate the game room. Why don't we plan to have dinner around seven?"

"Okay. See you later, Jessica."

The room was rather plain but comfortable. Twin beds with clean white candlewick bedspreads stood against one wall, and across from them were two padded armchairs and a fireplace with a wooden chest full of kindling and firewood. A door led to the balcony overlooking the wooden bridge to the lounge porch and the lake beyond.

Kate unpacked, and discovered that the closet was big enough to hold several wardrobes. She gave her dress a hearty shake and decided that it wasn't too badly wrinkled. Then she put on her robe. As she placed Jessica's things in a drawer of the antique bureau, she eyed the plain black telephone on the stand between the beds. For a moment she imagined hearing it ring and picking it up only to hear that whispering voice again. She shook her head. That wasn't going to happen here.

After her shower, Kate was sitting on the balcony when she heard Jessica knocking at the door. The little girl burst into the room, spilling out her enthusiastic description of the ping-pong match she had just finished with her Uncle Adam, while from the hallway Adam reminded them both that he'd be by to take them to dinner in half an hour.

"Okay, Jessica, that means you'd better hop right into the tub," Kate said. "I'll run the water for you while you get undressed."

When the little girl had bathed, Kate helped her into her pleated skirt and white blouse. "I think you'd better wear your new sweater, Jess, it may be chilly. And do you want knee socks or tights?"

Soon Jessica was all ready. She asked Kate, "Do I look okay?"

"You look very nice," Kate assured her.

"So do you," Jessica said. "I like that dress."

Kate glanced into the mirror. She had to admit she liked this dress too. The deep mossy shade set off her fair coloring and enhanced the green of her eyes. She enjoyed the feel of the soft wool challis against her skin. As she put her medallion on again and then slid her feet into her slingback pumps, she was secretly glad that Mohonk had a dress code for evening wear. Adam never sees me in anything but slacks and a sweater, she thought. I wonder if he'll like my dressed-up look—or maybe he won't even notice.

There was a tap at the door, and Jessica opened it while Kate put the room key into her purse and snapped off the lights. They stepped into the corridor.

Adam smiled impartially at the two of them. "You both look very nice."

And so do you, Kate said silently to herself as they walked toward the stairs. As usual he was wearing a V-neck sweater, this one a rich burgundy, over a crisp white shirt. His soft gray wide-wale corduroy jacket topped charcoal wool trousers and the whole effect was one of casual elegance.

The dining room was enormous, a brightly lit expanse of white cloth-covered tables and straight-backed wooden chairs. At the entrance Adam handed his table ticket to the man at the desk. "We'd like a table by the window, please."

"Let me see, Mr. Cordell," the man replied, scanning his list. But Kate had no doubt that they would be sitting by a window, and in a few moments a waitress was ushering them to a table overlooking the lake.

"I guess it's too dark to see much now," Adam said to Jessica, "but we'll have a great view for breakfast."

The waitress handed each of them a copy of that evening's dinner menu, and explained the system. "Just use that pencil in the cracker basket to circle the items you want, and I'll be back in a moment to collect your menus."

Adam raised his eyebrows at Kate. "Reminds me a little of hospital menus. I think that's the only time I've ever circled my choices."

Another waitress appeared at his side. "Can I get you something to drink?" she asked with a smile.

Adam said in surprise, "I thought Mohonk didn't have a bar."

"Oh, no, sir, drinks are available, but only during

dinner. We have beer, or I could show you the wine list, and we have a complete selection of cocktails.''

Adam asked for the wine list, and meanwhile he and Kate helped Jessica fill out her menu. She chose the vegetable soup and baked chicken, carefully drawing circles around each item. The waitress collected their menus and Adam ordered a carafe of house wine and a glass of milk for Jessica.

As they ate, they talked over their plans for the following day. Jessica was still eager to climb up to Sky Top. ''And you said they have horses here, Uncle Adam,'' she reminded him.

''So I did,'' he admitted. ''Tomorrow morning I'll call and make reservations for us to go riding after lunch. How's that?''

''Great,'' Jessica told him. ''I hope I have a black horse named King.''

Adam and Kate both laughed. ''Well, I can't promise you that,'' her uncle told her. ''Now, what would you like for dessert?''

''Can I have anything I want?'' Jessica asked.

Adam smiled at her across the table. ''Why not?''

She chose a sticky concoction topped with chocolate sauce and whipped cream and pronounced it delicious as she spooned her way to the bottom of the dish. Kate and Adam sipped their coffee and as he gazed fondly at the little girl Kate realized again how attractive he was.

When they left the dining room, Kate suggested, ''Let's wander around and see the rest of the hotel. I brought along the floor plan that was in our room, so we'll be sure we won't get lost.'' She gave Jessica a grin.

Everywhere they went, the public rooms of the hotel were filled with fabulous furniture. They weren't museum quality antiques, but functional pieces from an earlier era—caned loveseats, wicker settees, plump velvet-upholstered armchairs, oak end tables, and handsomely carved plant stands. Kate was impressed that all of it was obviously there to be used. Each informal seating area had an inviting, comfortable look.

When they got to the Lake Lounge where tea had been served that afternoon, they noticed some activity. A trio of musicians was setting up while hotel employees rearranged the furniture, pushing some of the heavy tables and chairs away from the center of the room. The bulletin board outside the lounge told them that the Saturday night dance would be starting before long.

Adam led the way through the lounge and out onto the porch. "How about a short walk before we call it a night, Jess?" he suggested. The three of them went down the porch steps and along the path toward the boat dock.

The almost full moon cast a shimmering reflection on the water, and the canoes tied to the dock rocked gently in the evening swell. Jessica clung to Kate, obviously tired but unwilling to give in to it. "Could I feed the fish again, Uncle Adam?" she asked.

"Not tonight, honey. I think they must be asleep, and I think my favorite girl should be too."

Jessica managed a tired smile, and soon they moved off the dock and headed back into the hotel. "I'll help you get ready for bed and then your Uncle Adam will come and read to you," Kate told the girl as they climbed the broad staircase toward their room.

After a chapter of *The Wind in the Willows*, Adam said to Jessica, "I think it's time for you to close your eyes and go to sleep."

"Are you leaving me?" the child wanted to know.

"It's a little early for Kate to go to bed, Jess. So we'll wander around the hotel for a while. We might go downstairs, but we won't be far away. You sleep tight, honey, and Kate will be back in a little while."

"And I'll be right here in the other bed when you wake up in the morning, Jess," Kate told her. "Night, night."

"Good night," Jessica said through her yawn as she

snuggled down under the blankets, Baby clutched in her arms.

Kate followed Adam out of the room, closing the door softly behind her. "I think I ought to stay nearby for a while," she told him, "just to make sure Jessica gets to sleep all right."

"But surely you're not planning to stand around in the hallway," he said, smiling at her. "Why don't you come and have a drink with me in my room—it's only a few doors away."

Once inside, Kate moved to the open balcony door and looked out. "It's really lovely here. I feel as though I've stepped into another world."

Adam laughed. "Well, I'd prefer it if this other world had a comfortable bar to sit in instead of encouraging guests to sneak drinks in their rooms like naughty kids."

Adam poured their drinks, and they took their glasses out to the balcony. The silence between them grew, and Kate felt a little silly staring out at a pitch-black night pretending there was a view. Still, she felt awkward about being inside Adam's room with him. Fingering the medallion hanging from her gold chain, she said, "I think this trip was just the right thing for Jessica. She's been bubbly and full of plans all day. You made a good choice in coming here."

"Yes, even with its idiosyncracies, this place is what I had in mind." He saw Kate shiver. "You must be freezing—you don't even have a jacket. Come on inside and I'll build a fire."

"One thing they've got here is great firewood," Adam said after they'd retreated indoors and he was hunkered down in front of the fireplace. "It's so dry you could practically start a log burning with a match. I wish I had some of this at home." He replaced the firescreen and then sat down in the other armchair. "Kate," he went on, "I hope you don't feel you have to be with Jessica every single second we're here. You're entitled to some time to yourself, so please let me know if there are some of these activities you'd rather not take part in.''

"Oh, no," Kate protested. "It all sounds like fun. I'm just in the mood for an old-fashioned country weekend." She took a final sip of her drink, then put her glass on the table and stood up. "Well, I guess I'll check on Jessica and make sure she's asleep."

Adam stood up as well. "But it's too early for you to go to bed yourself, isn't it? Let's wander downstairs and see what this country weekend place has to offer on Saturday night."

After a quick peek at the soundly sleeping little girl, the two of them walked down the broad staircase. Music filtered up the stairwell as they approached the ground floor, and once there they could see through the open doorway of the Lake Lounge that the Saturday night dance was in progress. Several older couples were dancing to an upbeat tune from the sixties, the women in long plaid wool skirts and the men in sport jackets, a few in ties. As Kate and Adam went in they noticed the couple whose daughter Jessica had met that afternoon. They were standing near a table that held a punch bowl and many little glass cups. Next to the punch bowl were several trays of potato chips and pretzels.

"Well, I guess this is it," Adam said, suppressing a grin. "Let's go over and say hello to June and Hal."

As they made their way to the refreshment table, Kate wondered how Adam knew these people's names. Then she remembered that she'd left him with Jessica and her new friend, feeding the fish. He must have introduced himself.

The other couple smiled as Kate and Adam approached. "Hi," Adam greeted them. "You haven't met Kate Jamison. Kate, this is Hal and June Bergman."

After a round of hellos and handshakes, Hal said,

"So, are you enjoying Mohonk? This is your first time here, right?"

Adam nodded and Hal went on, "Oh, it's a great place. We come up for a few days every fall. We're big on hiking and this year we've really lucked out with the weather—it's been terrific. I only wish you guys had showed up sooner, because Peggy hasn't had too many kids to play with. But maybe tomorrow morning the girls could spend some time together before we leave —we're heading home after lunch."

"That would be nice," Adam agreed, "but I more or less promised Jessica that we would walk up to Sky Top in the morning. She's eager to see the tower close up."

"No problem," Hal said, glancing at June who nodded in agreement. "That's a great walk, and the view is the best in the area. We wouldn't mind doing it again ourselves before we take off. What do you say we all go up there together? We can meet after breakfast, say around nine-thirty."

"That sounds fine," Adam said. Then he turned to survey the dance floor, where a number of couples were just finishing up a fox-trot. "This is quite something. Do they do this every weekend?"

"Yeah," Hal said with a fond smile, "isn't it great? This is such a nice, old-fashioned, friendly place, and it's fun for people like us to dance without hearing all that loud disco or whatever the kids listen to." The trio started in on the Tennessee Waltz and Hal turned to June. "Come on, honey, that's our song."

He took her hand and led her onto the floor. As they whirled off, Adam looked at Kate. "Would you like to give it a try? There's no sense standing around like a couple of wallflowers."

Kate thought, My God, I haven't waltzed since seventh grade. I hope I don't trip over my feet. But as she put her hand on Adam's shoulder, she realized there was nothing to worry about. I should have known—he's a wonderful dancer, she thought. He guided her effortlessly through the formal patterns of the music, and soon she was swept up in the pure pleasure of moving gracefully through the traditional rhythms. The trio changed beats then without a break, and they were dancing in four-four time, and then suddenly the tempo increased and the tune was a polka. Adam obviously assumed that she knew the steps and, silently blessing those torturous hours of social dancing in junior high, Kate swung right into it along with him. Five minutes later, flushed and laughing, they retired to the sidelines.

"Whew," Adam said with a grin. "I haven't done that for years. You're a good dancer, Kate."

Did he sound surprised? Kate wasn't sure. "All the credit goes to my partner," she said, pushing her hair off her forehead. "That was fun."

Hal came up beside her. "Boy, you two really cut a mean polka. How about changing partners for this one?"

After a sedate fox-trot around the floor, they all met near the refreshment table. "I don't know about you," Hal said to Kate and Adam, "but I'm ready for a break. Grab some cups and follow me."

Kate noticed that Hal and June were carefully spooning ice into their cups, ignoring the pinkish fruit punch in the bowl. June whispered, "Just get some ice and come on out on the porch."

When they got outside, Hal had pulled four of the rocking chairs into a little group in front of the railing. He pulled out a silver hip flask. "Hope Canadian Club is okay with everyone. Beggars can't be choosers." He poured a generous measure into each cup, raised his own, and said, "Cheers. Here's to new friends."

They sipped their drinks and looked out over the lake, while they exchanged information about themselves. It turned out that the Bergmans lived on Long Island. Hal was in the wholesale jewelry business, and June was active in the local hospital volunteer association, and ran a nature walk program in the elementary school. Peggy was their only child.

After a bit Hal and Adam went back for more ice. June leaned closer to Kate. "I couldn't help noticing that your last name isn't the same as Adam's. You kept your maiden name, I take it."

Flustered, Kate replied, "Oh, we're not married." Realizing that this didn't sound quite the way she wanted it to, she went on, "I work for Adam. That is, I take care of Jessica in the afternoons. I'm doing a graduate degree at Columbia."

June looked puzzled but interested. "Oh, I see. Adam's divorced?"

Kate wished the men would hurry up and return, so she wouldn't have to go on with this particular line of conversation. "Well, yes, he is. But you see, Jessica's not his daughter, she's his niece. His brother and sister-in-law were killed in a crash and he's her guardian."

"Oh, the poor little thing," June said. "But I bet he's glad to have you to help. What does a single man know about bringing up a little kid, especially a girl? I gather he doesn't have children of his own."

"No, he doesn't." Kate tried to think of another topic to talk about, but June pressed on.

"Well, he seems like an awfully nice guy, and the two of you make a nice couple. But I can't help thinking that this kind of ambiguous situation is hard for a girl Jessica's age to deal with. Now, I know this is none of my business, but wouldn't you all be better off if you and Adam just went ahead and got married? I mean, I'm sure he'd want you to keep on with your studies so you wouldn't be giving up anything, and I just think a child needs some stability and regular family life. I may be old-fashioned, but I think making it official would clarify things for everyone."

Kate looked at the woman in astonishment. She began to protest, "But it's not like that at all—" At that moment Hal and Adam returned.

"You women look like you've been having a real heart-to-heart here without us," Hal said with a chuckle. "Watch out, Adam. When my wife gets going, you never know what's going to happen."

Hal poured another drink for everyone. Then he perched on the arm of June's chair and gave her a squeeze. "My little Junebug. Would you believe we've been married twelve years next month? And still just as much in love as ever."

"Oh, Hal," June protested laughingly, "they don't want to hear about that."

"Why not? I'm not ashamed to admit it. I don't know how she puts up with me, all I know is I'm really a lucky guy." He took a swallow of his drink and then set the glass on the balustrade. "Come on, honey, let's get out on the dance floor and show some of these old-timers how it's done."

Kate leaned back in her chair. Hal and June were nice, well-meaning people, but she was grateful for a brief respite. She was grateful, too, that Adam didn't seem to feel he had to fill in every moment with talk. They sat for a bit in companionable silence. Then Adam abruptly asked, "Would you like to dance again?"

Kate nodded and they returned to the lounge. June's questions had made her self-conscious, and she was aware of how the two of them looked to the other dancers. They certainly weren't cheek to cheek, but they were definitely together. She felt his strong arm pull her closer to avoid collision with an elderly couple who acted as though the dance floor were their own. *Why do I care what anyone here thinks?* Kate said to herself. *I'm having fun.*

"Well, folks, we're going to take five, as the saying goes. But we'll be back so don't go away." The musicians put down their instruments, and Kate and Adam walked to the edge of the dance floor.

"Can I offer you another little drink?" Hal's friendly tones came from behind Kate.

"Oh, I don't think so, thanks," she said quickly. "Not for me. I've got to get upstairs and into bed or I won't be able to hike anywhere tomorrow. This country air is making me sleepy."

"Okay, sleep tight," Hal said with a wink. "See you guys in the morning."

They said good night to June and left the lounge. Adam walked up the stairs with Kate, and outside her door he said, "I hope you sleep well. Good night, Kate."

Tiptoeing into the room, Kate pulled up the covers over Jessica's sleeping form. She hung up her dress and got into her nightgown. As she stood brushing her teeth, she thought that everything had gone very well so far. But June's questions and helpful advice had made her a little uncomfortable, and she couldn't help feeling glad that the Bergmans would be leaving the next day. If she'd felt more at ease with Adam, they could have enjoyed June's misinterpretations together as a joke. But I think you'd better not bring it up, Kate counseled herself. Adam's reactions were unpredictable, and he might be annoyed at anyone discussing his personal life. As she climbed into bed and snuggled down under the blankets, she thought that June wasn't likely to say anything untoward in front of Adam. She was definitely the type for girl talk only.

Chandeliers gleaming with tall candles bathed the Lake Lounge in their warm glow as Kate stood in the wide doorway, a mist rising up over her gossamer evening slippers and the hem of her emerald-green velvet ballgown. The flickering taper in a nearby wall sconce played its light across her fair skin and showed her her reflection in the elaborately framed old mirror. Her hair, pinned up in the style of the period, framed her delicate features in a silken red-gold cloud as she stood there in the low-cut gown with its high-puffed sleeves, tight bodice, and narrow waist above the billowing long skirt.

The formal strains of the music wafted across the room and Kate could see shadowy couples swirling around the floor. In front of her was a man, tall and handsome in his velvet jacket, the ruffled silk of his shirt shimmering at his wrists and neck. The girl in his arms was beautiful. Her elaborately coiffed hair was the color of a raven's wing and she looked up at her partner with lustrous brown eyes surrounded by a fringe of long dark lashes. Only the sneer on her lovely lips spoiled the perfection of her features.

Suddenly the man looked up and caught sight of Kate. He released the girl he was holding and she vanished into the swirling mists behind her. He took a step toward Kate, staring full into her face. With a sense of certainty she knew the man was Adam, and she glided into his arms. He held her close and Kate felt she was floating as they whirled through the flickering shadows.

Then somehow they were climbing a steep path in the forest. Sweet-smelling pine boughs brushed against her billowing skirt and moonlight filtered through the branches overhead. Adam had her hand in his, pulling her along with desperate haste.

They reached the edge of the cliff. Adam turned to face her, and suddenly his arms were crushing her to him in a passionate embrace. Kate felt his heart thudding wildly through the softness of his shirt and an equal urgency surged within her. His mouth found hers and Kate yielded willingly to his devouring kiss. "Oh, Kate, I've found you at last," he whispered. Her arms tightened around his neck as she lifted her face to his, welcoming his burning desire.

Kate woke up. Her heart was beating rapidly and for a moment she looked uncomprehendingly around the unfamiliar room. It was very early; Jessica was still sleeping soundly on the other bed. Kate felt the hot flush of embarrassment on her cheeks. What could have made her dream such a thing? She didn't feel that way about Adam at all. And he certainly didn't feel that way toward her. She blushed again at the memory and thought, I'll just put it out of my mind. It's too absurd to think about.

She dozed off and when she woke again it was to see Jessica standing by the window. When the child saw that Kate's eyes were open, she hopped up on the bed and gave her a hug.

"Oh, Kate, I love staying in this hotel," she confided. "It's just like a sleepover. Don't you think it's neat?"

Kate smiled at her enthusiasm. "Yes, Jessica, I do," she said. "What time is it?"

"Fifteen minutes to seven," the child told her after looking at the travel clock beside Kate's bed. "Can't we get up now?"

"Yes, I guess so." Kate rubbed her eyes and sat up. "Why don't you brush your teeth and start getting dressed?"

Kate leaned back against her pillow as Jessica scurried into the bathroom. She was glad the child couldn't see her face as the memories of her dream came flooding back. Why had these images invaded her sleeping mind? Her cheeks burned as she tried to tell herself that she couldn't imagine the reason. I've got to stop thinking about it, she told herself sternly. Otherwise I won't be able to look Adam in the eye without blushing.

Jessica emerged from the bathroom, already nearly dressed, and Kate said, "As soon as you're ready, you can write a note to your Uncle Adam while I get dressed myself. Tell him we're downstairs in the coffee room. Then we'll slip it under his door as we go by."

"Okay." Jessica nodded importantly and started pulling on her jeans. "But what should I write it on?"

Kate waved toward the writing desk against the wall.

"Open up the front of that desk, and you'll see some writing paper inside. Just use one of those sheets for your note."

Twenty minutes later they were both ready. Jessica handed Kate her note and Kate nodded approvingly. "You did a nice job with this, Jess. It's hard to write without any lines, isn't it? Now let's go and you can put it under the door."

Out in the hall Jessica carefully slid the paper into Adam's room, and then raced ahead to the stairs. The Lake Lounge had been transformed once again, and now had a long table with coffee cups stacked on it. Kate took a cup and got a glass of milk for Jessica. Then they walked out onto the porch. The lake sparkled in the sun, and everything had a freshly washed look. Jessica peered down into the water. "Look, Kate, the fish are waiting for breakfast!"

"I thought they might be," Kate said as she gave the child a nickel. Soon Jessica was absorbed in dropping the pellets of fish food in just the right spots for the smaller fish to have a chance of reaching it.

Kate was just sipping the last of her coffee when Jessica came to say she had finished giving the fish their breakfast. "Let's go look at the horses, okay, Kate?" she begged eagerly, and Kate couldn't help giving in to her enthusiasm.

They left the porch and walked back through the hotel toward the front door. A young man was stepping into the elevator and Kate thought he looked somehow familiar. Turning, she caught another glimpse of him as the elevator door slid shut. She gasped. The man had looked like Walter! She had taken a couple of steps toward the elevator when she heard Jessica calling to her from the main entrance. Don't be silly, Kate, she thought, you couldn't have caught up with him anyway. And you're letting your imagination run away with you—how could that have been Walter, all the way up here at Mohonk? It's ridiculous. But as she hurried to join the little girl, she couldn't help casting another uneasy glance back over her shoulder.

The two of them walked down to the stable and stood outside a small corral where five horses frisked in the cool morning sunlight.

As Jessica cautiously approached the edge of the corral, one of the horses snorted in her direction, and then pranced away. "I think he likes me," the girl said to Kate. "Can I ride him this afternoon?"

"Well, I don't know, honey, but we can ask."

The horse trotted back around the corral and looked at Jessica. Then he flared his nostrils and whinnied before galloping off again.

"We'd better get back to the hotel, Jess. Your Uncle Adam is probably looking for us by now." The little girl stood, still transfixed by the sight of these marvelous creatures close up. "Come on, honey," Kate insisted. "You can tell your uncle all about the horses when we see him."

When they arrived back at the main building, Adam was standing irresolutely near the entrance to the main dining room. His face lit up when he saw them. "Oh, there you are. I was wondering—"

"Oh, Uncle Adam," Jessica burst out, "we saw some horses, and one of them sort of snorted at me. Don't you think that means he likes me? Can I ride him this afternoon? I think his name might be Spotty 'cause he's got a bunch of brown spots all over him."

"Take it easy, Jess," Adam said with a laugh. "Why don't we get some breakfast?" He led them into the dining room and as they walked to their table, he told Jessica, "I can't promise you that you can ride that spotted horse, honey. We'll all have to ride the horses that the wranglers think are best for us. But I'll bet you can give your friend a pat on the nose, and maybe they'll even have a carrot or something you can give him for a treat."

Breakfast consisted of a help-yourself selection of

juices, muffins, and boxes of cereal, as well as a menu of hot items. "Look at these tiny cereal boxes, Kate," Jessica said with delight when they got to that end of the buffet. "Aren't they neat? Let's see, which kind should I have?"

When they'd finished breakfast, they left the dining room, running into the Bergmans near the entrance. After cheery good mornings, they agreed to meet on the veranda in about half an hour. Then Kate, Jessica, and Adam went to their rooms to get ready for the morning's hike.

Chapter 11

THE PATH TO Sky Top was wide and covered with small pieces of black rock. Jessica and Peggy ran on ahead and then came racing back to report on the great rocks or neat gazebos stuck out on overhangs.

In half an hour they were at Sky Top, the tower rising in front of them. "Hey, you guys. It's really neat up here. You can see real far," Jessica called down to the adults from the top of the tower.

"Great!" Adam called back. "I'm coming right up."

They all climbed up the interior stone staircase and soon were standing on the open observation deck on top. The view was every bit as spectacular as the brochures had promised. Hills and mountains rose from the edges of grassy pasture land, the vivid green of the grass contrasting with the more somber shade of the evergreens and the brilliant blaze of orange and red leaves. The blue sky was dotted with fleecy white clouds, and the whole effect was one of an incredibly realistic painting. Below them were the many chimneys and turrets of Mohonk Mountain House and its sparkling lake nestled between the mountain and the cliffs.

"Well, this is really impressive," Adam told June and

Hal. "I can see why you were willing to do this walk again."

When they had all clambered down from the tower, June said, "Why don't we take Sky Top Path down to Mohonk Path? Then we'll end up near the Artist's Lodge and we can cut across to the gardens and the greenhouse."

By the time they'd reached the gardens the sun was nearly overhead. Jessica asked Kate, "Can me and Peggy go to the stables now? She's going to show me her horse."

Kate threw Adam a questioning glance, but he shrugged his shoulders, so Kate told the girls to go ahead. Certainly they weren't interested in the flowerless fall gardens or even in the greenhouse. And one thing Mohonk did provide was a feeling that kids on their own wouldn't get into any trouble. As the girls ran off, she heard Peggy telling Jessica, "You ought to ride Rusty. Tell them he's the one you want."

"Is he the white one with the brown spots?" Jessica asked.

"No, that's Victor. He's mean."

By the time they all headed back to the hotel for lunch, Kate felt as if they'd seen a good portion of the grounds. Hal and June insisted that they all share a table in the dining room, and when the meal was over the two little girls said a sad good-bye.

They turned to go upstairs and Adam said to Jessica, "Be sure to wear your jacket, I don't want you to get too cold on the ride."

The child's face lit up. "Riding! I almost forgot!" She dashed up ahead of Kate and Adam, her momentary sadness dispelled.

Down at the stables it turned out that just the three of them would be going out with a guide. Adam explained to the wrangler that Jessica was not very experienced, and he put her up on Rusty, a reddish-brown, stocky horse with a patient look in his eyes. The wrangler said,

"Don't worry, sir, Rusty is used to kids, and he really never wants to go faster than a slow trot. I'm sure the little girl will do fine with him."

One of the stable hands led out a tall brown horse whose coat gleamed with health, and held the reins while Adam mounted. The wrangler said to Kate, "We've got a nice lively little pinto and she could use some exercise. I think you'll like her."

By the time everyone's stirrups were adjusted, the wrangler had mounted a big, rawboned chestnut mare. "By the way, my name's Carl," he told them. "I thought we'd go up Mossy Brook Road, and then make a long circuit, coming back by way of North Lookout. It's a pretty ride, and not too hard for the little girl."

"Fine," Adam said, and they set off, Carl in the lead, then Jessica, and then Kate followed by Adam. As the path broadened out, Kate's horse was obviously itching to move a little faster, and Kate took her around in a circle to settle her down. Adam came up beside her.

"Everything okay?"

"Sure," Kate said with a laugh. "We're just deciding who's in charge on this ride." After a moment, she moved up next to Jessica, and the little girl turned to her with a beaming smile.

"Oh, Kate, isn't this great?" She looked straight ahead again, sitting up tall, and holding the reins just the way the wrangler had shown her. "I love riding!"

The trail sloped upward through the trees, and soon it was as if the buildings below didn't exist. They could have been riding through uninhabited wilderness, except for the well-maintained surface beneath their mounts' feet. After a while the path leveled off. Carl looked back.

"There's a nice, long, smooth stretch here if you folks would like to have a canter. I'll stay with Jessica and Rusty, and we'll catch up with you at the meadow up ahead."

Kate and Adam edged past the other two horses. The

pinto could hardly wait, and needed just the barest nudge of Kate's foot to take off up the trail. Kate felt the wind rushing through her hair, and heard the steady thud of Adam's horse behind her. Soon he had come up almost neck and neck with her, his big mount's long legs covering more ground than the pinto's. The tall brown horse clearly was the kind that liked to be the leader. But the pinto didn't like to be beaten either, and they thundered along the broad path together. Kate gave herself up to the exhilarating speed and the feel of the horse moving rhythmically beneath her. They emerged from the trees into a wide sunny meadow and circled it, reluctantly slowing to a walk.

"Wow, that was great!" Kate exclaimed, brushing her red-gold hair back from her face and leaning over to pat her horse's neck. "You're a good girl, Sheila."

"You ride well, Kate," Adam said. "There are a lot of things I don't know about you, it seems."

Kate looked at him curiously, and then kicked Sheila into a gentle trot around the edge of the meadow. What had he meant by that?

Once they were all at the meadow, Carl said to Jessica, "You're doing a fine job with your horse, young lady. Would you like to try going a little faster for a while? I'll go on up ahead and wait, and you can have Rusty trot on the road toward me."

Jessica looked eager but nervous as she nodded to Carl and gripped her reins tighter. "You might have to give Rusty a slap with your reins, ma'am," Carl instructed Kate. "He's not much inclined to get going unless he smells the barn up ahead."

"All set, Jess?" Kate asked gently. She could see the child's knuckles beginning to whiten as she gripped the saddle horn and reins together. Jessica nodded and Kate said, "Give Rusty a kick."

It took much more than a couple of kicks from Jessica to get the old horse going, but finally he started off. His trot had a slow rhythm reminiscent of a rocking horse, and before Jessica had gone more than a few yards she'd taken her hands off the saddle horn and was looking very proud of herself, sitting up and holding the reins.

When they reached the barn, Carl helped Jessica dismount. "Gosh, that was fun," she said blissfully. Then she gave Rusty a pat. "You were great, Rusty. You're a really neat horse."

Carl moved back toward a basket in the corner and returned with a small apple in his hand. "If you'd like, you can give this to him as a treat," he said, offering the apple to Jessica. "Just hold it in your palm and keep your hand flat."

Jessica didn't flinch as the horse's big lips swept across her outstretched hand, gobbling up the apple. "Look at that," she said, pleased with herself. "He liked it a lot."

"He sure did," Adam agreed. Then he thanked Carl for the ride before the three of them trooped back to the hotel. A number of people were hanging around in the lobby, and Kate stiffened as she caught sight of a man who had just turned away from the desk. There he was again, and this time she was sure it was Walter.

"Something the matter?" Adam asked her.

"Not exactly," she said slowly. "It's just that I think that man over there is Walter—you know who I mean."

She glanced down at Jessica, but the girl was already asking, "Who's Walter?"

"Someone your Uncle Adam knows," Kate told her.

Adam was looking around the lobby and now he said to Kate, "I don't see him."

Kate peered toward where she had seen the man, but he was not there. Scanning the room, she saw no sign of him at all. It was as if he had vanished. "I can't imagine what happened to him," she said unhappily.

"Well, I don't really believe it *was* Walter," Adam said. "It seems pretty unlikely. But if you see this guy again, point him out to me."

Kate nodded, and as she went up the stairs she thought, I'm sure Adam is right. It can't really be Walter staying here at Mohonk. But the incident had left her feeling unsettled, and the sense of foreboding that temporarily had left her now returned. Even here I can't seem to entirely escape the shadow that hangs over the house in Edgar's Landing, she realized uncomfortably. But Kate steeled her mind against the feeling. She wasn't going to let these nebulous fears spoil the good time they were all having. When she got back to Edgar's Landing would be soon enough to worry about the strange happenings that seemed to threaten the little girl she had vowed to protect.

When Adam tapped at their door, both Kate and Jessica had showered and changed. "How nice you two smell—all fresh and clean," Adam said as he bent to give Jessica a hug.

The three of them walked downstairs, and Adam said, "We have lots of time before dinner—let's check the bulletin board and see what's going on."

Jessica wandered into the lounge where a family was playing Parcheesi at one of the tables. She returned and said wistfully to Kate, "I wish we'd brought one of my games. I'd like to play a game now."

The young man at the Guest Services desk, overhearing her, said to Adam, "You know, we have board games that our guests can borrow, if you'd like to do that."

After looking over the assortment, Adam and Jessica decided on Monopoly. They got it all set up on a table and soon were absorbed in buying and selling and passing Go. When it was almost seven o'clock, the game of course was far from over. Jessica was eager to leave it all set up to be continued after dinner, but Kate felt certain that this wasn't possible. However, she got a pencil and paper and began to write down each player's assets. "This way," she told Jessica, "we'll know exactly where we all were if we get a chance to play some more." Then they returned the game and made their way to the dining room.

By the time Kate and Adam were drinking their after-dinner coffee, Jessica's eyelids were drooping. "She's had a long exciting day," Adam said to Kate as he carried the dozing child into the elevator. "She'll hardly stay awake long enough to brush her teeth."

Kate opened the door to the room and Adam deposited Jessica on the bed. "Just come down to my room when you've got her into bed," he said to Kate. "I'll see you in a few minutes."

As Kate helped the little girl into her nightgown and squeezed toothpaste onto her toothbrush for her, she wondered why she didn't feel more tired herself. Jessica had awakened her at the crack of dawn, and she wasn't used to so much physical activity. But she wasn't a bit tired—in fact, she felt strangely exhilarated.

"Good night, Jessica," she whispered, tucking in the blankets around the child. "Sleep tight."

Leaving the bathroom light on, she went out and closed the door softly behind her. Walking down the hallway, she knocked at Adam's door.

"She's sound asleep," Kate told him as he let her in. "And I bet you're kind of tired yourself. This is supposed to be a restful vacation for you, after all. I thought maybe I'd just go down and sit in front of one of the fires for a while."

"Oh. Well, I had thought maybe we could go for a walk, but if you'd rather be by yourself for a while, I can understand." He sounded disappointed.

"Oh, no. I mean, a walk would be fine. It was just—"

"Don't worry," he told her with a laugh. "I'll let you know when I'm tired."

Downstairs, they stepped out onto the porch. The full moon cast a cool, brilliant light over the lake, and the tall trees and the dark clouds scudding across it from time to time lent a touch of drama and mystery. "I don't think this is real," Kate told Adam. "It's a stage set they provide for the guests."

"Well, let's walk along the cliff," Adam replied. "Then we'll get the full benefit of the show."

They crossed the wooden bridge and made their way along the steep path. On the tumbled rocks Kate slipped and Adam caught her arm. "You'd better hold onto me," he told her. "Jessica would never forgive me if anything happened to you."

His strong hand was warm on hers and he kept hold of it even after they'd reached the level path and Kate was in no danger of tripping. He seemed almost unaware of it, as if he'd simply forgotten to let go, and after a moment he said, "Why are you doing a Ph.D. in English, Kate? What are you going to do with it once you have it?"

"Those are hard questions," she said lightly. "I guess I'm doing it because I enjoy it. As for what will happen after I'm finished, I really don't know. There's not much demand these days for English professors."

"I guess that's true. But it's important to be doing something you care about, no matter where it leads. What about your family—are they proud of what you're doing, or would they rather see you married and having babies?"

Surprised at the question, Kate replied, "Well, my dad died several years ago, but I like to think he'd be pleased with how I'm living my life. And my mom— well, she doesn't entirely understand what the attraction is for me in researching something that was written two hundred years ago, but she's willing to accept that it's what I want. I'm an only child, so I'm sure she'd like to see me settled down and producing grandchildren, but she doesn't push me about it." *Why am I being so forthcoming?* she wondered. *Was it because this was the first time he'd acted interested in her as a person? Or am I just under the spell of the mountain air and the full moon gliding above them?*

"And what about you?" she asked. "How did you decide to become a graphic designer?"

"Oh, that was easy," he replied with a laugh. "I started out to be an artist, and when I found out I wasn't good enough, graphic design was the next best thing."

She looked up at his strong face shadowed by the trees. "What do you mean?"

"Ever since I was a kid, I'd dreamed of being a painter, but after a couple of years of trying it, I realized I would never be more than just competent. I didn't have that special magic that it takes." He glanced at her and smiled. "Don't look so upset, it wasn't a tragedy. I like what I do and I think I'm good at it. And I wouldn't have been happy being mediocre."

"But you still paint," Kate said. "I saw some of your work upstairs that day I was searching the house for Jessica." In her mind's eye she saw those strangely unhappy faces again. Perhaps she shouldn't have said anything about them.

But Adam went on cheerfully, "Oh, sure, but I do it just for my own pleasure. Or therapy, maybe. It's a good way to get things out of my system." They angled onto another path that led through a stand of tall evergreens. Adam held Kate's hand a little tighter as he asked casually, "What did you think of them?"

What should she say? She couldn't avoid the question with some lame reply about not knowing much about art—he obviously cared what she thought. After a moment she said slowly, "I thought they seemed both angry and sad, and I found them a little disturbing. But they're powerful—those faces have haunted me."

He stopped walking and turned to face her. "Have they?" he asked gently. "I'm sorry—I didn't mean them to. They haunted me for a long time." His gray eyes held her gaze. Then he turned away and started toward a gazebo that clung to the cliff's edge above the sandy beach. He drew her inside and they sat side by side on the bench, looking out over the water.

Neither of them said anything, and as always when she felt uncertain, Kate was twisting her gold medallion back and forth on its chain. Then she realized that Adam was watching her, and she dropped her hand to her lap.

"That medallion is really lovely," he said. "I've noticed that you almost always wear it." He reached over to lift it in his fingers, and Kate felt the warmth of his hand as it brushed her throat. "But I haven't been able to figure out why the initials are K.S. instead of K.J.," he went on. "Isn't Jamison your maiden name?"

"Oh," Kate said with a laugh, "K.S. was my great-grandfather, Karl Swensen. This is his watch fob, and my grandmother, his daughter, gave it to me for my sixteenth birthday. I guess it is a little confusing."

Adam smiled at her. "I see—that explains it. I thought perhaps you'd been married . . ."

"No," Kate said quickly, "I haven't."

"That surprises me—you must have had lots of opportunities." Was it her imagination, or did he sound jealous?

"Well, not lots," she told him lightly, "but I did think about it pretty seriously last year. There was a guy I was really involved with. But when it came to actually marrying him, I just felt I couldn't. He was very nice and smart and all that, but sometimes I looked at him and wondered what I was doing with him."

"Smart girl," Adam teased her. "You were just waiting for a better offer, weren't you?" He ruffled her hair and Kate felt her face grow warm. She was thankful for the gazebo's concealing shadows. Then he went on in a more serious tone, "I'm sure you know I was married."

Kate nodded. "Mrs. Higgens told me."

"Well, I guess neither one of us was really ready for marriage—it's too bad we didn't take the time to know each other better before we plunged into it." He laughed shortly. "What Ginny really wanted was to be the wife of a rich and successful man so she could play lady of the manor. How she ever imagined that I was that man I don't know, but it didn't take her long to let me know how disappointed she was." He paused and gazed out over the moonlit lake. "I was hurt and angry when she left me and made it clear that she'd never cared for me, only for what I could give her. At the time I didn't have much, but she certainly took everything she could get."

Kate was astonished at this flood of self-revelation. It seemed so unlike Adam. "Where is Ginny now?" she asked softly.

His eyes met hers and he gave her his crooked smile. "I have no idea. It's all in the past and there's no reason for us to keep in touch. In fact, I haven't even talked about it for quite a while—I don't know what made me start in tonight."

He stopped speaking and they both sat in silence for a few moments. Suddenly Kate shivered and Adam said, "You must be cold." Before she could protest, he shrugged off his suede jacket and draped it around her. His arm still lay across her shoulders as if by accident. "Better?" he asked. When she nodded, his grip tightened, pulling her closer against the warmth of his body.

It was so quiet. The only sounds were the gentle lapping of the water against the shore and the rustling of the night breeze through the trees. Then Kate heard an owl hoot. Almost immediately they saw the large winged shape coming toward them across the lake.

"Look!" she exclaimed. "There it is! I've never seen an owl before except in a zoo."

They stood and moved quickly out from under the gazebo's roof, trying to follow the bird's flight. "I see it," Adam said. "Over there." Standing behind her, he put his hands on her shoulders and turned her in the right direction, then pointed up toward the stand of evergreens. "See, he's just landing at the top of the tallest tree."

Kate watched as the owl settled on the flimsy tip, making it sway slowly back and forth. Its body silhouetted against the bright moonlit sky evoked a sense of primitive magic. She held her breath as it flapped its wings and rose from its perch, gliding away through the trees until it was lost from sight.

They stood motionless for another moment. Then Adam turned Kate slowly toward him. She looked up into his eyes. His strong arms pulled her close and his lips met hers in a tender kiss. Her hands slid up along his back as her body melted against his. She could feel his heart thumping through the soft fabric of his sweater, and her own was pounding in response.

Adam drew back and cupped her head in his hands. Holding her still for a moment, he looked deep into her eyes, and then crushed her to him again. This time the urgency of his passion flooded through her and she clung to him with equal intensity. They were consumed in this moment that seemed to have no end.

Jessica was fast asleep when Kate crept into their room and undressed in the darkness. She gently pulled up the covers over the girl's shoulders before she climbed into her own bed. Tonight she knew there would be no dreams.

When she woke the next morning, Jessica was standing by the balcony door, peering out through the glass panes. "Wow, Kate! I can't even see the lake," the little girl said. "Come and look."

Kate slipped out of bed and went to the door. Fog curled up over the floor of the balcony and drifted across the glass. She could barely make out the little bridge near the hotel where she and Adam had walked the night before. Staring out at the impenetrable gray mist, Kate felt a shiver of apprehension, though she couldn't understand why.

As she got dressed, Kate wondered how last night would affect the way she and Adam behaved toward one another. But when he tapped at their door and they started down to breakfast, it was as if nothing at all had happened. Adam was polite and friendly, just as he'd been since they got to Mohonk.

Kate didn't quite know what to think. Did Adam regret what had happened between them? Had he just been carried away by the moonlit night, and did he now want to erase the memory of their romantic interlude? A wave of embarrassment threatened to engulf her. But then she thought, wait a minute. Maybe that's not it. Maybe he's just being cautious. After all, he was burned once and he may want to take time to think things over. Besides, he's very aware of Jessica's needs and he may not want her to see any change in our relationship unless he's sure it's a permanent one. And I suppose he's right about that. Kate resolved to take her cues from Adam and just let things move at his pace.

As they entered the dining room, Kate stopped short. Sitting at a table near the front was Walter! But as Kate looked more closely, she could see that it wasn't really him. In an undertone she said to Adam, "That guy over there in the blue shirt is the one I thought was Walter. But I was mistaken."

Adam glanced across. "I can see the resemblance, but it certainly isn't Walter."

He didn't go on, but Kate heard the unspoken criticism. He obviously thought she was letting her imagination run away with her.

The fog was just as thick and cold by the time they finished breakfast, so Adam suggested they stay indoors for a while until it had time to lift. Jessica was eager to continue the Monopoly game and soon Kate had arranged the board and bank to duplicate the way they'd been when they quit the evening before.

Kate had been doing well in the game when they'd left off, and now through a series of lucky throws and shrewd investments, she was collecting money from both Adam and Jessica on almost every turn. Jessica didn't seem to mind. The game was new to her, and she enjoyed putting up as many houses as she could and looked forward to reading her Chance cards. Kate helped her as much as she could, but the dice just weren't rolling Jessica's way.

Luck wasn't with Adam either, and he appeared to be on the verge of bankruptcy. Kate felt more and more uncomfortable with him and took refuge in talking mostly to Jessica and avoiding his eyes. He continued to act polite but distant, and by now she was sure he intended this as a message that Kate couldn't help reading. He must really wish he hadn't behaved so impulsively last night. It made Kate feel like a fool but there wasn't much she could do about it.

Two turns later Adam was broke. Kate suppressed a gleeful smile as she raked in the last of his money, but she couldn't resist saying teasingly, "Another victory for women in the world of high finance."

She thought he might laugh or at least smile, but instead he said in a biting tone, "You needn't gloat about it. Remember, this has happened to me before—only the last time I managed to keep my house."

Shocked at his implication, Kate stared at him as a hot flush of anger crept up her neck. Before she could think of a suitable response, Jessica said, "I don't feel like playing anymore. Can't we go outside? I want to take that walk like before."

Adam glanced through the window. "It's still pretty foggy," he told the girl, "but I think that sounds okay. It's our last chance for a walk before we leave. We can't go all the way to Sky Top, though."

"No, I mean around the lake." Jessica jumped up, eager to be off. "You're coming too, right, Kate?"

"Sure, Jess, I'll come." Kate was still angry, but there was no reason to take it out on Jessica and spoil her pleasure. "I guess that sweater you're wearing will be warm enough, but I've got to get my jacket."

"I've got to get mine, too," Adam told the girl as he

finished putting away the game pieces. "But you can go on outside and we'll be down in a few minutes."

As Kate and Adam walked up the stairs, Kate realized that two could play at the game of being aloofly correct. And that way she wouldn't give him the satisfaction of knowing he'd hurt her feelings.

By the time they got outside, Jessica was nowhere in sight. "She shouldn't have started without us," Adam said, "but I'm sure we'll soon catch up to her."

You didn't make that very clear to her, Kate thought. But she said nothing.

They found the path without difficulty, and followed it along past the cutoffs to the Sky Top Path and the Labyrinth. They could see the trail at their feet, but the mountain on one side and the lake on the other vanished into misty shrouds a short distance away. The fog seemed to muffle all the nearby sounds, and Kate felt as though they were encased in a damp, gray world.

A figure loomed out of the mist in front of them, and Kate gasped in surprise. But it was only a solitary hiker coming the other way around the lake. With a crisp hello he passed them, and they were alone again in their fog-bound world.

"Shouldn't we have caught up with Jessica by now?" Kate asked.

"I'm a bit surprised we haven't come across her by now," Adam admitted. "But I'm sure we'll hear her, if not see her, very soon."

They trudged on farther, and soon came to the spot where Jessica had been climbing up on the rocks beside the trail the first time they'd taken this path. There was no sound of scrambling young feet above them, but Kate called, "Jessica?"

She listened intently for a reply that didn't come. Maybe she's hiding and wants to jump out and surprise us, she thought. So she said to Adam in a loud voice, "I wonder where Jessica is. Where could she be?"

Catching on, Adam responded in an exaggerated

voice, "I don't know. Jessica, where are you? I just can't imagine where she might be."

They moved on along the trail while Kate waited for the small figure to jump out from behind a tree or rock and say "Boo!"

By the time they'd reached the far end of the lake Kate was beginning to worry. "I don't like this," she said to Adam. "She must be lost or hurt or something. She wouldn't let a joke go on this long. If she were hiding, we'd have heard her giggling by now."

"Well, I'm sure she'll turn up," Adam told her, but he, too, sounded concerned.

Not long before they would have reached the bathing beach, they saw an elderly couple swathed in mufflers and tightly buttoned coats strolling toward them. "Have you seen a little girl?" Adam asked them.

"No, we haven't seen anyone," the man replied.

"We did hear someone call, though, a few minutes ago," the woman added.

"Oh, that must have been us," Kate explained. "We thought she might be hiding."

"Well, other than that, we haven't seen or heard anything," the man assured them. "Quite soothing, this silence, isn't it?"

The couple moved on along the path, leaving Adam and Kate staring at each other. "She can't have come this far," Kate said. "We would have caught up with her by now. Let's go back to where the rocks are. Maybe she was hiding and didn't hear us."

They retraced their steps around the bend of the lake. "Jessica! Jessica! Where are you, honey?" Kate called anxiously as they reached the rocky outcroppings above the path. "We're ready to go back, Jess. Come on out." But there was still no scuffling of feet, no answering call, no little-girl giggle.

Adam walked to the crest of a rock slanting up from the trail. He jumped across to another group of rocks and moved along well above Kate's head. "She's not up here," he called down to her. "I don't think she came this far. She must be back along the way we came."

Instantly in her mind's eye Kate saw a vision of the child hurt and unconscious somewhere among the rocks. This image soon gave way to a chaotic whirl of other thoughts, each one scarier than the last. Had it really been Walter after all in the hotel lobby? Could he have done something to Jessica? Or had the child herself panicked for some reason? Kate felt just the way she had on that terrible day when Jessica had disappeared from her bed—frantic and helpless at the same time. Could Jessica have had another of her nightmare fantasies? And if she had, where would she have run to escape?

Adam jumped down to the path, and the two of them started slowly back. The wide, well-maintained trail now seemed to Kate to be a sinister place filled with hundreds of hidden dangers. They looked behind fallen logs and peered down the little gullies leading to the lake. Kate searched every gazebo, not only going inside the open structures which couldn't have hidden anyone, but scanning the rocks that formed their bases. As they approached the starting point of the path, cold fingers of fear clutched Kate's heart. Where could Jessica be?

Then she saw the sign to the Labyrinth. "That's where she must be," she exclaimed. "Don't you remember how eager she was to explore up there? And you told her this was the last chance for a walk before we left. I'm sure she tried to climb that way. Something must have happened."

Kate moved toward the entrance between two steep rock faces, but Adam's voice stopped her.

"I'm sure you're right," he said decisively. "I'll start up that way. You go back to the hotel and explain what's happened. They can send some of their people to help."

Kate nodded, her face white and drawn. Then she hurried off in the direction of the hotel, while Adam turned into the narrow cleft of rock.

A moment or two later Kate stopped. Surely that was Jessica's voice she had just heard, thin and fearful. "Uncle Adam!" The muffled sound came again through the fog. Adam must have found the child. And that meant she couldn't have gone too far into the Labyrinth itself. Kate paused indecisively. It would be foolish to go on to the hotel with Jessica so near. It would make more sense to go back to the Labyrinth and find out what had happened. If she still needed help from the hotel, at least she would know what kind of help it should be. But maybe with Kate's assistance Adam could extricate the girl from whatever problem she'd gotten herself into.

Kate returned to the entrance of the Labyrinth and began to pick her way over the rough stones. The rock surfaces were slippery with condensing fog, and Kate skidded over them, banging her shoulder painfully against a jutting corner of rock. The place was spooky, even frightening, with its cramped passageways between the sheer rock faces. Even on a bright day it would be dark and gloomy in here; in the fog it was a threatening maze.

Then she heard Jessica's voice, sounding much nearer. "Don't make me, Uncle Adam! I'm afraid!"

Kate rounded a bend where the passageway widened, and slipped on the loose stones underfoot, sending a rattling noise bouncing between the rock walls. Ahead of her she saw Jessica huddled on a ledge of rock high above the small canyon's floor. Standing on a huge flat boulder, and staring at Kate with a look of annoyance, was Adam. Only a few feet separated Jessica's rocky ledge from the surface where Adam stood, but between them was a long sheer drop to the jagged tumble of rocks below.

As Kate watched, Adam turned to Jessica and held out his arms. "Come on, Jess, it's not really very far.

Just take a deep breath and jump. I'm right here to catch you."

Kate stifled a gasp of horror as Jessica gathered her courage and leaped across the chasm into the safety of her uncle's strong grasp. He held her tight for a moment, and then the two of them clambered carefully down the far side of the boulder. Adam sat down on a rock and the little girl climbed into his lap and clung to him, her face still stained with tears.

"Is she all right?" Kate asked softly.

"Yes," Adam replied briefly, "just scared."

Jessica raised her eyes to Kate's face. "I couldn't get back down," she said with a sniffle. "It was easy climbing up, but then I couldn't find out how to go back, and I was scared to jump across. I called and called."

"Oh, Jess," Kate said, "we were looking for you. But you were brave to jump when your Uncle Adam told you to."

"I thought I was going to fall down on the rocks and get killed," the child said.

"But you didn't, did you?" Adam said, giving the girl a hug. "Come on, let's walk back and get ourselves something hot to drink."

Jessica was subdued as they went slowly back to the hotel, and she clung to Kate's hand on one side and her uncle's on the other. They went into the gift shop and sat on stools at the counter to drink their hot chocolate, and by the time they were finished it was nearly time for lunch. During the meal the little girl's spirits revived and she seemed to have forgotten her adventure in the fog. "Can we go down and say good-bye to Rusty?" she asked as they left the dining room.

"Sure, honey," Adam answered.

"I think I'll go up and get Jessica's and my things packed," Kate told him.

Glancing out through the balcony door while she folded her clothes and stowed them in her small suitcase, Kate noticed that the morning mist had partially burned off, and weak sunlight now shone on the lawns and the lake below. And when they went outside to get into Adam's car, she could see a break in the layer of clouds over the valley.

On the way back to Edgar's Landing, Kate and Adam spoke little to one another. She and Jessica played car games until the little girl dozed off. Adam was listening to a tape of Mozart concertos, so Kate gazed at the passing scenery and before long they were turning onto Alder Drive.

Kate put her suitcase in her little car and then gave Jessica a hug. "See you tomorrow, honey." To Adam she said politely, "Thank you very much for the weekend. It was nice of you to invite me along." With a wave to Jessica she got into her car and backed down the driveway.

Once inside her apartment, Kate put away her things. As she opened a can of soup and put it on to heat, she thought about the trip to Mohonk. She hoped that the strain between her and Adam wouldn't make it impossible for her to keep taking care of Jessica. She needed the money; the job was important to her.

Unbidden, the memory of his kisses swept over her, and then, overriding it, came the echo of his bitter words. I'm just not going to think about it, she decided. There's no need to let him influence what I do. I really love Jessica, she realized, and I think she needs me. As she turned away from the stove, an odd tremor of fear crawled down her spine. Kate knew she could never leave Jessica while the unnamed threat still hung over the child.

CHAPTER 12

TUESDAY AFTERNOON WAS crisp and brilliant, and Kate felt full of energy when she picked up Jessica from her tap dance class. She had already collected Red from the kennel, and he was overjoyed to see his people again. "We're going to stop at the store and get some material to make your Halloween costume," she told the little girl. Jessica had at last made up her mind to be a black cat, and Kate hoped the weather would hold through the next day so she could wear her black tights and a turtleneck without freezing. They bought enough fabric to make a tail and a hood with ears and then drove up the hill to Adam's house.

Jessica watched with fascination as Kate cut out the pieces for her hood. "Will you go and get the stapler, honey? We're not going to sew this together. Staples will hold it just fine," Kate told her.

The little girl carefully stapled up the seam. Then Kate helped her draw two cat ears on a piece of cardboard. They cut them out, and Jessica covered every millimeter of each ear with black felt pen. When the ears were attached, Jessica tried on the hood and gazed at her reflection in the mirror.

"Oh, Kate, it's really neat. But what else am I going to wear?"

"Well, you can wear your black tights and those old ballet shoes you've been using for slippers. And then we'll see which of your turtlenecks is the darkest color."

Jessica quickly got into her tights, and then pawed through her collection of tops. "I think the dark blue one will work best," Kate told her.

"But it's not black!" Jessica said. "It won't look like a black cat."

"Well, honey, it's close enough." But seeing the disappointment in the child's face, Kate went on, "I'll tell you what. When I come tomorrow, I'll bring my black turtleneck, and you can wear that. It will be kind of large but you can wear another shirt under it. In fact, that might be better, in case it's a cool evening."

"Oh, thanks, Kate!" the child cried. Then she asked, "Can we see how the whiskers are going to look?"

Kate took out her eyebrow pencil and drew dainty cat whiskers on Jessica's cheeks and at the corners of her eyes. Then she used lip gloss to give her a small pink kittenish mouth. Jessica was thrilled. "How did you do that? I look like a real cat!" she exclaimed. "This is going to be the best costume I ever had."

Kate sat back and looked at her. It did look good. "Now you have to practice some good meows," she told the girl.

"Or I can purr," Jessica said with a giggle. "Can I leave my costume on to show Uncle Adam?"

"Sure, I guess so," Kate replied. "Now let's go downstairs. I have to get supper started, and you have to do your homework."

As Kate was peeling carrots over the sink, the phone rang. It was Ms. Burns. "I'm Camilla's mother. You know, Jessica sometimes walks home with Camilla. A group of the kids are going to go trick-or-treating together tomorrow evening around six o'clock, and we wondered if Jessica wanted to join them. I feel it's a good idea for them to go in groups."

"Well, sure, I think that sounds fine. But I was planning to go with her myself."

"Oh, yes!" Ms. Burns sounded shocked. "Of course the parents are going, too. But it's just more fun for the children if there's a whole bunch of them together. So why don't you and Jessica meet us around six at the corner of Alder and Brook Lane, and then we'll all go along that way."

"Fine," Kate said. "Thanks for calling, and we'll see you tomorrow."

She told Jessica about this plan, and the girl seemed happy to go along with it. "Camilla told me in school today that she's going to be a witch," she informed Kate. Then she put away her homework and began to set the table while Kate gave Red his dinner.

While they ate their own dinner, Jessica tried to think of ways to act as catlike as possible. Kate said, "It's a good thing Red is such a nice dog, or he might chase you, and you'd have to spend the night up in a tree." Jessica giggled and slid from her chair to give the dog a hug, carefully avoiding his enthusiastic licks so her whiskers wouldn't get smeared.

Then Red raised his head and barked, and a moment later Adam walked into the kitchen. "Look, Uncle Adam!" Jessica ran to him and twirled around to show her costume from every angle. "Isn't this a great costume? I'm supposed to be a black cat. And guess what —tomorrow I'm not going to wear this blue turtleneck because it really isn't black. Kate's going to bring me one of hers so I'll be all black just like a real cat. And look, I even have whiskers!"

"You look terrific, Jess," he said, "just like a Halloween cat."

Kate carried Jessica's applesauce and cookies to the table. She said to Adam, "Ms. Burns called and invited Jessica to go trick-or-treating with Camilla and some other children tomorrow at six. I told her yes—I hope that's okay."

"Fine. But you'll have to take her—I can't be home that early tomorrow. I'll be here when you bring her back." He sounded abrupt, almost harsh. Kate turned to look at him, but he was bending over Red, scratching his ears. He didn't even say hello to me when he came in, she realized.

"You have your dessert, Jessica, while I do a few things at my desk," Adam said, and then walked out of the room.

He seemed more unfriendly than before, Kate thought, but Jessica didn't seem to have noticed anything amiss. She chattered happily as she finished her supper and helped Kate clear the table. When they had finished the dishes, Adam came in and said, "Jessica, tell Kate good night and then run up and get into your nightgown. I think we have time for a game of checkers before bedtime."

Without even a glance in Kate's direction he went out of the room again and she could hear him going up the stairs. Jessica gave her a hug and said, "Don't forget the black turtleneck tomorrow, Kate."

Kate promised that she'd remember and then, gathering up her things, let herself out of the house.

Driving home, Kate couldn't keep from thinking about Adam and the way he was acting. Things seemed even worse now between the two of them. If only he were an easier person to talk to, Kate could just tell him that she was perfectly willing to forget the entire weekend at Mohonk and pretend it had never happened. That was obviously what he wanted, and then they could get back to the civilized relationship of employer and employee they'd had before. But she knew that kind of open communication with him wasn't possible now.

By the time she reached home, Kate was fuming. How dare Adam act this way? He was just as responsible for this situation as she, maybe even more so. And they were both adults—surely he could manage to control himself and behave like a regular person instead of being so rude.

As she slammed around in her tiny kitchen area, she wondered how much more things were going to deteriorate. He wasn't far from being actively insulting, and Kate didn't know how she would manage to keep her temper if it got to that. But eventually she calmed down and was able to see that she had some control over the situation herself. I'll just stay out of his way from now on, Kate decided. I'll be ready to leave as soon as he gets home in the evening. She could have kicked herself for standing there like a dummy tonight and giving him the opportunity to order her out of the house. But I won't let that happen again, she thought grimly. I don't have to take that from him.

The next day at twelve-thirty, Kate and Amy were comfortably ensconced in their favorite Chinese restaurant near the university. Amy poured the tea, and when they'd ordered, she said, "Now tell me all. How was the weekend?"

"Well, it's an amazing place," Kate told her. "It's awfully expensive, of course—I think it's about a hundred dollars a night per person and that doesn't include the horseback riding. But the food is boring. The grounds are huge, and they're really beautiful, especially with all the fall colors and everything, and a lot of people go there for the hiking and sort of a back to nature feeling. We met people who go there every year. I'm glad to have had the experience, because I sure couldn't afford it on my own, but on the other hand, once was probably enough for me. I guess the guy at the gatehouse when we got there summed it up. He told us, 'Welcome to the nineteenth century,' and he was right!"

"Come on, Kate," Amy said with a laugh, "that's all very interesting, but you know that's not what I meant. What happened with Mr. Tall, Dark, and Handsome?

Tell me the important stuff. Was he just as mysterious as ever?"

"Mysterious is absolutely right," Kate told her. "Not to mention arrogant and rude."

"What do you mean?" Amy asked, her eyes aglow with interest.

"Well, when we first got there," Kate began slowly, "he seemed like a different person. He was relaxed and charming and we were all having a lovely time. And he seemed kind of interested in me—you know what I mean. Then, the second night, we went for this long walk, just the two of us. He asked me all kinds of questions, and he really opened up too, about himself and his ex-wife and all kinds of personal stuff. And after all of that, he kissed me." Kate blushed slightly as she added, "I guess you could say it was a fairly passionate scene."

"I knew it!" Amy exclaimed. "But then what happened?"

"I guess he changed his mind," Kate told her, trying for a flippant tone. "The next morning he acted very cool. And then after breakfast the three of us were playing Monopoly—it was too foggy to be outside—and when I won, he made this truly insulting remark."

"What did he say?" Amy's eyes were wide with interest.

"I can't remember his exact words, but the implication was that I was a conniving golddigger just like his ex-wife and I was after him for his money."

"What?" Amy was outraged.

"Oh, yes," Kate assured her. "Then last night when he got home, it was more of the same. He treated me like the scullery maid who didn't know her place, and he could barely bring himself to acknowledge my presence."

"What a turkey," Amy said in disgust. "But, Kate, what do you think is going on?"

Kate shook her head. "I guess he regrets the whole incident. And he's letting me know it was an aberration.''

"But that doesn't make any sense," Amy protested. "He may not want to fall in love with you, but you're a perfectly nice person. Why should he act so unpleasant?''

"I don't know, but I think I'd have quit today if it weren't for Jessica. I've really gotten attached to her, and I feel as if she needs me.''

"That's it!" Amy exclaimed. "He *wants* you to quit—he's trying to drive you away because you're too close to Jessica.''

"You mean you think he's jealous of my relationship with her?" Kate thought for a moment and shook her head. "No, that doesn't feel right to me. I don't believe that's it. He's been happy that Jessica likes me—he's told me several times.''

"But that's not what I meant," Amy told her. "Didn't you tell me Jessica has a lot of money and Adam is her guardian? Well, what if he's got plans for that money himself? He wouldn't want someone as smart as you around to figure out what was going on.''

"Oh, Amy, come on. They have rules and regulations about these things—he'd have to have a pretty elaborate plan to fool the bank and the trustees and whoever. I wouldn't even be involved in that anyway.''

"Forget embezzlement," Amy said impatiently. "Didn't you read that stuff in the paper about someone who tried to arrange a fake kidnapping of some rich kid? I bet that's what he's up to. He's trying to either have Jessica kidnapped by some friend of his so he can get the ransom money, or else he's trying to have her killed so he'll inherit it all.''

"Really, Amy," Kate laughed. "This isn't a Dickens novel or something—this is real life in the twentieth century. That just sounds absurd.''

"No, no," Amy insisted. "What about all those things that have been happening to her? You told me yourself it seemed as if someone was trying to kill her.

Truly, Kate, I'd be afraid to be around there very much. Maybe you really ought to quit."

Kate smiled. She couldn't resist teasing Amy just a little. "But if it's true, you wouldn't want me to leave that helpless orphan alone at the mercy of her wicked uncle, would you? That's not what they do in books."

Amy looked unconvinced by Kate's joking tone. "Well, maybe you're right, but I'd sure be scared if I were you."

Kate refilled their teacups and, determined to change the subject, asked Amy about her Thanksgiving plans. As she had expected, Amy had lots to say. "You won't believe this, Kate, but not only are Mark's parents coming, all three of his sisters and their husbands and kids are going to be in the East for one reason or another, and Mark has decided that they should all come to our house for a big family gathering. Secretly he just wants to show off the house. Anyway, when he told me, I said to him, 'I hope you don't think I'm cooking turkey and all the trimmings for twenty-seven people' or whatever the number is. I told him I'm not in any shape to do it this year—not that I ever would be. At least he doesn't think they can all stay with us—just his parents will be there, and he said it was no problem, his mom would do all the cooking." She gazed earnestly at Kate. "Can you imagine? I've just finished setting up my new kitchen the way I want it, and now everybody will be pitching in helpfully and putting things away in all the wrong spots. But anyway, I plan to just look pathetic and helpless and stay out of the kitchen entirely. How bad can it be, after all?"

They laughed together and went on to talk about the baby, and soon it was time for Kate to leave. "Goodbye, Amy, it was great to see you."

"Bye, Kate," Amy said, giving her a hug. "And remember what I said. Just be careful."

Kate smiled. "I will."

Driving up the West Side Highway toward Edgar's Landing, Kate thought over her lunch conversation with her friend. Really, she said to herself with a smile, Amy sometimes comes up with the most absurd ideas. But Amy frequently did take a melodramatic view of life. She wanted this saga of Kate's to turn into a gothic thriller, so she'd just arranged the pieces to fit.

Still, Kate was glad she'd talked to Amy. Somehow, having her friend sympathize about Adam's rudeness took some of the sting out of it. And at least Amy believed Kate was right about Jessica being in danger, even if her theories were a bit bizarre.

Kate decided to pick Jessica up at school. Then the two of them could drive to the farm market in Ardsley and buy a jack-o-lantern pumpkin. They'd also have to buy some candy to have in the house. There would be plenty of time to carve the pumpkin before Jessica had to get into her cat costume for trick-or-treating.

Once they got home, Kate lugged the pumpkin inside while Red jumped around, eagerly sniffing. "No, Red, this pumpkin isn't for you! Now, Jessica, I need you to draw a jack-o-lantern face so we'll have a design to follow while we carve. Why don't you get a piece of paper from the shelf and figure out what you want your pumpkin to look like?"

"Oh, I think he should have teeth," Jessica said, and then pondered the rest of the face while she drew a circle on the paper.

When she was finished, Kate looked at it and said, "That's nice. I'm glad you're having a friendly looking jack-o-lantern to greet people."

"Kate, do you think we could give him ears?" Jessica asked.

"Well, I've never done that before, but I don't see why not. Help me spread newspaper on the floor and we'll get started." Soon they had carved a toothy grin, a triangular nose, and eyes with eyebrows. "Now, let's see," Kate said, squatting back on her heels and eyeing the pumpkin. "Where do you think the ears should go?"

"On the sides," Jessica answered with simplicity.

Pointing with the tip of the knife, Kate asked, "About here?"

Jessica nodded and Kate contemplated how to best fashion ears on a pumpkin head. Finally she decided that triangular plugs pulled partway out would come closest to the desired look. When they were finished, Kate got out a candle, set it inside the pumpkin, and lit it.

"Let's see how it looks in the dark," Jessica said enthusiastically and ran to turn off the kitchen light.

The two of them watched as the flame took hold and a warm glow lit up the pumpkin's face. Even Red seemed taken with the effect. "Great!" Kate said. "Let's put it out on the front porch. Open the door, Jess, and I'll carry him out."

Jessica ran down the sidewalk and checked on the jack-o-lantern's placement, and eventually they came up with a location which pleased them both. Kate reminded Jessica that she'd better eat soon so that she'd be ready to go out at six.

After a quick dinner of scrambled eggs, Jessica pulled on her black tights and one of her own long-sleeved sweaters. "Did you remember to bring me your black turtleneck?" she asked Kate anxiously.

"Sure I did," Kate replied, and produced it from her big purse. "Hang onto the sleeves of your sweater and I'll help you get it on."

With the addition of the hood with ears, the black tail, and the ballet slippers, Jessica was transformed. Once again Kate gave the little girl eyebrow-pencil whiskers and a pink kitten mouth. "Meow," Jessica said in a squeaky voice while she admired herself in the full-length mirror.

"You look really great," Kate told her. "It's time to go."

Kate and Jessica descended the stairs, Red padding along behind them. "Meow," Jessica said to him. The dog looked at her curiously, but he seemed willing to join in whatever the game was. Jessica looked up at Kate and shook her head solemnly. "Poor Red. He doesn't get to have a costume and he can't go trick-or-treating."

Smiling, Kate said, "Well, he's wearing a dog costume. And we'll give him a doggy treat after we get home."

The dog looked mournful when he realized they were going off without him. "See you later, Red," Kate told him as they went out the front door. "Jessica, be sure to blow out the candle in the jack-o-lantern. We can light it again when we come home."

"Do we have to?" Jessica begged. "He looks so great."

"Yes, he does. But we don't want another fire." Involuntarily Kate glanced at the blackened remains of the garage. Repressing a shudder, she added, "He'll be waiting for us when we come back."

Jessica and Kate met Camilla and her mother and a couple of other kids at the corner. "Now, children," Ms. Burns said in her no-nonsense voice, "we aren't going to eat *any* of our treats until we get home. Do you understand? No matter what it is or where you got it, you can't eat it until your parents have had a chance to look it over. Okay, let's go. And we're all going to stay together."

They set off and soon were joined by a dad with a first-grader dressed as a pirate and a toddler whose bunny disguise consisted of her blanket sleepers, a cotton wool tail, and a set of ears. At each house the children trooped up to the door crying "Trick-or-treat!" Sometimes the person who opened the door simply dropped candies into the outstretched bags. But at other homes there was more of a Halloween spirit, and there were many exclamations of astonishment and mock fear at the array of scary and funny costumes.

"Kate," Jessica confided as she returned to the sidewalk, "that lady thought I really was a cat!"

Wasn't it nice that kids could still enjoy the harmless pleasures of Halloween? Kate thought, as Jessica ran ahead to catch up with the kids at the next house. She remembered back to all the fun holidays she'd had as a kid with her mom and dad. How happy and secure her own childhood had been. I'm glad I can pass on some of that to Jessica, she said to herself. She's so eager and full of enthusiasm for life.

As they turned into the far end of Brook Lane and the last block of houses, Ms. Burns said to Kate, "Well, I think this has all worked out quite nicely and the kids had fun, didn't you think?" Before Kate could respond, she went on, "I always like to go early and get back early. When it gets later, there's always the danger of running into teenagers. And you know how they can be. They're often so rough and mean that they scare the younger children. Besides, I like to be home when those kids come around. I want to be there so I can see what they're up to."

Kate nodded noncommittally, and when they reached the corner she said good-bye, remembering to thank her for suggesting that they go trick-or-treating together.

" 'Bye Camilla, 'bye Ricky, 'bye Samantha, 'bye Teddy," Jessica called. She clutched her trick-or-treat bag in one hand and slipped her other hand into Kate's as the two of them walked along Alder Drive to the house.

Adam's car was in the driveway, and they heard Red's eager bark as they walked up the front porch steps. "Don't forget to light the candle in the jack-o-lantern," Jessica reminded Kate. "Hi, Uncle Adam. Look at all my treats!"

Kate got matches from the fireplace and went outside to illuminate the pumpkin face. "Come on, Kate," Jessica called from the kitchen. "You have to look at my treats with me."

Suddenly realizing that she hadn't put out anything for the trick-or-treaters who would appear at their door, Kate went into the kitchen, opened the package of lollipops she'd bought, and dumped them into a bowl. Adam stood at the table looking through the mail, and kept his eyes on the circulars in his hand.

She put the bowl on the hall stand near the front door, and went into the living room to collect her bag. He wasn't going to get another chance to abruptly toss her out; she'd leave first.

The doorbell rang, and Adam went to answer it. "My goodness, a skeleton and a ghost," he said in mock alarm. Jessica ran out to look at the costumes of the kids at the door.

Kate pulled her sweater off the hook in the kitchen and wrapped her scarf around her neck. But when Jessica came racing back in, she looked crestfallen. "You can't go yet," she told Kate. "I still have all my treats to look at. Don't you want to see them?"

Adam wandered into the kitchen and still didn't say anything to Kate. With a flash of irritation, Kate thought, why do I care what his problem is? I'd like to be with Jessica while she finishes up her Halloween, and I can ignore him just as well as he can ignore me. She smiled at the girl and sat down at the kitchen table. "Let's see what you got."

Jessica dumped the contents of her trick-or-treat bag onto the table. First she sorted them into two piles, one of the treats she didn't like and the other of the ones she wanted to eat. She pondered over the assortment of chocolate bars and little packets of jelly beans and candy corn.

"How many can I have?" she asked her uncle.

"Oh, I guess two of the big ones or three of the little

ones," he told her. "Then you can save the rest for another day."

As the girl considered which of the sweets to eat right away, Kate said hesitantly to Adam, "I'd feel better if I opened up these things that aren't sealed and just took a look at them. I mean, you hear a lot of stories . . ."

"Sure, go ahead if you think it's necessary," he said brusquely.

Kate began to unwrap the chocolate bars. Just then Jessica said, "Oh, look, this is one of those skeletons that you throw on the wall and it creeps down. I think it glows in the dark too! If I can just open it—" She tugged at the resistant plastic bubble encasing the little figure on its cardboard backing. At last it parted and the sudden release surprised her. Her hands flew apart and she knocked some of the newly opened chocolate bars onto the floor under the table. She and Kate bent to retrieve them but Red was there first. He wolfed down two or three of the larger pieces before Adam sternly called to him.

"Red! No! Leave it alone, Red."

"Oh, no," Jessica wailed, "he ate some of my treats!"

"Never mind," Kate told her, "you've got plenty more."

"Bad dog!" Adam told his pet. "Go and lie down."

Red slunk into the living room, still licking his lips, and thumped to the floor. By this time Jessica had chosen a KitKat bar and a packet of candy corn and was enjoying every mouthful. "Want some candy corn, Kate?" she offered generously, and when Kate took one, she watched and then said, "Aren't they good?"

"Delicious," Kate said. "I always liked candy corn."

Jessica held out the packet to Adam and then halted, her arm outstretched. "What's the matter with Red?" she asked. "Why's he making that noise?"

Adam rushed into the living room, followed by Kate and Jessica. Red lay on the floor, his legs jerking and twitching, his eyes staring glassily, and his mouth frothing. They stared at the dog for a moment, unable to move. Then Adam snapped, "I've got to get him to a vet right away. Open the door, Kate." He bent and tenderly lifted the large animal in his arms and carried him out and down the front steps. Kate hurried ahead of him and opened the passenger door of the Datsun.

"Put the seat back down," Adam told her in a brittle voice. Then as he laid the pathetic creature gently on the flat seat, he said, "Call the emergency animal hospital in Yonkers and tell them that I'm bringing in a poisoned dog."

Kate walked slowly back to the house. Jessica stood white-faced and trembling in the doorway. "What happened to Red? Why did Uncle Adam take him away?"

"He got sick, honey," Kate said carefully, "and I'm afraid it must have been from the candy he ate. I don't want you to eat any more of it, Jessica."

"But, Kate," the child said with quivering lips, "I heard Uncle Adam say Red was poisoned. Is he going to die?"

"I don't know." Kate spoke as gently as she could. "We'll have to wait and see. But your Uncle Adam took him right to the doctor so let's hope he's going to be okay."

Jessica stared at her for a long moment and then burst into tears and flung her arms around Kate, burying her face against her. "I don't want Red to die!"

CHAPTER 13

IT WAS ALMOST midnight when Adam returned alone
from the animal hospital. Kate met him in the front hall
and began to ask how Red was, but one look at Adam's
face told her all she needed to know. He spoke shortly.
"Red is dead. They did their best, but there was no
chance of saving him."

"Oh, I'm so sorry," Kate told him. "Jessica will be
heartbroken. What a terrible thing."

"Yes." Adam looked haggard. Kate wondered if he
had had time to realize all the implications of what had
happened. She nerved herself for what she had to say.

"I'd better tell you—I called the police after you left.
It seemed to me that it must have been the candy he ate
that made Red sick, and I thought they ought to be told
about it. I told Jessica she wasn't to touch any more of
it, and when Detective Roper came I gave all the candy
to him. And I also gave him a list of the streets we
visited tonight, as well as the names of the other children who went trick-or-treating with us. He promised to
call all of them and warn them—"

Adam cut her off. His voice was coldly furious as he
said, "I know what the police said and what they've
done so far. I called them myself from the hospital and

found you'd already talked to them. I've heard the whole story and I don't particularly want to hear it again."

Kate clenched her fists to keep from screaming. She'd been distraught ever since poor Red had been poisoned, and she'd had to keep her own emotions tightly in check to avoid upsetting Jessica any more than she already was. She wanted to release her own tension, but instead she said in a controlled tone, "I guess you don't understand. What this means is that someone was trying to kill one of the children."

Adam stared at her, his face a frozen mask. "The only one that got killed is my dog."

He continued to stare straight ahead as Kate, after one shocked glance at him, gathered up her things and let herself out of the house.

Bewildered and frightened, Kate drove home. Quickly she got ready for bed and then huddled under the covers, unable to sleep. She felt she was living in a nightmare—she couldn't seem to grasp hold of what was going on. Every time she thought she had things in focus, the lens turned and a new picture appeared out of the kaleidoscope of events. Kate was used to being in control of her life, and this amorphous network of circumstances left her feeling frighteningly vulnerable.

She tried to concentrate, to find a perspective that would provide a rational explanation for all that had happened since the hit-and-run accident. For she was convinced that that had been the beginning. And she acknowledged to herself that she was equally convinced of one terrifying fact: someone was deliberately trying to kill Jessica. Nothing else could explain the extraordinary train of near tragedies the child had been subjected to. And when you look at it like that, she told herself, it's clear that the person who is trying to kill Jessica must be the hit-and-run driver. Who else could possibly have a motive to murder a little girl?

Why did no one else see this as the explanation? But

Kate knew the answer—it was because no one else thought that the hit-and-run driver could possibly know that Jessica had seen the incident in which Rosemary Donegan had been run over and killed. In fact, Kate felt sure that both Adam and Detective Roper, the only other people Jessica had confided in, were uncertain about whether she had actually seen the incident at all. Kate herself had no doubt that the child had told the truth. But she had to admit that it was hard to see how the driver could have known who Jessica was.

Unwillingly, Kate faced the thought that had crept into her mind. She'd dismissed Amy's words so lightly the day before, but was it possible that her friend was right? Adam was cold and unpredictable, as Kate well knew. Was it conceivable that he was trying to kill Jessica in order to get control of her trust fund?

Don't be ridiculous, she said to herself, alarmed at her willingness to entertain this thought. You told Amy it was absurd, and it is. But in spite of herself, she began going over everything that had happened, seeing it all in this new light. Could Adam be using the hit-and-run driver as a decoy? What if he'd seized on that event as the perfect cover for his own attempts to kill Jessica? Reluctantly, for she'd hoped to rule Adam out entirely, Kate admitted that it was possible. He could, for instance, have waited for Jessica to go into the garage for her bike and then started a fire and closed the door. He knew she would be going bike riding with her friend that day.

Kate turned over restlessly and pulled the blanket closer around her neck. Was this chain of ideas even remotely plausible? It seemed to her that it was. Horrifying as it sounded, Adam could easily have introduced the poisoned candy into Jessica's trick-or-treat bag. And now that she'd begun to think about it, what about that strange incident on their last day at Mohonk? Adam had looked so annoyed when Kate had come into the Labyrinth instead of going on to the hotel as he'd told her to. Was his annoyance simply because she'd interrupted Jessica's concentration on making the jump? Or was it because Kate had made it impossible for Adam to engineer an "accident" in which Jessica would tragically fall and break her neck?

Now wait a minute, Kate thought. You have to look at this rationally and examine all the evidence. Adam couldn't possibly have been the man in the car who tried to pick up Jessica and Louise—Jessica would have recognized him. But insistently another part of her mind supplied the answer. That could really have been a stranger in need of directions—or it could have been a completely unrelated attempt to molest two little girls.

Angrily Kate sat up. Her head was throbbing and she got up and padded into the bathroom for a glass of water and some aspirin. Her imagination was really getting out of hand. But disturbing memories kept claiming her attention. Adam had been so eager to tell her about Jessica's fantasies, whereas as far as Kate could tell, most of Jessica's stories had been at least close to the truth. And his reaction tonight had been so strange. He'd been grief stricken about poor Red, but he'd also seemed implacably angry. Kate couldn't help wondering whether his anger had been not so much because Red had died but because Jessica hadn't.

The faint gray of dawn was in the sky before Kate finally dropped into an uneasy sleep.

Late in the morning, Kate woke up and dragged herself out of bed. Heavy-eyed, she made coffee and got dressed. There was no question of working on her thesis today—she felt that her mind was barely functioning. She made a list of errands she needed to do and groceries to get at the store, and went out to perform these mindless activities. Picking up a local paper, she returned to her apartment. After she'd put away her purchases, she realized that she was hungry and it was time for lunch.

Kate made herself a sandwich and sat down to eat and

read the newspaper. When she got to the editorial page, she was riveted by the headline: "Children—Our Endangered Species?"

It was a lengthy and impassioned piece, focusing primarily on poisoned trick-or-treat candy, and asking what this kind of evil, directed haphazardly at any unlucky child, reflected about today's society. The writer referred to poisonings in other parts of the country, but mentioned particularly an incident in Edgar's Landing, and Kate shuddered as she realized this was the candy that Red had eaten. The editorial went on to discuss other instances of violent acts against children, such as the still unsolved hit-and-run death of Rosemary Donegan. "What can we expect of future generations when our children see the lack of concern we have for their safety and protection? How can we be surprised if they feel no respect for property, morality, and life itself if this is the example we provide?" The editorialist wound up with a plea to everyone in the community to attend a public meeting at which ways of safeguarding children would be explored.

Kate shivered involuntarily as she came to the end of the article. Of course people were frightened by the crimes that seemed directed at their children. They believed they were random incidents, part of the increasing violence of society as a whole, and they were terrified that their own innocent children might be next. It was intolerable to think that little kids might be killed simply walking to school or participating in traditional childish pleasures like Halloween trick-or-treating. But, Kate thought with a sense of despair, if I'm right, Jessica is the only child who's really in danger.

In the cold light of day, Kate reconsidered her suspicions of Adam and his designs on Jessica's life and fortune. I must have let my own hurt feelings influence my judgment, she thought. There's a big difference between having an unpleasant personality and being an honest-to-god killer. It would make a good plot for a novel, but in real life, wouldn't I know if he were really that crazy? Wouldn't my instincts let me know I should be frightened of him? And I'm not frightened, she reflected. I'm angry and insulted, but he doesn't make me afraid.

But with chilling certainty Kate knew she was right. Someone was trying to kill the little girl she was supposed to be taking care of.

Still moving in slow motion, Kate got into her car and drove to Edgar's Landing and Adam Cordell's house. She let herself in, and for a moment listened for Red's bark of greeting before realizing with a pang that she would never hear that cheerful sound again. She walked into the kitchen and looked at the clock. It was nearly time for school to let out. Perhaps she ought to walk up and meet Jessica today, and walk with her to tap class. She didn't want to overprotect the little girl, but on the other hand, she herself would feel better if she made sure Jessica got safely to the church.

As she stood there, gazing blankly out the window, Kate caught a movement out of the corner of her eye. Was that someone skulking around among the bushes at the back of the yard? She stiffened, then peered intently toward the tangle of overgrown branches, but she could see nothing unusual. I'm sure that was a man out there, she thought. I'd better go and take a look.

Quelling the tremor of fear, she opened the back door and went outside. Oh, Red, I wish you were here now, she thought uneasily. She poked around among the bushes but she found nothing at all. As she returned to the house, she decided that it had been her overwrought imagination playing tricks on her. Still, I'll feel better if I go up and make sure Jessica is okay.

Locking the front door behind her, Kate missed the familiar feel of Red's leash in her hand. Only now was she realizing how integral a part of her everyday life the dog had become. On the way up the hill, she found herself turning to find the source of every little sound she heard. I guess I'm just nervous and jumpy because of what happened last night. Poor Jessica, Kate thought. I wonder how she's dealing with Red's death.

Kate reached the school just as the students were streaming out. She spotted Jessica and Louise deep in conversation. "Hi, girls," she said to them. "I thought I'd come and walk over to tap class with you."

"Okay," Jessica told her without surprise. "We saw the weirdest movie in school today."

"Yeah," Louise joined in. "Wait till you hear about it."

It turned out that the film had been on dental hygiene.

"Did you know you're supposed to brush your teeth after you eat anything sweet? Every time," Jessica solemnly informed Kate. "If you don't, your teeth get all this yucky stuff all over them. It's really disgusting!"

"Yeah, it's gross," Louise said and both girls giggled.

They went on to talk about how one of their classmates' dad had come in and played math games with them that morning. Kate noticed that Jessica seemed somewhat subdued, but the little girl didn't mention Red or anything about the night before.

After tap class, Kate and Jessica waved good-bye to Louise and headed up the hill toward the Cordell house. "Did Red really die?" Jessica asked almost as soon as they were alone together.

"Yes, he did," Kate said, and immediately the little girl's eyes filled with tears.

"It's not fair!"

"No, honey, it's not. I'm real sad about it too. I missed him today. I kept thinking he should be along when I walked to school to meet you. And I know you'll miss him too." She gave Jessica a hug and stroked her hair.

"I wish he didn't die," the child said through her tears.

For the rest of the way, Jessica was silent, and as they turned onto Alder Drive Kate asked her, "How would you like it if I taught you to play double solitaire this afternoon? It's a card game I liked to play when I was your age."

"Okay," Jessica told her.

When they got up on the front porch, Kate unlocked the door and Jessica ran inside. As she was pulling her key out of the lock, Kate looked over and noticed something sticking out of the mailbox. She lifted the lid. Jammed inside was Baby, its head completely smashed in. Oh my God, Kate thought in horror. Quickly she stuffed the doll under her jacket and took it inside. While Jessica was upstairs changing her clothes, Kate hid the brutalized doll on the top shelf of the hall closet. I hope she doesn't ask for Baby before bedtime, Kate said to herself. And by then I'd better have figured out something to tell her.

Mechanically Kate went through the afternoon's activities, playing with Jessica and fixing dinner, while her mind went over and over this latest terrifying discovery. And the more she thought about it, the more worried she became. There was something so horrid about the look of that twisted doll. Visualizing the pathetic plaything once again, Kate felt certain that the damage had been done deliberately in an act of wanton cruelty. It's just mindless destructiveness, she tried to convince herself, but she didn't really believe it. The perverted and vicious act held more meaning than the mere shattering of a favorite toy. Baby's destruction was a message, and in helpless fear Kate realized what it was. The doll represented Jessica, and its caved-in head was a symbol of what someone wanted to do to the little girl.

Kate was concentrating hard on hiding from the child her growing concern. It wasn't until they sat down to dinner that she really looked at Jessica and saw the dark shadows under her eyes. The little girl's face was pale and drawn, and as soon as dessert was over Kate got her ready for bed. Jessica clung to Kate's hand as she tucked her in. "Where's Baby?" she asked fretfully.

"I don't know," Kate temporized. But before she had to say anymore, Jessica fell asleep, her fingers gradually loosening their hold on Kate's.

Downstairs Kate poured herself another cup of coffee and wandered into the living room. She felt jumpy in the big house without Red's comforting presence. All the small unexplained noises seemed louder and scarier than ever, and she wanted to turn on all the lights to banish the disquieting shadows.

Irresistibly drawn to the hall closet where she'd hidden Baby, Kate took out the battered doll and stared at it. Could this have been done by the hit-and-run driver? His attempts on Jessica's life had been thwarted and his frustration must be mounting. Smashing a toy so violently was the act of a twisted mind out of control.

But how could he have gotten hold of it? Kate tried to remember where and when she'd seen it last. Jessica had taken Baby out on the porch to see the jack-o-lantern before they'd gone trick-or-treating yesterday evening. Maybe she'd left her there. But didn't she have Baby with her when she'd finally gone to sleep last night? In her mind's eye Kate saw the lump under the covers next to the child—that must have been Baby. And surely Jessica hadn't put the doll outside this morning before going to school.

Kate's hands were shaking, and she put the doll back at the top of the closet. Whoever did it must have been here at the house. The thought made her sick. He had climbed the porch steps and found the doll and . . . The realization she'd been avoiding hit her like a blow— Baby hadn't been on the porch. Whoever had done this had been inside!

She remembered the figure she'd glimpsed today in the back yard. Was it Walter? She had no idea. But she remembered how easily that policeman at the fire had opened a window off the porch. She hadn't even mentioned that to Adam. At the time, there had been too much confusion and later it had slipped her mind. What if the man in the yard, whoever he was, had watched her leave, and then found his way inside and waited for them? He couldn't have known that she and Jessica were on their way to tap class after school and wouldn't be back until much later. She imagined how his impatience and fear must have grown as more than an hour went by. And finally, unable to accomplish his purpose, he'd struck out in rage at the symbolic child before he'd left.

But what if he hadn't left? He could still be somewhere in the house, hiding. Desperately, she wished for Red. He would have let her know immediately if anyone were here. Her heart pounding in fear, Kate ran up the stairs and into Jessica's room. She let out her pent-up breath as she saw the child still safely asleep in her bed. Then she heard a noise downstairs. A door was opening.

Kate crept toward the banister and looked down. Adam was standing in the hallway below.

He looked at her in alarm as she came down the stairs, her trembling visible. "What's the matter? Is Jessica all right?"

"Yes, she's asleep. But there's something I have to talk to you about."

"Okay," he said. "But could we sit in the living room and have a drink with our discussion?" Without waiting for her reply he moved toward the liquor cabinet and Kate noticed that his steps were weary.

Kate fetched what was left of Baby from the hall closet and followed Adam into the living room. "I found this in the mailbox today," she said without preamble.

He stared at the pitiful broken plaything with a puzzled frown. When he said nothing, Kate went on soberly. "I find it terrifying. And Jessica hasn't seen it yet—she was so exhausted, she fell asleep without it. I don't know how she'll react when she finds out."

Adam took a sip of his drink. "Well, of course she'll be upset. She must have left it outside, and I know it's her favorite doll. But I'll tell her—someone probably stepped on it by mistake and we'll take it to the doll hospital to get it fixed.''

Kate shook her head. "Don't you understand? This doll proves that someone is trying to kill Jessica." In a rush of words she poured out her suspicions and her reasons for thinking Jessica was in danger.

"Are you trying to tell me that you think someone broke into this house this afternoon in broad daylight?" Adam's voice was incredulous.

"The trees hide the house pretty well, as I'm sure you've noticed. And the day the garage burned down, that young cop opened one of these windows"—she gestured in their directon—"in two seconds flat. I'm sure I could do it myself. It's not the least bit implausible." Kate heard a rising note of irritation in her voice and tried to calm down. "I should have called the police when I saw that guy in the back yard. For all I know it was your weird friend Walter."

"For heaven's sake! He's just a pathetic social misfit. I'll get the windows fixed if it will make you feel any better. But I really think that calling in the police about a broken doll is going a bit far. You seem to think that the police are the answer to everything."

Kate's green eyes blazed at him. "No, I don't. But at least they pay attention to what's really going on and I can count on them to care if someone is in danger!"

Trying to keep the discussion under control, Adam got up and poured himself another drink. He said quietly, "It seems to me that you're a little overwrought. I really do appreciate your concern about Jessica's safety—I know you're conscientious and care a lot about her. But I'm afraid your fears are going to be communicated to her and I just can't let that happen to her. She's come so far." He looked at Kate, an unreadable expression on his face. "I don't think she could handle it."

Kate stared at him for a long moment, then shrugged

her shoulders helplessly. "I'm sorry I couldn't explain myself in a way you could hear," she said at last as she picked up her bag and grabbed her jacket. "Good night, Adam."

Kate was still keyed up by the time she got to her apartment in Yonkers. She reran their conversation in her mind. Was it possible that he was right, and that she'd let her imagination overwhelm her sense of reality? For a moment Amy's suspicions of Adam flitted through her mind, but she dismissed them. From the first day she'd met him, she'd seen how his face lit up when he saw the child and how much he obviously cared for her. So why was he being so obdurate about what Kate told him? Why was he refusing to see that her explanation of the events of the last few weeks was the likeliest? And why did he insist on acting as though no threat to Jessica existed?

Kate didn't know the answers. All she felt sure of was that she was the only person who stood between the little girl and her nameless pursuer.

CHAPTER 14

AROUND ELEVEN O'CLOCK the next morning, Kate's phone rang. It was Adam, sounding businesslike and a bit rushed. "I've just found out that I have to go to Connecticut this afternoon and stay there overnight," he told her. "I'll be meeting with clients this evening and again tomorrow morning, so I'm not quite sure what time I'll be back. Will you be able to stay the night with Jessica?"

"Well, yes, I guess so," Kate replied. Was I planning to do anything tonight? she asked herself. No, I can't think of anything. Sounding more definite, she said into the phone, "Sure, that will be fine."

"Good. I'll be going to the house before I leave to pick up some clothes, and I'll know by then where I'm going to be staying. I'll leave the phone number for you on the kitchen table, just in case you need it." He paused and then went on, "I didn't know about this when Jessica went to school this morning, so please explain to her what's happening and tell her I'll see her tomorrow."

"Okay," said Kate. Determined to be polite, she added, "Have a good trip."

Just before three, Kate pulled into the crowded school parking lot. She got out and walked toward the building, scanning the throng of noisy kids who streamed out through the doors. As she looked for Jessica, she felt a tug at her arm. "Hi, Kate," Jessica said. "I knew you were here—I saw your car."

At least that repulsive chartreuse color has some redeeming value, Kate thought wryly. There's not another one like it in the parking lot. "I decided to give you a ride home today," Kate told Jessica with a smile.

"But I wanted to play with Louise," the girl protested.

"Well, that's okay," Kate said. "Why don't I take both of you to our house, and Louise can call her mother and ask if she can stay and play with you?" This was fine with the girls, and they hopped into Kate's VW.

It was a clear crisp day with gusts of wind blowing the drying leaves off the trees in flurries of fading color. The girls were eager to play outside, but Kate felt uneasy at the idea of letting Jessica out of her sight. "I'll tell you what," she suggested. "We'll get out the rakes and rake up all the leaves in the yard. There are plenty to make a nice big pile, and then you girls can jump in it."

They agreed enthusiastically, and soon all three of them were outside. Jessica and Louise weren't the most skillful rakers, but eventually there was a huge heap of dry leaves in the middle of the yard, and Kate stood back to watch as the kids jumped and rolled in it, scattering the neat mound all over again. They threw them into the air and shrieked with glee as the wind tossed the crackling leaves around their heads.

She heard the phone ring in the kitchen and went inside to answer it. "Cordell residence."

There was silence at the other end. "Hello?" Kate said. "Who is it?"

After a short pause the voice she had come to dread spoke in a whisper. "I'll huff and I'll puff and I'll blow your house up.'' It stopped and then repeated even more softly, "Blow your house up, blow your house up.'' The sound trailed off, and the echoing noise of the open phone line seemed to wait expectantly for Kate's reaction.

Trembling, she slammed down the receiver and stood in the kitchen, clasping her arms close to her chest as if she were chilled to the bone. Then, pulling herself together, she went outside and called to Jessica and Louise.

"Girls! I think that's enough playing outdoors—it's getting a little cold.'' She glanced at the sky. Now that daylight savings time was finished, the days were much shorter, and already the light was going. "Come on in now.''

The girls ran up onto the small back porch and waited, giggling, while Kate helped them brush off all the little pieces of dry leaves that were caught in their hair and clothes. Then they all trooped inside and Kate bolted the back door securely.

"Can we play Parcheesi, Kate?'' Jessica wanted to know. "And will you play too?''

"That sounds like a good idea,'' Kate said. "Why don't you get out the board? And you'd better turn on a light in the living room—it's kind of dim in there.''

They settled down on the floor, rolling the dice and moving the little men around the pathways to "home.'' Kate found herself feeling jittery and tense, and she realized that she kept expecting the phone to ring again. There was something so unnerving about these snatches of nursery rhymes, twisted to sound hostile and threatening, and whispered in that soft unidentifiable voice. She hated being at his mercy like this, for she was sure he knew perfectly well that she wouldn't let the phone ring unanswered.

Kate glanced at her watch. Louise's mother would be coming soon to pick up her daughter. I'm glad I don't have to drive Louise home today, Kate thought. After yesterday, she didn't think she'd be able to return to the house once she'd left it empty. The vulnerable feeling, the fear that someone might be waiting inside, was just too strong. She resolved to call a locksmith on Monday, if Adam hadn't already done so, and get secure latches fitted on the downstairs windows.

Going to turn on the front porch light, Kate saw a car pull into the driveway. She opened the front door as Janet Black got out of her car and came up the steps.

"Hi, come on in," Kate greeted her. "We've just finished up a Parcheesi tournament."

"Brr," Janet said. "It's chilly out there. And I just can't get used to it getting dark so early. I guess winter's really upon us." She said hello to Jessica and went on, "Okay, Louise, are you all set? Get your stuff together —we have to hurry home, I left the dinner in the oven."

Kate helped Louise collect her school bag and lunch box. "Did you have a sweater?" she asked.

"No, just my jacket," Louise said as she struggled into it. Soon she was ready to leave, and after a flurry of good-byes, Kate closed the front door behind them.

The house seemed suddenly silent except for the gusts of wind that occasionally rattled the windows in their old wooden frames. Kate found herself talking to dispel the lonely feeling. "Gosh, Jessica, I haven't even thought about what we're going to have for dinner," she said. "We won't eat for a while, but let's go in the kitchen and see what we can find."

Kate opened the refrigerator and surveyed its contents. "Well, there are always eggs," she said. "We could have scrambled eggs and bacon, I think there's bacon in here, yes, here it is, or we could have—"

"Kate," Jessica interrupted her, "there's someone at the back door."

Closing the refrigerator, Kate looked at the glass upper section of the door. But it was dark outside and she saw only reflections of the light from the kitchen. "I don't see anybody, Jess," she began. Then she heard the thudding noise the wooden steps made when someone ran down them. Her heart seemed to stand still. There had been someone outside the door!

Jessica was saying in a puzzled way, "That's funny. I saw a face by the glass. I wonder why they didn't ring the doorbell."

"Could you see who it was, Jessica?" Kate asked, trying to keep her voice calm.

"No." The little girl shrugged. "It was a grown-up but I couldn't see him very well."

Kate stepped to the door and flipped on the outside bulb, but she saw no one in the small lighted area. Leaving it on, she turned to Jessica. "Do you think it was a man?"

"Oh, yeah, I think so."

Kate made her decision, and moved toward the phone. As she dialed the police and waited for someone to answer, she thought, it may be foolish and hysterical to call the cops again, but right now I really don't care.

"This is Kate Jamison at Mr. Cordell's house on Alder Drive," she said into the phone. "We've had a prowler up here and I'm alone in the house with Mr. Cordell's young niece. Would you please send someone up to take a look around outside and make sure he's gone?"

The voice on the other end said cheerily, "All right, Ms. Jamison, one of our men will be up there right away."

Kate thanked him, and hung up to find Jessica staring at her with round eyes. "Did you call the police?"

"Yes, I did." Kate tried to sound brisk and matter-of-fact. "I don't like the idea of someone prowling around the house and peeking in the windows at us. People aren't supposed to do things like that. So the police are going to come and make sure the man went away. And if he sees a police car, he'll know he can't come back and bother us." But as she spoke, she thought, I can't very well ask the cop to stay the night with us. There's nothing to stop this guy from returning later on. Her brave words to Jessica sounded hollow and unconvincing to her own ears.

When Kate heard the police car drive up, she looked out the front window to see a tall young patrolman clomping up the steps. She let him in and explained what had happened, and he nodded. "Okay, Ms. Jamison, I'll go outside and take a good look all around the house."

But of course he found nothing. Ten minutes later he returned and said, "I don't see any sign that anything's been tampered with, so I really don't know what to tell you. It could have been some kid. We haven't had any other reports of prowlers up in this neighborhood. I guess the best thing is for you to make sure all the doors and windows are locked and your curtains are drawn. You might want to leave these outside lights on too, to discourage anybody from hanging around. And we'll try to keep an eye on things. I'll put your house on my list so the guys in the cruiser will make a point of driving down this street on their rounds. And of course if you see anybody again, be sure to call."

He put his cap back on and looked as if he were ready to leave. At that point Kate realized that she couldn't face the thought of spending the night alone here with Jessica. She walked out onto the front porch with the patrolman and said, "Listen, Mr. Cordell is out of town until tomorrow, and I really don't feel comfortable staying here with the little girl by myself tonight. So I'm going to take her to my apartment in Yonkers, and we'll both sleep there. I'll try to call Mr. Cordell as soon as we get there, but in case I don't reach him, maybe I should give you my address and phone number, just so somebody will know where we are." He nodded and took out his notebook. She gave him the information and then went on, "Anyway, the house will be empty tonight, so I guess whoever drives by to check on it should know that. And could you please be sure to tell

Detective Roper that we won't be here? He's been up here before, and he said he was going to drive by and keep an eye on things on his way home. I don't want him to think something is wrong if he doesn't see any lights."

"Fine," the policeman said as he finished jotting in his book, "I'll take care of it. Well, good night, ma'am." He walked out to his car and Kate went back inside.

"Guess what?" she said to Jessica. "We're going to go and spend the night at my apartment."

"A sleepover?" Jessica's eyes lit up. "Oh, neat! I get to see where you live."

"Right." Kate smiled at her, relieved that the girl seemed unaware of the real reason for this change in plans. "Let's go up and get your nightie and tooth-brush."

It took only a few minutes to bundle Jessica's things into her case, and Kate was glad to turn out the lights and leave the empty, brooding house behind. When they reached her apartment and went inside, she was struck by the sense of friendly familiarity the place gave her. Jessica darted around, exclaiming over Kate's pictures, her books and papers, and the cozy intermingling of kitchen, bedroom, and working areas. "It's like a whole house all squashed up in one room," she told Kate, and Kate realized that the child had probably never lived in an apartment. This small studio must seem almost like a doll house to her.

Kate picked up the phone and called the number Adam had left for her. She didn't want him to be worried if he tried to call her at his house. But when the motel switchboard tried his room, there was no answer. Kate debated leaving a message, but then decided it might just complicate things. She could try to call him later.

"Are you getting hungry, Jessica?" she asked. When the child nodded, Kate said, "Me too. I think this is a

special occasion, so shall we go out to dinner like two
ladies?"

The little girl responded with enthusiasm, so they put
on their jackets again. Kate drove the three blocks to a
small, cheerful Italian restaurant where lots of families
were always eating at the round tables. She'd been there
a number of times, and enjoyed the owner's concern
that his customers be really satisfied by eating more
than they needed. She ordered linguine with clams for
herself, and suggested that Jessica might like the spaghetti with meatballs. But the owner, who was taking
their order, thought Jessica would much prefer the
ravioli—"I make it myself, so you know it's very good"
—and the girl was happy to go along with him. When it
came, she was charmed by the little packets stuffed with
meat.

"How did he make these, Kate?" she wanted to
know. "I don't get how he puts the meat inside."

"I don't know either, honey," Kate admitted. When
the owner came to clear their plates and ask if they had
enjoyed their meal, Jessica asked him how the ravioli
was made, and while Kate sat and finished her glass of
wine, he took the girl into the kitchen with him. When
she came back to eat her ice cream, she tried to tell Kate
all about it. "It's really neat in there," she said, "but
it's really hot, too. And they have all these machines
that make the different foods, like spaghetti and ravioli.
You should go and see it, Kate, 'cause I can't explain it
very well."

Kate promised that she'd take a look the next time she
ate there, and then with many thanks and good-byes
they were ready to leave.

Kate drove back and left her car in the parking lot of
her building. As the two of them walked toward her
apartment door, she could hear the phone ringing inside. But by the time she'd gotten her key into the lock
and pushed the door open, the ringing had stopped. She
picked up the phone anyway, but there was no one on

the line. That's always the way, she thought—I suppose those were the eleventh and twelfth rings I heard, and whoever was calling has decided I'm out for the evening. Then she realized that it might have been Adam. I'd better try him again, she thought. But once again the operator rang his room without success. This time Kate left a message for him with her phone number and a request that he call her. Anything lengthier was bound to get garbled.

Jessica asked if they could watch some TV and Kate went to turn it on. The familiar strains of the "M*A*S*H" theme music drifted out of the box and Jessica said, "Oh, great! I love 'M*A*S*H'!"

"Okay, honey, if that's what you want." There wasn't much else to choose from anyway, Kate thought. The two of them sat on Kate's hide-a-bed, and Jessica pulled the multicolored afghan over them and snuggled up next to Kate.

As they sat there, Kate's gaze wandered around her snug little nest. She'd never really appreciated the place before. It's got a solid wood door with a sturdy deadbolt lock, and the windows are not only too high up to be reached from the ground, they're covered with wrought-iron grillwork on the outside, she told herself with a sense of satisfaction. And not the least of its virtues is that it's so small, no one could possibly be hiding in it. She relaxed with a small sigh. It was nice not to worry about answering the phone and having some jerk try to scare her, too. She was glad she'd decided to bring Jessica here for the night.

Kate turned her attention back to the television. Once again things were working out for the best at the 4077. She was pleased to see that this episode was one of the ones with a happy ending for all—it might have been hard to explain the ambiguous kind they sometimes had.

"Can I watch another show?" Jessica said pleadingly.

"Well, I guess so." Before the words were out of her mouth, Jessica had the TV section of the paper in front of her.

"Oh, boy. 'Dukes of Hazzard' is on. Let's watch that, okay?"

Inwardly Kate groaned. She wasn't sure she could sit through an hour of car chases, male chauvinism, and tasteless jokes. But Jessica was giving her one of those imploring looks, and Kate nodded her assent.

Just after the first commercial break there was a knock at the door. Relieved to have an excuse to leave the Duke boys, Kate turned down the volume and called, "Who is it?"

The man's voice outside told her he was from the police. Kate opened the door as far as the safety chain allowed and looked into the well-lit hallway. A young man in a policeman's cap and jacket stood there smiling at her. "Hello, ma'am, I'm from the Yonkers Police Department. They asked me to come by and see if everything is okay here."

"What?" Kate was puzzled.

"Well, I don't know much about it, but I understand they got a call from the Edgar's Landing force that you had some sort of problem up there earlier tonight, and so I'm supposed to see if you and the little girl are all right."

"Oh, well, that was nice of them. But everything's fine. Thanks for stopping by."

The young man looked worried. "Well, uh, well you see, ma'am, I'm supposed to come in and check things out for myself. I'm sorry to bother you, but I have to put it in my report. I won't be more than a few minutes." He stared at her with a nervous expression.

"Okay," Kate told him. "Wait till I take off the chain." As she pushed the door closed, she thought with amusement that they must have sent their newest recruit to take care of this easy job. Obviously he didn't have much experience; he lacked that confident, self-assured manner that most cops developed.

The young policeman stepped quickly into the apartment, closing the door behind him, and Kate got a good look at him for the first time. He was about medium height with a stocky frame, and his pale blue eyes darted rapidly around the room. He flicked a glance at Jessica but the child's eyes were still glued to the action on the screen in front of her. As he walked into the kitchen and looked around, Kate thought his movements were oddly jerky, almost skittish, for such a solid-looking young man. He shoved open the bathroom door and checked to make sure there was no one there either. Kate watched him, thinking that he really took his job seriously. But there was something about him that made her uneasy and she wished he would hurry up and leave.

The policeman moved back into the living room and stood next to the couch, his pale gaze flitting nervously from the door to the phone. Kate looked at him, waiting for him to say something. Suddenly her eyes took in what he was wearing. The hat and jacket looked like a policeman's, but those navy corduroys couldn't be part of a uniform. And where's his gun? she wondered. Then she noticed the patch sewn on his sleeve. It said Edgar's Landing Police Department. But hadn't he told her he was from Yonkers? She was sure he had.

She took a step toward him and was about to speak. Suddenly there was a knife in his hand and with one long stride he was beside Jessica, one hand clutching her arm and the other holding the knife at her throat.

Kate stopped, frozen in horror. Oh, my God! He's going to kill Jessica. Kate's mind raced as she glanced helplessly about the tiny apartment and then looked back at the man with the point of his knife nearly touching Jessica's delicate skin. "Don't move, honey. It's going to be all right," she said to the girl, trying to soothe that small trembling figure. Then to the man she said in as calm a voice as she could manage, "Look, just take whatever you want. I've got some money in my purse. Just take it all and leave. Please."

"No, no," the man said in a soft voice. "We're all going for a ride. But it's cold outside. Get your coat, Kate, and Jessica's jacket."

Numbly Kate moved to obey him, her eyes still locked on the position of his knife. This is incredible, she thought. That smooth silky voice sounded genuinely concerned for their comfort, and that somehow made it more terrifying. Then, as she turned with Jessica's jacket in her hand, she realized with a sickening jolt that he had used both of their names. He knows who we are, she thought, and then she heard him whispering.

The young man leaned down close to Jessica's head, but his pale blue eyes watched Kate. "Little girls shouldn't tell tales out of school. Now you'll have to be punished."

Kate's blood ran cold. It was him—the voice on the phone. And he was the hit-and-run driver. Before she could think further, he said in his silky voice, "We'll have to take your car. Do you have your keys? And don't forget your purse. You know it's wrong to drive without a license."

Through the walk out to her car Kate kept thinking frantically, there must be something I can do. But the sight of Jessica's thin shoulder in his firm grasp kept her from acting on any of the half-formed ideas she came up with. When they reached the lime-green Rabbit, he ordered Kate to the driver's seat while he and Jessica slid into the back. Though his tone was gentle, he never slackened his hold on the child.

Naturally Kate had trouble starting her car. As she pumped the accelerator and repeatedly turned the key in the ignition, she both cursed and blessed the old machine. Maybe all this racket would bring some neighbor out to see what the problem was. Or maybe she'd flood it and wouldn't be able to get it going at all. But no concerned or even angry faces appeared at any of the windows facing the parking lot, and the car started on her third try.

Kate turned around in her seat to look out the rear window as she put the car in reverse. Backing the car out as slowly as she could, she thought of all those exploits on television. Was there some way she could crash into the cars behind her and get Jessica out while the man was still stunned? But seeing the little girl's face frozen in fear, she realized that he'd have plenty of time to cut her throat and run away before she could get out and reach the girl herself.

Jessica's eyes were enormous, and her skin looked a sickly green in the lights of the parking lot. Achieving a semblance of a smile, Kate said to her, "Try not to worry, Jess. I'm here. And we're just going for a ride."

"That's right," said the silky voice from the back seat. "Up hill and down dale. Jack and Jill went up the hill to fetch a pail of water. Jill fell down and broke her crown." His voice sank as he repeated, "Broke her crown. Broke her crown."

A shaft of light from the street lamp gleamed for a moment on the young man's chest and Kate automatically read the nameplate above the badge. It said Roper. How can that be? she wondered. But the young man's words broke into her thoughts. "You've backed up far enough now. Just go up here until you hit Broadway and then go north."

Kate followed his instructions mechanically. How could he have Detective Roper's jacket. Suddenly she knew—he's Roper's son. The one the detective said was still finding himself. Richie, that was his name. She opened her mouth to utter the word and then closed it. Maybe she shouldn't let on that she'd figured out who he was. There was no way of knowing how he'd react, and the chances were better that he'd let them go if she didn't reveal to him that she knew his identity.

After turning onto Broadway, Kate looked in the rear

view mirror. He looks scared. Maybe I can talk him into forgetting the whole thing, she thought with a surge of hope. He'd probably be relieved to get out of this mess. If only I can get him to believe we'll pretend it never happened and won't tell anyone about it. But as she tried to form a way of putting it that would sound reasonable and wouldn't upset him, he began to speak again.

"Little Jack Horner sat in a corner, eating his curds and whey. Along came a spider and sat down beside her and said, 'What a good boy am I.' "

The low singsong cadence of the mixed-up rhyme was like a fingernail scratched across a blackboard, and Kate felt her back teeth begin to ache. There was no way she could talk to this kid; she wouldn't have a clue of what to say or how to start.

They moved north through Yonkers. Kate's mind swiftly ran through the countless stories that she'd seen in movies and read in thrillers. What could she do to get Jessica out of his grasp? She dismissed out of hand the fancy driving techniques of the James Bond types. Apart from the fact that she didn't have any idea how to do them, her car wasn't equipped for such stunts. But even more important, she was sure that the young man in the back seat would harm Jessica if Kate tried anything rash.

Maybe she could do something that he wouldn't notice. If she ran a red light or gradually increased her speed she'd eventually attract the attention of a cop. Then she could turn on her hazard lights to alert him that something was wrong. The flashing police lights and blaring siren might unnerve the young man enough to make him bolt from the car and run instead of staying there to hurt them.

Kate stepped on the gas and watched the speedometer needle edge upward. From the back seat came the gentle voice again. "Don't do that, Kate. Remember Polly Flinders? Her mother came and caught her and whipped her little daughter. I don't want to whip you. Or your daughter.''

Could he see her instrument panel or was he just guessing? Kate knew it didn't matter. Keeping her eyes on the road and pretending she hadn't heard him, she gently eased the pressure on the accelerator. She'd better be careful. If he got it into his head that she was trying to trick him, he might lash out at Jessica. And she realized that so far he seemed to understand that if he hurt Jessica, he'd lose his hold over Kate. She'd have to preserve this delicate balance until the situation changed. He seemed to have a definite idea of where they were headed, and once they got there, Kate could only hope that she would be able to create an opening for Jessica to get away. But the child hadn't moved or spoken a word since they'd gotten into the car. It was almost as if she were in shock. If Kate told her to run, could she do it?

CHAPTER 15

KATE CONTINUED TO drive carefully north on Broadway. Soon she passed the small green and white sign announcing "Village of Edgar's Landing." She looked desperately around for a police car, but of course none was in sight at the moment. What would I do even if I saw one, she asked herself. I wish I'd just stayed here in Adam's house, and then none of this would have happened. But she knew even as she thought it that it wasn't true. Richie Roper would have found a way to abduct them just as easily in Edgar's Landing.

As she passed one of the few bars on this part of Broadway, two couples came out, chatting and laughing. Could she somehow signal to them and attract their attention? It won't work, she knew despairingly. Even if somebody noticed us, they wouldn't know anything was wrong. They'd see a young man in the back seat with a child who looks ill, and they'd probably think we're on our way to the hospital.

Her thoughts raced in circles as she rejected one useless idea after another. Behind her the young man began to chant slowly. The familiar tune gave Kate the creeps —"Rockabye baby in the treetop, When the wind blows the cradle will drop. When the bough breaks, the cradle will fall, And down will come baby . . ." Like a broken record the thin voice went on, "Down will come baby, Down will come baby . . ."

The repeated words shocked Kate. Could he possibly know that Jessica's doll was called Baby? Surely not, but then the implication was that he was referring to Jessica. She was the baby in the song. Kate shuddered and glanced into the rear view mirror. His eyes were staring straight at her from the reflecting glass, as if he'd known she'd have to look at him and had waited to see her reaction. As she watched, he smiled slowly.

By now they had passed through the quiet residential section of Dobbs Ferry, and Kate braked as she came down the hill to the main intersection where Broadway turned left to follow the river. The Grand Union parking lot was half full of evening shoppers doing their marketing after work. But no one looked twice at her little chartreuse car. The light was red, and as she waited for it to change she tried again to come up with a plan of some sort. But her mind just kept going over the same thoughts again and again, and she couldn't seem to get hold of anything that would help.

When the traffic light turned green, Kate put the Rabbit in gear and started slowly through the large intersection. A couple of cars passed her going the other way, and then she saw coming toward her a sporty little white Datsun. She stifled a gasp. Could it be Adam, back early from Connecticut by some miraculous chance? The Datsun was moving rapidly through the intersection and as it passed her, Kate turned her head slightly and tried to peer at its driver. But it was dark inside the other car and she couldn't be certain. She thought it was Adam, but then she wondered if she were clutching at straws, trying to convince herself that help was at hand. And even if it were Adam, she acknowledged to herself, he didn't seem to be looking at me. She checked the rear view mirror, hoping to see the white car turn around and come after her, but it was accelerating up the hill toward Edgar's Landing, and showed no sign of slowing down. A wave of terrible disappointment washed over her, and for a moment she wanted to simply give up. With a sense of foreboding she knew there could be no escape.

But the image of Jessica's strained white face renewed Kate's resolve. She'd told Jessica that everything would be all right, and by God, she'd do her best to carry out that promise. From now on she wouldn't waste her energy searching vainly for help that wouldn't arrive. The only person who could save the two of them now was Kate herself.

She kept on driving at a steady pace through the quiet darkness. Only in the centers of the little towns was there any sign of life and activity. Where is he taking us? she wondered as they crossed the line into Tarrytown. How long is this going to go on?

Glancing back at the young man, who had been silent for some time, Kate saw that he was staring out the side window. His face looked blank and vacant. She let herself hope that perhaps he was so lost in the confusion of his twisted thoughts that he'd forgotten what he was doing and why they were there.

But his arm was still draped across the back of the seat, the knife still firmly held only inches from Jessica's neck. And as they passed the entrance to the thruway he leaned forward and spoke to Kate.

"When you get to Main Street, turn right on Neperan," he instructed her softly. Kate was dismayed to realize that, far from slipping away into a tortured world of his own, he seemed to know exactly what he was doing.

In a couple of minutes they'd reached the intersection and Kate turned as he'd directed. As she climbed the hilly road, she thought the area looked familiar, though it was hard to tell in the dark. But when the road began to wind through Marymount College and then started to descend, Kate's heart sank. They were going to Tarrytown Lake. She glanced into the rear view mirror to see if she could decipher his expression. He looked pleased with himself, almost smug. Then she knew she was right. The lake was the only place in this heavily populated area that was sufficiently isolated for whatever he had in mind. And at that hour on a November night it would be dark and deserted.

Again from the back seat came the whisper she'd learned to dread. "Who killed Miss Robin? I, said the sparrow, with my little bow and arrow, I killed Miss Robin."

Kate's blood ran cold, and fear crawled like icy fingertips up her spine. He hardly could have made his intention plainer. She tried to block the low muttering from her mind as he went on.

"Who saw her die? I, said the fly, with my little eye, I saw her die."

The road dropped, and soon the water appeared on their left, dark and sinister as it lapped gently at its banks. The young man with the knife told Kate to slow down. Now the narrow road passed between the two sections of the lake. At a bend where the soft dirt shoulder sloped directly into the water, the voice ordered Kate to turn out her headlights and pull off the road.

Now Kate knew his plan. He was going to drown them and probably try to make it look like an accident. But if he didn't want to arouse suspicion, that meant that he wouldn't be able to use his knife. Jessica was still huddled on the back seat, not saying a word. He must think she's too scared to move or fight back. And for all I know, he may be right. In any event, he'll have to deal with me first, she thought.

Kate switched off her lights, and as the car moved slowly onto the shoudler, she readied herself for the struggle that would mean her life and Jessica's. Her mind groped toward a plan. Stopping the car, she pulled on the handbrake and thought, As soon as he moves away from Jessica, I'll—

The blackjack slammed against the back of her head, and everything went black. Kate slumped forward over the steering wheel. Jessica screamed, her voice a high thin wail of terror. The man grabbed her roughly by the arm and got out of the car, yanking her angrily after him.

Just then the high beams of a car coming down the hill toward them lit up Kate's car for a moment. The young man stopped, his movement arrested by this new element, and then quickly shoved Jessica back into the car. She cowered on the floor of the back seat as he snarled, "Keep your mouth shut, little girl!" Then, caught in the oncoming lights, he stood looking out at the water as he waited for the car to go by.

But instead, it slowed and stopped a few yards from Kate's Rabbit. He stared at it truculently as a tall man got out of the driver's seat. His face was in shadow as he advanced a step and called out, "Excuse me, I think I'm lost. Can you tell me how to get to the thruway?"

Richie Roper didn't answer, and the man walked toward him, repeating his question. And before he could react, the man was behind him, and a strong arm was around his neck, choking him.

Struggling for breath, Richie raked the knife in his hand along the man's forearm and tried to jab his elbow into the man's stomach. He nearly succeeded in breaking away before the man kicked his feet out from under him. As Richie went down, he grasped the man's arm and dragged him off balance. The man fell heavily to his knees on top of him, one knee driving into his midsection and forcing out his breath in a hissing rush. Taking advantage of Richie's momentary inertia, the man grasped him by his jacket and dragged him upright against the car. He jerked the younger man's jacket down over his shoulders, immobilizing his arms, and shoved him roughly into a sitting position against the rear wheel of the VW.

The back door opened and Jessica hurled herself into the man's arms. "Uncle Adam!" She clutched him as if she would never let go, heedless of the blood that smeared his clothes. "Uncle Adam, that man hit Kate! Is she dead? I don't want her to be dead!" The tears that she had held back so long gushed out, and her small body was racked with heartbreaking sobs.

Adam's face paled with anger. Quickly he looked toward Kate, still unconscious in the front of the car. He set Jessica gently on her feet beside him, then bent to pick up the knife that the boy had dropped. For a moment it seemed he might turn its blade on the young man. With an effort of will he stopped and carefully folded the blade back into the handle. Dropping it into his pocket, he moved toward Kate, but headlights coming along the lake road caught his attention. He walked quickly out onto the pavement and waved with his good arm to flag the driver down. The car stopped and Adam walked toward it, calling, "We need help!"

The driver cautiously rolled down his window and, aware of the disheveled picture he presented, Adam halted a few feet from the car.

"We need the police and the paramedics. There's an injured woman in that car, and a little girl who may be in shock." The two young men in the car looked curiously toward the VW, and Adam realized with relief that these were potential allies. "That kid on the ground is the hit-and-run driver from Edgar's Landing. I could sure use your help."

Now the young men were intrigued and a little awed. "Hey, man, you're hurt," the driver said, and his buddy craned his neck to see.

"Yes, he knifed me," Adam said. "But I'm okay— I'm more worried about the woman. Will you drive into Tarrytown and tell the cops what's happened? I want to turn this over to them as soon as I can and get some medical attention for the woman and the girl."

"Hey, yeah, man," the driver breathed, "you got it."

The other one leaned forward even farther. "How about if I stay here with you and help you guard this dude? He ain't going anywhere if I'm standing over him."

"Good idea, man." The driver nodded his approval. "Dominic here may look like a teddy bear, but he can be a mean sonuvabitch when he wants to."

"Great," Adam said, meaning it. As Dominic got out and closed the car door, he added to the driver, "But for God's sake, hurry!"

The driver nodded again, and with shrieking tires shot off up the hill toward Tarrytown.

Kate heard two male voices, and for a moment she couldn't understand what they were saying. Then one said clearly, "Hey, man, you ought to put a bandage on that arm or something—there's a lot of blood." It all came flooding back to her, and she painfully raised her head and tried to open the door of the car.

Adam noticed her movement and hurried over to her. "How do you feel, Kate? Don't try to move."

She looked up at him. "What happened? Adam?" Suddenly she was panicked. "Where's Jessica?"

"She's fine, she's right here," he reassured her. "Just take it easy for awhile."

She couldn't take in anymore, and shut her eyes again. A few minutes later she sensed flashing lights through her closed eyelids and realized that she'd been hearing sirens. One of the paramedics came over to her.

"How do you feel, miss? Do you think you can get out of the car?"

She nodded, and he helped her out, then began asking her questions. He told the other paramedic to bring a stretcher, but Kate protested that she was perfectly able to walk. As she made her way slowly toward the ambulance, she saw that Richie Roper was sitting in the back seat of one of the police cars. Repressing a shudder, she climbed into the back of the ambulance and sat down. The paramedic shone a light into her eyes and performed various other tests.

Finally, on her solemn promise to see a doctor the next day, he agreed that she could go home.

Adam stood near one of the police cars, talking to a uniformed officer. Jessica stood next to him, clutching his hand. Kate made her way to them and put her arms around the girl, who clung as if she would never let go.

"Oh, Kate, I was so scared!" she whispered.

Kate nodded and said, "So was I, Jess, but it's all over now."

The officer opened the squad car door and motioned to Kate to sit down. When she did, Jessica climbed into her lap and the two of them listened as the officer took Adam through his story. The policeman said hesitantly to Kate, "Ms. Jamison, I know you've been through a lot, but we need to know how all this got started."

For a moment Kate thought in protest, Not with Jessica here! But then she realized that the girl had gone through the whole ordeal with her. She needs to hear it wrapped up—it can't be left dangling for her. So Kate explained briefly the events of the evening, beginning with the face at the kitchen door and ending with her stopping the car at the edge of the lake. "I don't know what happened after that," she finished. "I guess he hit me—I'm just so thankful that he didn't do anything worse."

"Well, we're all thankful that Mr. Cordell realized something was wrong and took the action he did." The policeman looked at her closely and said, "We'll have to go over some of this with you again, Ms. Jamison, but I think that's probably enough for tonight."

Another police car pulled up next to them, and Kate saw that its insignia said "Edgar's Landing." She watched as Detective Roper got out. He looked terrible—pale, his shoulders bowed, the image of a broken man. He glanced around and saw Adam. As he walked toward them slowly, Kate wondered what he would say.

"I don't know what to tell you folks," he began. "I can't explain—I feel it's all my fault. If I'd realized, if I'd been able to help him . . ." His voice trailed off and he looked at Jessica with tears in his eyes. "I'm just glad it wasn't worse, that everyone's okay. I don't know how I'd feel if I were you, but I have daughters myself and—" He looked down at his feet. "There's no way to blot this out and pretend it never happened. All I can say is thank God you got here when you did, Mr. Cordell. It won't help much if I tell you I'm sorrier than I can express about all this. I just hope you can find it in your hearts to forgive me—and Richie too."

There was a long pause. Then he looked at Kate and at Adam. "I'm going to go over and see Richie now. No matter what's happened, he's still my son." Kate's heart went out to him as he turned and trudged toward the other squad car where his boy sat handcuffed in the back seat.

CHAPTER 16

KATE WOKE SLOWLY, feeling the crisp cool sheets against her cheek. She opened her eyes and saw the glow of a small lamp reflected in the dark of the window pane. She heard someone breathing evenly beside her and turned her head to see the small mound of Jessica's sleeping form in the big bed. She wondered idly where she was. Then in the dim light she saw the carved posts at the foot of the massive bedstead in Adam Cordell's bedroom.

Kate raised herself on her elbow and heard Adam's voice. "How are you feeling, Kate?" He was sitting in the rocking chair across the room, keeping watch over Kate and Jessica. Or at least that was how it seemed to her.

"I feel okay, I think," she replied to his question.

"Can I get you anything to eat or drink?" he asked.

After a moment, she answered, "I am a bit hungry, I guess."

Before she could go on, he stood and said, "I'll go down and fix you something." He headed out the door and down the stairs.

Kate sat up, vaguely remembering that she and Jessica had crawled into bed when they'd reached

Adam's house. He had said in tones that brooked no argument that he wouldn't allow Kate to go home alone to her apartment. And Jessica had seemed to need Kate close to her after the night's terrible events. Her jeans and sweater were folded neatly on a chair across the room, and she realized that Adam's warm flannel bathrobe was spread over her side of the bed.

Wrapping herself in the big robe, she padded down the stairs and into the kitchen. "I'll be glad to—" she began, but he cut her off brusquely.

"You shouldn't be walking around. Just go sit down in the living room in front of the fire," he told her. "I'll be in soon."

Kate did as she was told, and as she stared into the flickering flames, she tried to make sense of all that had happened. In a few minutes Adam carried in a tray and handed Kate a glass of wine and a plate with a grilled cheese sandwich on it.

"Thank you," she said quietly. "This looks like just what I need." She bit into the warm food. Adam sat down in the armchair across from her and she noticed how tired he looked. He had changed into jeans and his sleeves were pushed up, revealing a big gauze bandage on his left arm. "What happened?" she asked. "How did you get hurt?"

"Richie scraped me with his knife, but it looks worse than it is," he told her.

Kate sat silent for a moment. There was a lot she didn't understand, and she felt she had to know. At last she asked, "Adam, how did you find us?"

He looked suprised. "I saw you at the light in Dobbs Ferry—I thought you realized that I had. But I was afraid to do anything then. I could see there was someone in the back seat with Jessica and I didn't want to precipitate any craziness. So I followed you and waited for a chance to get closer without alarming him. I was pretty worried—he didn't give me much opportunity."

Kate looked puzzled. "But you were in Connecticut,"

she persisted. "Why did you decide to come back?"

"Well, that's a little more complicated," he said slowly. "I got worried when I called the house and no one answered. So I called the police to ask them to check on you and they told me you'd taken Jessica to your apartment, and they told me why. Then I called your place and got no answer there either. At that point I just had a feeling that things were coming to a crisis and I'd better be here when it happened. So I got in the car and drove back."

"But—" Kate shook her head. "I still don't understand. Was Richie the hit-and-run driver?"

"Yes," he told her. "I was able to put the pieces together after I talked with the police. Of course, no one knows for sure whether Richie ran over the Donegan girl deliberately or whether it really was an accident. But after it happened, he seems to have gone off the deep end. He apparently knew another child had seen him, and through some things his father said, he worked out that it was Jessica. So he started his campaign of harassment, with the phone calls and so on. It's unclear when he decided he wanted to kill Jess, but he was definitely responsible for the fire and for the poisoned Halloween candy. Of course, as you know, the Ropers live quite near here, on Brook Lane—you must have gone there with the children trick-or-treating."

Kate's face paled. "My God," she breathed. "That means I actually saw him. How could I not have known there was something wrong?"

Adam smiled at her gravely. "Don't blame yourself for that," he said. "Richie has apparently had problems for a long time, and no one, not even his parents, knew how serious they were. You remember the story Mrs. Higgens passed on to you, about the little boy who was tied up in the woods last year?" Kate nodded, and he went on, "Well, it seems Richie did that too. He has a thing about punishing young children."

A shudder of fear and revulsion swept over Kate. He

had come so close to killing them both, and no one would ever have known who did it or why. She could hardly believe that the long nightmare was really over at last.

"But what about Walter?" Kate wondered aloud. "Was he involved at all?"

"No, he wasn't," Adam said. "He's certainly a strange fellow, but he really is just a social misfit who doesn't know how his actions look to other people. That's what I thought in the first place, but I checked up on him just to make sure and convinced myself he wasn't the one who was threatening Jessica."

"But I thought you didn't believe me," Kate protested. "All the time I was saying Jessica was in danger, you acted as if it was all my imagination."

Adam stood abruptly and walked to the fireplace. Kneeling to add another log, he said, "I know. I was wrong. And I came so close to losing both of you." He paused and then turned to look at her. "How can I make you understand? At first I didn't believe that there was any threat to Jessica. I'd had a year of dealing with her fantasies and fears, and I was determined not to give them any support. I thought she needed to put them behind her. But after a while I began to think you were right, though I couldn't figure out how or why these things were happening." He paced restlessly across the hearth, then went on in a low voice, "Of course, after we came back from Mohonk I couldn't discuss any of this with you. You seemed so angry at me, and I was afraid that anything I said would make you leave."

Kate looked at him in astonishment. "But I wasn't the one who got angry—you were. You acted so cold and distant that morning, as if you wanted to forget what had happened the night before." She felt her cheeks burning, even though her words could hardly make things worse.

His gray eyes held hers. "Oh, Kate. I couldn't forget that night. And I wouldn't want to. But I knew I had taken advantage of you. After all, I had more or less forced you to go up there. I thought . . ." His voice trailed off.

Kate stared back at him. Could he really believe that she had responded to his embrace because she was afraid she'd lose her job if she didn't? It seemed impossible. But, she thought, maybe his experience with his former wife has made him distrustful of women in all kinds of ways. Aloud she said, "You didn't take advantage of me at all. Whatever I did was because I wanted to."

"I guess I've made a mess of things all along the line." His voice sounded oddly muffled. "But at least we're all safe at home now."

"Well, not exactly," Kate told him with an attempt at a laugh.

"Oh, Kate." He looked searchingly into her eyes. "This is your home, if you'll have it."

She stared back at him, her eyes wide with bewilderment.

"I love you, Kate." He held out his arms to her and she moved into them with a sense of rightness. He clasped her close, and as his mouth met hers, Kate knew she'd found her Mr. Darcy at last.